Dear Abigail,

Thanks for your interest.

Jeff Athur

Gloucester, MA

6 June 2019

OVERRUN

The Battle for Firebase 14

Jeffrey H. Ahlin

authorHOUSE®

AuthorHouse™
1663 Liberty Drive
Bloomington, IN 47403
www.authorhouse.com
Phone: 1 (800) 839-8640

This is a work of fiction. All of the characters, names, incidents, organizations, and dialogue in this novel are either the products of the author's imagination or are used fictitiously.

Published by AuthorHouse   07/26/2016

ISBN: 978-1-5246-1767-7 (sc)
ISBN: 978-1-5246-1768-4 (hc)
ISBN: 978-1-5246-1766-0 (e)

Library of Congress Control Number: 2016910988

Print information available on the last page.

A fictional account of the struggles to initiate, implement, and defend a firebase in the north-central highlands of South Vietnam. Where are America's POWs and MIAs? Where is US naval pilot Dennis Pike?

Jeffrey H. Ahlin, CDR, DC, USNR-R

OVERRUN
The Battle for Firebase 14

Whatever happened to Dennis Pike? How does a highly decorated naval aviator and his aircraft vanish off the face of the earth?

CDR Jeff Ahlin

Lt. Dennis Pike, on the flight deck of CVA-63, the USS *Kitty Hawk*, 1969

This Vietnam story about the USS *Kitty Hawk*, Firebase 14, and Lieutenant Commander Dennis Pike is dedicated to all those lost in action during that war and to their families—the survivors. The real heroes were the young brave marines, rangers, and South Vietnamese and American soldiers in the jungle, mountains, valleys, and firebases and the airmen and support crews serving on the ships in the Gulf of Tonkin and on air bases in Asia and throughout Vietnam.

Immense and long-term suffering has been borne by the families of the combatants of North and South Vietnam, the United States, and their allies. Too many families have suffered from not knowing what happened to their loved ones in combat. What really happened to America's POWs and MIAs who were not returned at the end of the Vietnam War?

This story is also dedicated to the strength and resolve shown by the American and Vietnamese relatives of those missing in action in that Southeast Asian conflict. This strength has been critically important for the healing process.

Many challenges for the Pike family still lie ahead—even after more than forty years of not knowing what happened to their loved one. They have already shown that they are up to the task. Dennis and his 58,213 fellow warriors from America lost in the conflict are not forgotten by family, friends, or shipmates.

Preface

This is a historic narrative of events that took place over forty years ago in Vietnam. Although many of the events were real, much of this book is fiction and speculation. The actual writing of this story began thirty-eight years ago; a recent call from a colonel who worked at the Pentagon compelled me to finish the book.

In a roundabout way, this is a story of admiration. *Overrun* not only reflects esteem for the many brave servicemen who retold firsthand reports of their intimate fears and challenges while in the jungles of Vietnam, but it also especially demonstrates the admiration for my friend Dennis Pike and his family. Dennis was looked up to not only for his skill as a highly trained fighter pilot but also for his devotion to his navy family in his air group, the Golden Dragons (VA-192), on the USS *Kitty Hawk*. His fidelity to and adoration of his wife and children was legendary. He always spoke very highly of his family whenever he had the chance. He was a rock of stability in a war of inconsistencies.

It was my very good fortune to have friends on the ship, including my roommates, Marine Captain Chuck G. and Lieutenant Jim A., who were always very loyal and faithful to their families. Whenever I went on liberty, it would be with Dennis, Jim, or Chuck. Chuck was one of the two marine captains on the ship and the marine detachment's executive officer. Although I was single at the time, their faithfulness and attitude toward women was always encouraging to me. Jim eventually became a well-known orthodontist and almond grower in Northern California.

Dennis was lost over Laos when a violent vibration caused his aircraft to crash into the jungle in March 1972. It is still unclear whether his aircraft was hit by triple-A antiaircraft fire or a surface-to-air missile or suffered a mechanical failure. The Plexiglas cover was blown off the aircraft, as observed by his wingman, but no one saw an opened chute. Dennis and his Corsair aircraft were never located. Last year, a farmer from the area turned in his helmet, which he had found in a small stream. Dennis's last name, Pike, was neatly lettered across the helmet in all capital letters. It brought home to me the realization that Dennis and many of his fellow naval, marine, and air force aviators have never been properly thanked for saving the lives of many men in the marine and ranger units up and around the firebases in the central highlands and A Shau Valley of Vietnam in the winter of 1969–70. These brave aviators risked everything in some very inclement weather and difficult flying conditions, including bursting flak shells, surface-to-air missiles, and antiaircraft fire, to come to the aid of their fellow soldiers and to protect the civilian population in South Vietnam.

The pleasure of meeting the rest of the Pike family has always eluded me. In the Vietnam era, Dennis had two little girls and a son. These children must be in their forties or fifties by now. They should be very proud of their father; he was always very proud of them.

This story begins over four decades ago. It is intended as a tale of hope and speculation about the fate of Lieutenant Pike and the many other US servicemen who might have been left behind in Vietnam. It is a novel about the experiences of several dedicated men and women serving in Vietnam and the Tonkin Gulf. After I talked once with Mrs. Pike about the possibility that Dennis might have survived, the pain in her voice caused me to discontinue all speculation. Even after I mentioned an experience of a possible sighting at the Stomatologic Institute in Moscow, she was very uncomfortable discussing the possibility that Dennis may have survived. The call I received from the colonel at the Pentagon, along with the new knowledge from the colonel that the Russians had taken some of our pilots and many parts of our aircraft to Russia, convinced me to finish this project.

The Vietnam War, 1969–1975

Key
- U.S. and South Vietnamese offensives
- Ho Chi Minh Trail
- Major U.S. bases
- Neutral countries bombed by U.S.

0   100 mi
150 km

N
W — E
S

Foreword

Overrun is a work of fiction. It is based on the experience of several brave warriors who participated in the Vietnam War during the years 1969–71. Most of the author's time was spent serving as one of four staff dentists on the USS *Kitty Hawk* (CVA-63). During my time aboard the ship, I developed a close friendship with one of the men from Flight Squadron VA-192, Lt. Dennis Pike. Dennis was lost and his A7-E Corsair II disappeared over the Laotian jungle in March 1972.

Firebase 14 is a fictionalized compilation of several firebases in the central highlands and the A Shau Valley and near the seventeenth parallel, which was then the border of North and South Vietnam. All the names have been changed, including the name of my deceased friend, Lieutenant Commander Dennis Pike, who was promoted before he was lost. Abbreviations are used for my roommate, Dr. Jim A., and for my Vietnamese friend and colleague, Dr. David H. The names of the executive officer and the navigator on CVA-63 have been shortened to initials, but the names of the plastic surgeon at the Chelsea Naval Hospital and the department head of anesthesiology at University Hospital in Boston were not changed because they are all a matter of public record.

Accidents attributed to the USS *Kitty Hawk* actually did occur, but some of these accidents involved other ships operating in the Tonkin Gulf. Several reported incidents, such as a dangerous magnesium fire in the wheel well while the *Kitty Hawk* was in Subic Bay and racial tensions on the ship, were not included because the author was not involved in their reporting or resolution.

My experiences in Vietnam do not in any way compare to those of the brave men written about in this novel. The bulk of my active-duty time aboard ship at Yankee Station in the Gulf of Tonkin was spent performing oral surgical procedures and clinical dentistry aboard the USS *Kitty Hawk*. However, all the dialogue and situations included are from firsthand reports of friends and men who lived through the horror of conducting search-and-destroy and other missions in Vietnam. Purposely left out were the mundane stories of rear echelon supply troops, whose experiences, although the men served bravely, could not compare to the personal challenges, grief, and hardships of the marines and soldiers who served in the jungle.

Nor could any of my experiences compare to those of the brave fighter pilots who flew very dangerous missions in all types of inclement monsoon weather and fog in the mountainous regions of Vietnam, Laos, and Cambodia. Much of the North Vietnamese antiaircraft fire control and almost all of the surface-to-air missile equipment and technology were supplied and manned by Russian technicians. Unfortunately, much of the technology used against the United States in Vietnam by the Russians and Chinese was obtained, borrowed, or stolen from US corporations. America even built some of the factories that manufactured the weapon technology in the Soviet Union.

The experience of bringing a patient from the *Kitty Hawk* to a medical facility in Vietnam was quite real; all the reports from *Overrun* are a compilation of reports and fictionalized accounts related to me by dental and medical personnel who were involved with trying to save that firebase and others from being overrun. The story is presented as a first-person narrative for the sake of convenience and flow. Any errors or omissions from the actual reports of activities belong to the author and are in no way attributable to the many fine soldiers, sailors, pilots, and marines who helped me reconstruct and recreate these events. In addition, the novel adapts historical events and situations to support the plot and flow for the reader. Although many of the characters are based on actual service personnel, this book is a novel.

Most of the interviews conducted for this book occurred many years ago, when I first began the project in the 1970s and '80s. It was interesting to find that many of the people who had been quite forthcoming about their experiences in Vietnam thirty or forty years ago were now uncomfortable in recent interviews reliving the events that had shaped their lives.

Many of these fine men have gone on to remarkable careers, and some have been quite successful financially. However, other brave soldiers have drifted from job to job; some have resorted to drugs and alcohol to dull their memories. For many, their past experiences in Vietnam were not something they wanted to relive through remembering and discussing the events. It was not the author's intention to bring undue discomfort or to single out any particular individual. All the included sources were promised that their actual names would not be used. Most of the names included in this project are fictitious; any similarities to names of surviving military personnel are coincidental.

It should be remembered that many of the casualties of the Vietnam War belong to the survivors: the eighteen- and nineteen-year-old boys who became men in an instant; those who came back looking fine on the outside but were changed forever on the inside, eternally haunted by the horrors of war. Combat can leave an indelible mark on those who endure it.

The author's participation in actual combat was minimal, and there is no way that anyone can adequately describe what these brave men underwent. If the stress, tension, and terror that some of our young heroes lived through can be conveyed, perhaps some of the same mistakes that led to our involvement in the Vietnam War can be avoided in the future.

The views and opinions expressed in this novel are those of the author and do not in any way imply the endorsement of the US Navy, the Department of Defense, or any other agencies of the US government.

Prologue

Gloucester, Massachusetts, December 2012

It was a blustery, gray, early December afternoon. Although it was almost completely dark outside, wind-whipped whitecaps were visible in the harbor. That cold easterly wind carried a fine, salty spray across the front of our building. My office manager, Jane, called my operatory and announced, "Dr. Ahlin, there is a military officer here to see you."

It was 5:45 p.m., and my last patient of the day was almost finished. Since my commercial pilot friend Bill B. occasionally came to my office in uniform to check on me for lunch or dinner, I told Jane, "Have Bill wait in the reception area. I will be right with him after finishing this patient."

After a pause, Jane announced, "Ah, Dr. Ahlin, it's not Bill. It is a Colonel Konrad from the Pentagon. He is following up on an inquiry you made about a friend of yours from the USS *Kitty Hawk*."

My dental stool jerked backward as my body stiffened. *Good Lord, could this be news about Daniel Kirk?* I quickly finished up with my patient and hurried downstairs to introduce myself.

"Good afternoon, Colonel. What can I do for you?"

The colonel was in a dress blue uniform with plenty of ribbons over his left breast pocket. His military bearing was impressive and possibly intimidating to my staff and remaining patients who hadn't left for the day. He was over six feet two inches tall, and he stood ramrod straight. He had close-cropped dark hair with flecks of gray around the ears and sideburns.

His hat was tucked under his left elbow. His face was all serious business, but he addressed me pleasantly enough.

"Good afternoon, Commander. Is there a place where we can talk in private?"

"Yes, sir! Come this way." As I led the colonel into my private office and closed the French doors, I thought, *This military officer is a little short on pleasantries.* Although he seemed friendly, his demeanor immediately put me on the defensive and made me cautious.

"Colonel, could I get you a Diet Coke or a chilled water?"

The colonel's eyes bored into me, and he said, "No, thank you. I am here to follow up on what you may know about the circumstances of Lieutenant Commander Daniel Kirk."

The question was like a rifle shot over my head. All my senses were immediately alerted. The colonel wanted to hear and see everything I had about the missing aviator.

"Sir, I have no earthly idea what happened to my friend Lieutenant Commander Kirk." I dug out an old *Kitty Hawk* yearbook and retold the strange story about seeing his likeness at the Soviet Stomatologic Institute. I skipped the details of my interaction with the department head of oral surgery and the circumstances surrounding the discourse with the woman at the US embassy in Moscow.

He then stated, "Commander, some of our pilots and airmen were actually taken to the Soviet Union during the Vietnam War. The exact number is unknown, but we think there were six Americans taken, and they were all returned at the end of the war."

The colonel had force and conviction behind his statements. I had no cause or interest in questioning him, except I wanted to know whether he had any new information on my pilot friend. The tone of his voice and his demeanor led me to believe that his was the final authority in the case.

"Colonel, is there any new information concerning Daniel Kirk?"

"Commander, that pilot has been listed as killed in action, body not recovered."

The colonel then explained to me that there was an entire department in the Pentagon that kept in touch with the families of military personnel who had been killed or were missing in action. Although this came as a surprise to me, it was comforting to know that our military expended time and effort in this direction. The government's treatment of our returning veterans certainly has not been exemplary.

I recounted to the colonel the conversation I'd had with Mrs. Kirk twenty-seven years earlier, explaining that it was born out of speculation and hope for what might have happened to Daniel. "Sir, there is no way that I would know anything about what actually happened to him after his plane went down in Laos in March of 1972."

The colonel then proceeded to tell me that a farmer had found a US naval pilot's helmet in a small stream in Laos recently; my friend's name was neatly lettered across it. He had no further information on the helmet or where it had been found.

I dug out some old *Kitty Hawk* photographs from my files and turned again to the old yearbook I had pulled out, and we found some old arm patches that had been made up for our band, The Yankee Air Pirates. I didn't mention the Super 8 videotapes that Daniel had taken from his Corsair while on bombing or strafing runs or anything about his nickname—certainly nothing about the note I had received while boarding the train from Moscow to Helsinki.

The Kirk family was welcome to everything in my possession that might be of any significance to them. Although I had never heard directly from the family, the colonel gave me a commemorative bracelet with the date and location of the last known sighting of Daniel. The colonel also asked about my phone call to Mrs. Kirk several decades ago. I carefully explained again that I had no real idea what possibly could have happened to Lieutenant Commander Kirk and that everything was speculation and theory about his disappearance.

In addition, the colonel provided information about the Russians and the Chinese taking several parts of our downed aircraft to their respective countries. Even more surprising was his repeated mention of pilots being taken to the Soviet Union and China—and these pilots had all been released during the prisoner exchange and return of all prisoners at the end of the war! The question was still out there: where was Lieutenant Commander Daniel Kirk?

I had always thought that someone somewhere on this planet must know what had happened to Daniel. Then there was an even larger question: where were the almost seventeen hundred Americans who had gone missing in that distant Asian war and were still unaccounted for? Why would the Laotians, North Vietnamese, Chinese, or Russians want to continue hiding information they might have concerning the fate of our pilots or service personnel?

The colonel then asked about my family and my plans for full retirement, and we talked for a while in general about the navy and life aboard the *Kitty Hawk*.

"Sir, I hope to be able to comfort and treat my patients well into my seventies and eighties."

"Doctor, I certainly hope you can," he replied.

He was very respectful. We looked through a 1969 *Kitty Hawk* yearbook for additional documentation about Daniel. The visit was short but direct and to the point. He left without further comment.

*****

After the colonel had left, I changed into more comfortable clothes and went down to the kitchen in my home part of our office. I started to pour myself a Diet Coke. It was then I noticed that my hand, indeed my whole body, was trembling. Was it fear or the new information from the colonel?

I walked into my study and over to a file cabinet. It took me only a few moments to find the folder I wanted, labeled "USS *KITTY HAWK*." I sat down at my desk without turning on any lights; I could see through the gloom by the light in my kitchen. I thought hard about even opening the folder. It was like opening my life back four decades. Did I really want to relive these memories?

My mind was racing: Was it possible that the navy department actually had new information on Lieutenant Commander Kirk after all these years? What could possibly be buried in the Pentagon that might shed light on the disappearance of my pilot friend from the USS *Kitty Hawk*?

With that thought, I spread the contents of the folder across my desk. My cat, Tuppy, came over and jumped on the desk, even though she knew she wasn't supposed to be up there. She seemed to be trying to comfort me; I gave her a little pat under her chin and snapped on the desk lamp. Its bright light washed over my notes and drew me back decades to my first active-duty assignment on the *Kitty Hawk* and my time spent in Vietnam.

Images of Daniel Kirk crept into my mind as I remembered being instantly alert at that Russian dental school. The image of that patient on the screen who looked a lot like Daniel has haunted me for decades.

I had been called up for active duty on two more occasions, during Operation Desert Shield and Operation Desert Storm. Neither of these experiences had affected me nearly as much as my two tours in Vietnam.

Chapter 1

Disquieting and Foreboding, June 1969

Every muscle in my body was screaming, *Get off this plane!* After only a few hours of flight, the long metal bench that spanned each side of the huge aircraft had already taken its toll on my weary bones. There was row after row of seating for soldiers in the middle of the airplane, yet there wasn't one empty seat. It wasn't so much the hard, cold surface or the continuous vibration of the giant C-10 military aircraft as it gnawed its way through the atmosphere at thirty thousand feet. Nor was it the unrelenting whine of the four enormous jet engines that prevented all but rudimentary conversation. The seat that held me tightly and firmly felt like a trap. Looking over my shoulder and out the window, I could see nothing but blue. The sky appeared to touch the Pacific Ocean; it seemed to be one continuous, unending entity.

We had to be about halfway between Hawaii and the Philippines; it had been several hours since the departure from Hickam Field in Hawaii. The interior of the plane was cold, dark, and cavernous. The other three hundred or so men packed on this flight must have been fighting similar circumstances; my whole body felt numb. The engine noise and vibrations made hearing and participating in normal conversation all but impossible. Our immediate destination was Clark Air Force Base in the Philippines. My best guess was that most of these men were headed into a war zone in South Vietnam. Their facial expressions made it evident that many of them were not having an easy time on this flight; fear, numbing pain, despair, air sickness, and homesickness were all close to the surface for these men.

As one of the oldest men on the flight, twenty-six that month, I had orders to report to the commanding officer, dental department, the USS *Kitty Hawk*, CVA-63, no later than June 24, 1969. The orders contained not even the slightest hint of the nightmare and terror that would slowly evolve.

The orders were not very specific for the location of the ship, perhaps because of the need for secrecy. All I knew was that the orders meant western Pacific because of the Westpac designation.

While I was watching the face of an eighteen- or nineteen-year-old man on the opposite side of the aircraft, it occurred to me that it was not only physical discomfort he was feeling, but bone-numbing acquiescence. The face that stared back through the din had dark skin stretched tightly over a firm, handsome skeletal frame. The dark shining eyes said it all. They were cold, penetrating, and full of resentment. There was no hint of fear, pain, or even despair. It was abject resignation.

The casualty rates in Vietnam had been increasing monthly; how many of these men worried about getting home in one piece? The cold, boxed, somewhat stale bologna sandwich that served as lunch did nothing for our disposition. If anything, it furthered everyone's belief that upcoming circumstances were going to be completely beyond our control. Sheer exhaustion finally took over, and I succumbed to sleep. My thoughts drifted back to time with family and friends during my childhood. As I dozed off, dreams of early family life seemed pleasant. I remembered that my father was also about my age when he was in the US Army Air Force flying sorties over Germany, first in the Eighth Air Force based in England, then in the Fifteenth Air Force based in the Mediterranean. Dad's missions frequently took him over the mountains of northern Italy. I fell into a deep slumber, remembering my childhood.

*****

My earliest memories were quite humbling. The product of a woman with one semester of secretarial training and a father who was a high school dropout, I had very modest beginnings. My parents and I had always lived with relatives until around age six. You might say our family was dirt poor, even though it never felt that way growing up. After my brother Jonathan was born in 1946, my grandfather thought the family should move out from living with relatives and someday have our own home.

My granddad was quiet and reserved; he owned a small business selling specialty food items. The House of Herbs in Connecticut was one of his typical accounts. He worked hard growing his small enterprise and lived alone in a small one-bedroom apartment on the third floor of a walk-up in Medford, Massachusetts. His wife had passed away from cancer the previous year. Our family's one source of joy and pride was a farm my grandfather had inherited along with a small antique family home in the town of Sudbury, Massachusetts. This sixty-acre farm in Sudbury was taken by eminent domain in the early 1950s so the town could build a new high school. Granddad got so little money for the farm that most of the family complained. But he was philosophical and claimed, "Our ancestors probably took this land from the Indians for nothing."

After World War II, in 1949, Granddad said to his daughter, "It's time you folks had your own home." He then loaned my parents the $500 down payment on a very modest $4,900 house in Reading, Massachusetts. In addition, on several occasions, he had to make the $39 monthly mortgage payment.

My father, Phil, although not a high school graduate, had good practical skills. He had left school in 1932 at age sixteen in order to work and financially help support his family during the Depression. He worked at an entry-level position for Liberty Mutual Insurance Company in Boston and volunteered for duty in the US Army Air Force when America was thrust into World War II on December 7, 1941.

By 1942 rationing was in high gear in the United States. At first it was all rubber and petroleum products; then the ration list included coffee and sugar. At the time of my birth in June 1943, rationing had been extended to include canned soups and juices, meat, fish, and dairy products. Approximately twenty million "victory gardens" sprung up from nowhere; these gardens supplied almost one-third of all the vegetables consumed in America. My grandfather's farm in Sudbury helped supply some of those vegetables.

So many American men had gone off to aid in the war effort that millions of women and teenagers ages twelve to seventeen had volunteered to fill their ranks in the workforce. Unemployment was eliminated; the Depression was over, and "Rosie the Riveter" (illustrated by Norman Rockwell) made the cover of the *Saturday Evening Post* in May 1943.

The Imperial Japanese Army had conquered most of Asia and were conducting bombing raids on Australia. The first and largest raid on the city of Darwin commenced on January 19, 1942, and included 242 Japanese aircraft in a surprise attack. The Japanese bombed ships in the harbor, shore-based military installations, and the city's two airfields. The objective was to prevent the Allies from staging raids on the Japanese-held islands of Timor and Java. The city was only lightly defended, and the Japanese inflicted heavy losses with little damage to their own aircraft. It was a dark period of time for Australia and America and a difficult time to bring a child into the world.

My father and I met for the first time when he was released from active duty, after World War II, near my third birthday. Before age three, my mom, Phyllis, her twin sister Barbara, and Barbara's daughter Sandy were all the family I knew. Sandy was two years older, but she always felt more like a sister than a cousin. During the war years, we were very happy living in my uncle's small home in Plaistow, New Hampshire.

After the war, my dad told me a story about an aerial battle over Schweinfurt, Germany, that occurred shortly after I was born. On August 14, 1943, my dad was flying as a waist gunner in a bomber aircraft in a huge fleet of aircraft that was targeting armament and ball-bearing factories over the Ruhr industrial complex in the Fatherland (Nazi Germany).

He said this one battle was the most terrifying of his life. They were met by mountains of steel from hundreds of flak and antiaircraft guns. "The sky was black with flak," he said. In addition they were intercepted by swarms of 109 German fighter aircraft. "Some of those damn Krauts flew right into our bombers. They came so close on several occasions that it was difficult not to miss. I kept spraying .50-caliber machine-gun fire directly into their cockpits, and they still came at us!

"My gun got so hot that my hands were burning through my leather gloves, even though my hands had been cold. Holes were opening up in the fuselage where bullets and flak would tear through the cabin. The waist gunner on the other side of the aircraft was hit in the backside by flack that came right through my side of the aircraft. There wasn't much left of our tail gunner when we landed. His compartment looked like Swiss cheese. Parts of our tail gunner were scattered all around the compartment. What a bloody mess.

"None of us had seen or experienced anything close to that terrifying mission. Our pilot, Jock, said his upper body was so stiff and tense from trying to hold the plane on course that he couldn't really move them for several hours after the flight."

The American losses totaled sixty heavy B-17 bombers and six hundred highly trained airmen from the Eighth Air Force. It was the largest loss of aircraft and men in any single mission of the war. It was the first time that the US Air Force admitted to such horrendous losses.

My dad said he was just fortunate that his aircraft could limp back to the air base. Although his plane had been riddled with holes from German fighter pilot bullets and flak, somehow it still flew. The mission, as devastating as it was for the Eighth Air Force, did destroy several industrial armament and ball-bearing plants and highlighted the need for fighter aircraft escorts for the bombers. It was my third month of life.

My dad had trained and studied for a navigation and waist machine-gunner position in B-17 and B-24 bombers at Dickinson College in Carlisle, Pennsylvania, before his tour of duty with the Eighth Air Force overseas. The new B-24 heavy bombers were called "Liberators" and could fly nonstop for up to three thousand miles. They were powered by four twelve-hundred-horsepower air-cooled engines and could carry ten men, four tons of bombs, and five thousand rounds of .50-caliber machine-gun ammunition. They were made at the Ford Motor Company's Willow Run Assembly Plant, near Detroit, Michigan.

Each plane contained 1,225,000 parts, and at the height of production, one plane was assembled every fifty-five minutes! The plant in Willow Grove produced a total of 8,685 B-24s for the war effort. The manufacturing facility Willow Run, located between Ypsilanti and Belleville, Michigan, had been constructed specifically to build the B-24s. After the war, ownership of the plant transferred to Kaiser Motors and then to Ford's rival, General Motors. On June 1, 2009, General Motors announced that it was closing the plant as part of its bankruptcy proceedings.

Although the B-24 was the latest bomber developed to that point in the war, it was not without problems. The aircraft loaded with fuel and ordnance needed four thousand feet of runway for takeoff. The Model D weighed 71,200 pounds when fully loaded. It was hard to fly—thus the nickname "the flying boxcar." It was also notorious for gas leaks. If an airman lighted up a cigarette, his plane could explode. During World War II a total of 52,173 army air force men were killed or missing in combat, many of these from accidental deaths. During the Pacific campaign these planes earned the nickname "the Flying Coffin."

Although the Eighth Air Force (then the US Army Air Force, or USAAF) was the largest of all sixteen numbered air forces in the USAAF, it suffered a staggering number of casualties during World War II. Over half of the casualties of the entire USAAF came from the Eighth.

*****

My dad had quick reflexes, and his math skills were pretty good. He often flew as navigator or waist gunner wherever he was needed. Most of the time, his aircraft was flying sorties over the Ruhr industrial complex, the heart of Nazi Germany. He had a couple of close calls: once his shot-up plane had to crash-land back at his air base, and once he had to jump out over northern Italy after his plane was hit with antiaircraft fire and flak. The flak burst into razor-sharp metal shards that sliced through the wings and the fuselage of his lumbering bomber. He always said those planes were "tough, well-built and stubborn, but you sure don't want to try to land them in the mountains of northern Italy."

When my dad first came back home after the war, it was a terrifying experience for me, a happy three-year-old. Up until that time, my world and family had been limited to my mom, her twin sister Barbara, and my cousin Sandy. When my uncle and father came home and we met for the first time, we were complete strangers. After I acted up a bit, it took some explaining on my mother's part for me to get used to the intrusion of two very unfamiliar men in my life.

Several years later, around my tenth birthday, my curiosity got the better of me. "Dad," I asked, "how was it being shot down over enemy territory in the mountains of northwest Italy? How did you survive after jumping out of an airplane filled with smoke and fire?"

My dad needed to tell his story. His experiences later shaped my hope and prayers for my pilot friend on the *Kitty Hawk*, Lt. Daniel Kirk.

*****

My slumber was temporarily interrupted by a sailor handing me a small cardboard box containing a bologna sandwich and an apple. I made both disappear quickly and went back to my dream. The droning of the aircraft engines made sleep almost instantaneous. Sleep helped numb the pain in my backside.

*****

To my way of thinking, World War II, in the European theater, was Britain, France, Russia, and the United States against the enemy—the Germans and the Italians. Dad got pretty upset with this way of thinking and told me that it was Italians who had saved his life. After his plane was hit by flak and antiaircraft fire, it could not maintain altitude, and the cabin filled with smoke. Dad was the navigator. After quickly conferring with the pilots, the crew decided that bailing out was their best and only option.

"The aircraft was no longer capable of flight. There were too many holes in the underside of the plane, and the landing gear was a dangling mess. We were not even sure we could get out of the aircraft because of the erratic and violent lurches of the plane as it continued losing altitude. A couple of the crew were injured from the flak that penetrated the aircraft; others were injured by the violent vibration and lurching of the aircraft from the winds coming off the mountain range."

They were over the Apennine Mountains in northern Italy and had no idea precisely how high above some of the mountains they were actually flying. They had flown over Lake Trasimeno and were near a small town outside of Arezzo called Gello. Although he grabbed a sidearm before he jumped, Dad was reluctant to use it against a well-armed enemy, and on the way down in his parachute, he was pretty sure his fingers were too cold to even fire the weapon.

He mentioned that he wished his plane had been protected by the Tuskegee Air group of fighter pilots. This was an all–African American group of fighter pilots who served with distinction during World War II: they never lost a bomber they were protecting. The Tuskegee airmen painted the tails of their aircraft with a distinctive red paint. This African American pilot group eventually became known as the "Red Tails" and later in the war, because of their success in guarding the bombers, as the "Red Tailed Angels."

All of the crew bailed out. Dad said he saw one other crew member's chute on the way down, then nothing. The wind howled and blew icy-cold. He was scared and freezing on the way down, and it seemed to take forever to hit the ground. Much of the time, the wind blew him sideways. The cold, penetrating wind felt like it would freeze him solid before he landed. His chute got caught in some tree branches, and he had to fight and pry his way free in order to climb out of the tree.

On the way down in his parachute, he had two primary thoughts: surviving and getting back to his wife and new son. He came down in a very sparsely populated wooded area. There were no lights or roads visible. On the way down, he saw what he thought might be a building or church steeple in the distance. He was very cold, scared, and lost. He thought about praying, but he was too afraid God might not be on his side right at that moment. His primary concern was getting warm.

It was March. There was about a foot of snow on the ground, and it was bitterly cold. He thought if he could get to a high point on the landscape, he might be able to spot some of his crew. Climbing to the highest point of a low hill, he spotted the top of a church steeple. It was—although he didn't know this at the time—part of a small village in the distance. Perhaps that church steeple was God's way of answering his unspoken prayer.

As he crept toward the village, he knew he was in trouble. There were German swastika markings on some of the vehicles; in addition, he spotted a patrol of soldiers in the village that he was smart enough to avoid. He found a narrow, snow-covered road and started uphill to try again to spot some of his crew. After another hour, he could no longer feel his feet or his fingers. It was very slow going in the icy-cold weather and snowy road. He was starting to freeze solid. He was out of options. Giving himself up to the Germans with the chance of being tortured, however, didn't seem like a very good plan.

Rounding a bend on this narrow country lane, he spotted a small farmhouse. It looked abandoned and had no lights, but there was a very faint smell of a wood fire. Basically, he had no real choice: he could freeze to death in northern Italy or take his chances knocking on the door. After several minutes of his banging on the door with his closed fist and then his foot, it cracked open, and a loud voice, speaking Italian, made it clear that he was not at all welcome.

Dad knew he was out of realistic choices. He wasn't sure whether the owner would shoot him or just slam the door in his face. Dad also had no idea what the man had said because he knew only a few words in Italian, but he knew that whatever the homeowner was shouting, it wasn't friendly. When he tried to protest in English, the rather large Italian answered in a gruff, anger-laced voice, "Americano?" As my father quickly nodded his head, the truculent, burly homeowner grabbed him and pulled him inside. Now Dad was warmer but terrified.

This Italian family, which consisted of a mother, a father, an eight-year-old daughter, and a fourteen-year-old son, saved my father. They warmed, fed, hid, and sheltered him for about three weeks, until he was able to leave and rejoin up with US forces that were advancing through central Italy.

In my heart, this is what I later hoped had happened to my shipmate on the *Kitty Hawk*, Lieutenant Commander Daniel Kirk, when he came down over Laos in the spring of 1972.

*****

After the war, in my twelfth or thirteenth year, around the mid-1950s, my dad and uncle took a trip back to Italy to find and thank that Italian family. My father knew his approximate coordinates before jumping out of his crippled aircraft, and he remembered the name of the family and the name of the village outside of which the family's farmhouse stood, but he wasn't sure exactly where the farmhouse was located or whether it was still there. After all, nearly twelve years had gone by since his last "visit."

9

In addition, it was now summertime, and the landscape looked lush and green and totally different from that winter of 1944.

As my dad and uncle were going through the village, they found someone with some knowledge of English at the local fire station. Dad was a "call" or volunteer fireman in his hometown of Reading, Massachusetts, and always felt at home in fire stations. Wherever he went, firemen were always friendly and helpful. He claimed, "It's just in their nature because of their work." He would show them his badge and be immediately welcomed. The Italian fireman with some knowledge of English said he wasn't sure of the exact family, but he gave them the location of a family they could contact for more information.

*****

As my dad and uncle climbed uphill and approached an old farmhouse, Dad said it didn't look at all as he remembered it. The countryside was lush with shades of green and beautiful flowers everywhere. The sky was crystal-clear blue with fluffy clouds floating across the landscape. He thought he would at least try to inquire about the family.

He knocked on the door. It was opened by an attractive young woman who asked with pretty good English, "Is that you, Phil?" It was the family's eight-year-old daughter, who was now around twenty years old. My father evidently hadn't changed too much; she instantly recognized him.

The next part was difficult for them both; the reunion was bittersweet. The Nazis had tortured and killed her parents and brother while she hid in the woods. The enemy soldiers had rounded up all suspected collaborators and partisans and shot them before fleeing the area. The daughter said she could hear the pleading and cries of her family and neighbors as they were systematically slaughtered. My dad and uncle were heartbroken. My father carried that heartache, horror, and guilt with him for the rest of his life.

My dream drifted back to my college and dental school years in the 1960s. After college and during my third year of dental school at Temple University, I remarked to my father, "It would be terrific to specialize in one particular area of dental medicine."

Dad retorted, "Have you ever thought about getting a job?" College, graduate school, and then postgraduate school were probably just a little too much to comprehend for this brave, hardworking, and loving high-school dropout.

But his comments were constructive. Dad believed the world was politically uncertain. He had always wanted me to have a military career. He said, "In the navy you would have a steady income, a steady flow of patients, and a safe, clean, comfortable environment, and you'll be working for one of the finest organizations on the planet." It sounded pretty good at the time. The US Navy Reserve welcomed me as an ensign during my third year of dental school.

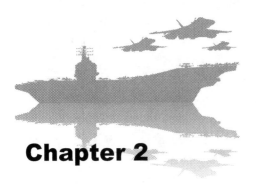

Chapter 2

CLARK AIR FORCE BASE, MANILA, THE PHILIPPINES, JUNE 1969

The change in pitch of the engines gradually pulled me from my slumber. As the aircraft began its descent over the Philippines, the country looked like a sparkling emerald jewel. My backside was so numb and yet when I moved, quite painful. It was difficult to appreciate the beautiful countryside. Everyone on the plane wanted to land and walk around for exercise.

It had been three weeks since I'd finished dental school and started active duty, and a few minor second thoughts about my so-called comfortable environment were starting to creep into my mind. Would this horrible flight ever end? At the time, exhaustion had overtaken too much of me, numbing my recognition of the mounting terror crowding into the corners of my mind. It was the type of feeling you can't really characterize as fear. It was a pervasive aura of unease. Perhaps it was just excess stomach acid reacting to the bologna sandwich.

Our arrival in the Philippines provided a break and respite from fatigue, but it did little to abate building apprehension. Most of the weary men were ordered to proceed to a holding area for their flight to Da Nang. About fifteen of us, both officers and enlisted men, were told to board a military bus just outside the terminal building. We were informed that the bus for Subic Bay would leave in thirty minutes. Under no circumstances were we to venture outside the main gate of the base. At the time, that statement seemed a little odd, but a shower and uninterrupted sleep were my uppermost needs to be addressed. The brief stop in Hawaii had done nothing to cure the numbness and discomfort of the fourteen or more hours of total flight time from Travis Air Force Base near San Francisco.

*****

The military bus we boarded resembled a faded blue rectangular metal box on wheels, completely devoid of any useful suspension. It looked like it might have been designed for transporting prisoners. Were uncomfortable metal seats the norm for all military vehicles? This bus was in rough shape. Clearly, it had been through many miles of hard driving with very little care and minimal maintenance.

The windows had no glass, but the heavy one-inch mesh wire screens provided no ventilation and seemed to trap the air in our humid, metal cage. It felt like sitting in an airless, sweat-drenched, metal jouncing box. Every bit of the vehicle's age pounded through my body. No one had mentioned that the bus trip to Subic Bay Naval Station was an additional three hours of travel over potholed, washed-out, sometimes gravel roads. In retrospect, the plane ride combined with this bus ride, made me never want to sit down again.

The air was heavy and full of moisture, almost suffocating; it was difficult to take a full breath. Every mode of transportation, every building, every walkway from Boston's Logan Airport to Clark Air Force Base in the Philippines had been comfortably air-conditioned. Now, within minutes my uniform was drenched from the fetid humidity. It felt like total immersion in a steam bath. Fortunately, my luggage was light: a duffel bag with a well-used banjo padded by loosely folded clothing.

The road to Subic Bay was narrow and tortuous as it meandered through a series of small villages. At times there was barely enough room for an oncoming vehicle to pass. The jungle seemed to come right up to the bus. Other than the oppressive heat and the unrelenting clouds of flies that were free to swarm through the bus, the back-numbing ride wasn't that much different from the one on the plane to Clark. An abundance of animal life, including strange birds, monkeys, palm rats, and other slithering creatures, didn't seem too distracted by our bus as we charged through the jungle.

As we passed an open field of rice paddies, a navy chief sitting behind me remarked, "Doc, the monument we just passed commemorated those lost twenty-seven or so years ago on the Bataan Death March during World War II."

He continued, "The battle for Corregidor was lost for three reasons. First, the Japanese had been there before. They knew where all our armaments were located because they had visited the site and made extensive notes before hostilities commenced on the seventh of December 1941. In addition they attacked with overwhelming firepower and numbers of troops. The Phillipino's and US troop contingent were completely overwhelmed. And most importantly, Doc, they threatened the patients and soldiers billeted in the Malinta Tunnels on Corregidor with extermination from howitzer fire directly into the tunnel. Our commanding officer had no choice in order to save the lives of thousands of soldiers and civilians in the tunnels."

I learned the chief had been a history major at the University of Wisconsin before joining the navy. This lanky thirty-something-year-old had a high forehead, narrow face, and penetrating dark eyes. He was sort of bookish-looking with a kindly demeanor. He said he wasn't a "lifer" but had been in the navy for over twelve years. I said nothing but knew he was in for at least his twenty. I found him interesting and asked him to tell me more.

He continued, "Camp O'Donnell had been a Filipino army post. After the US defeat at Corregidor, the Japanese needed an internment center for the terminus of the Bataan Death March, and this was it. Sixty to eighty thousand American and Filipino soldiers on Bataan were forced-marched seventy miles in sweltering heat from the southern tip of the Bataan peninsula to San Fernando, where they were packed and jammed into railroad boxcars without ventilation, food, water, or sanitation facilities. Many of the soldiers died on the trains during the slow, hot, interminable twenty-four-hour trip to Capas, the location of Camp O'Donnell.

"During the forced march, the Japanese tortured and killed many of their captives. The Japanese officers or their enlisted men bayoneted or beheaded prisoners who were ill or lagged behind; the other prisoners were forced to bury their dead along the road. I know. I had an uncle who died right after the Death March. When he stopped to help a fallen soldier, the Japanese beat him so severely that he lived only a few days at Camp

O'Donnell. It was hard to tell if it was malnourishment or the repeated beatings by the cruel Japanese that killed so many of the prisoners.

"Doctor, over twenty thousand Filipinos and American servicemen were tortured and killed at Camp O'Donnell before the US and Philippine armies liberated them on January 30, 1945. Later in that year, international officials declared that the physical abuse, torture, and murder of Filipino and American servicemen to be a war crime, and many of the perpetrators, including the Japanese commander, General Homma, were convicted and hung."

Listening to this history so early in my deployment felt like an ominous sign. The more he talked, the queasier my stomach felt. I looked over at the outline of my banjo in my duffel bag and wondered, *What the hell did I bring that for?*

Desperate to change the subject, I asked, "Chief, does this driver have a particular schedule to keep?" We were traveling way too fast for the narrow winding roads. My backside was turning from numbness to painful bruising.

The chief replied in a jaunty tone, "The military bus makes for less of a target while moving quickly. That wire mesh over the windows isn't for keeping out big mosquitoes. It's for rocks and possible grenades. You know, Doc, if you are headed in-country, be sure not to wear any uniform insignia in the bush. They make great shiny targets for the gook snipers and disgruntled marine psychos." He was probably just exaggerating, but this certainly brought up a lot of negative feelings; my stomach was starting to churn.

I replied, in retrospect quite naively, "It's of no concern, Chief. The *Kitty Hawk* will be home for the next couple of years. Vietnam will be on the distant horizon." Actually, listening to the chief, I was starting to realize I didn't have a clue as to what awaited me during this shipboard tour of duty.

The sailor in the seat in front of us popped his head up. "Jeez, Doc, that's pretty good duty. What admiral's daughter did ya have to screw to get a duty assignment like that?"

Was he joking? Was it good duty to be on a ship in a war zone? Unfortunately, future events would make it crystal clear just how good.

The bus trip to Subic Bay was tortuous, painful, and beautiful at the same time. We made one stop for a lunch break, and the Filipinos were gracious and accommodating. The light meal seemed to consist mostly of fruit and possibly vegetables. None of us were sure of exactly what we were eating, but it tasted delicious.

The beautiful young waitress seemed to go out of her way to be polite and make sure in pidgin English that everything was satisfactory: "Sailor, you please let me know if anything better I can do for you." All of us noticed her diminutive, alluring figure with perky breasts and an undeniably sexy voice.

Back on the road, we traveled along a very narrow highway that snaked and bumped through the jungle full of strange sounds, smells, and oppressive humidity.

At one point some huge prehistoric-looking birds flew by. "Chief, what the hell are those? They must have a five-foot wingspan!"

"They're just fruit bats," said the chief with a shrug, "and quite common. If you're ever in-country, you'll meet some jungle roaches that are big enough to take on those birdies for lunch."

He has to be freakin' kidding me! I thought. "At least they're not meat-eaters. You're making duty in Vietnam sound more unattractive by the minute."

He remarked, "Duty on a ship the size of the *Kitty Hawk* isn't too bad. Just don't expect to meet a lot of women on board. You'll have over five thousand men when the air wing is aboard but no women—although last year Miss Black America was on board to sing and entertain the troops. You'll have to go into Olongapo, Saigon, or Da Nang to find 'boom-boom' houses for female enjoyment."

"Uh-huh." I wasn't exactly sure what he was talking about, but I had a pretty good idea and nodded my head knowingly.

"The other nice thing about the *Hawk*," the chief continued, "is that you don't get too seasick on a ship that size. If any serious monsoon storms come up, the captain will make every effort to move the ship out of harm's way. The carriers are a little top-heavy, but they're fast. They can do over thirty knots, especially during flight operations when they turn into the wind."

The chief had a lot of good information about shipboard protocol. It was a relief that he had stopped talking about the Death March. He talked about boarding and leaving the ship, reporting aboard for the first time, and the names of various parts of the ship. It would have taken me a while to realize the scuttlebutt was the water fountain. Who would have guessed what a "meatball," "Gee dunk," "navy shower," or "Focsle" and "wardroom" were all about? This chief was pretty salty, but he was gracious in his introduction to shipboard life.

This was my first real discussion with any enlisted personnel, and it made me realize the value of navy chiefs and their indispensable wealth of naval knowledge. With only two weeks of officer training (some called it charm school) at Newport, Rhode Island, it was unsettling to be on the way out to join a warship in the fleet. It was truly amazing what I didn't know. It probably was unfortunate that I had slept through most of charm school at Newport. The discussion with the naval chief was the beginning of any *real* officer education. The chief, and later the marine sergeants, helped me and other new officers realize and appreciate the role of discipline and the value of serving in our nation's armed forces.

*****

Once the bus was inside the gate at Subic Bay Naval Base, everyone seemed to relax and breathe a little more easily. Much of Subic looked like many American small towns and villages. There were walkways, lawns, trees, and white picket fences along well-laid-out streets. All the yards were well maintained. In contrast to the partially paved, pothole-riddled "highway" we had just traveled, the streets were perfectly smooth, wide, and bordered by sidewalks and well-manicured lawns.

When we arrived at Subic's Naval Air Station at Cubi Point, we saw that the bachelor officers' quarters (BOQ or Q) had only the bare necessities. It was set back from the street and resembled an elongated cement college dorm. It had absolutely no architectural beauty but was well landscaped with shrubs and palm trees. To us, in our current worn-out, dead-tired condition, the Q looked like a five-star hotel.

My small junior officer's room contained a single bed, a small dresser with a mirror, and a small desk with a metal folding chair. The cinder-block walls were painted pale green, and the floor consisted of a yellowing, gray asbestos-type tile that no amount of polishing could bring back to its original luster. The pale-gray well-worn scatter rug next to the bed seemed to harmonize with the yellowing asbestos tile. In my current weary condition the room looked positively palatial.

Perhaps the senior officers' quarters had actual air conditioning, but away from the sweltering sun, it seemed a little cooler. A squeaky, temperamental ceiling fan kept the air moving. The comfortable surroundings kept my growing uneasiness and outright angst bottled up in the far reaches of my mind. After a lukewarm shower, it took me maybe three or four minutes to fall asleep.

I spent most of the next day, Saturday, trying to figure out how to get out to the ship. There was only one minor problem. The *Kitty Hawk* had just left Sasebo, Japan, and wasn't due back at Yankee Station in the Gulf of Tonkin in Vietnam for a few days. The air dispatcher assured me, "Sir, I will have you delivered to the ship in two days." He emphasized that the COD (carrier onboard delivery), a C-3 turboprop aircraft, was very reliable.

The dispatcher reserved a seat for me on the first COD flight to the *Kitty Hawk* out of Cubi Point Air Field. I was sure this seasoned first-class petty officer knew he was talking to a newly minted, nervous, and very green dental officer; it was a relief that he not only was respectful but also had a caring and considerate attitude.

It is so difficult to convey the nervous apprehension that was grinding at my gut. Outwardly, I hoped to remain calm, but inwardly, I felt that I was probably ready for ulcer medication.

Late that afternoon I found some badly needed exercise at the BOQ pool directly behind the officers' quarters. Although not luxurious, it looked clean and inviting. After a few laps, I was relaxing and reading under a beach umbrella when one of the other junior officers asked me what made for such interesting reading.

Chuck was a marine captain, detached from Vietnam, and was also on his way out to the *Hawk*, as the marine executive officer, or XO, replacement for the ship. He was from some small town in upstate New York and was very cordial. I was surprised to learn from Chuck that there were almost seventy marines on the ship, and their task was even more surprising: "running the brig, guarding the nukes and keeping the 'pukes' in line." They also provided security in port and while underway at sea.

Captain Chuck asked, "Doc, would you like to join us for dinner in town this evening? Three of us are going out for a little local cuisine." He continued, "Some of the local food is a little spicy, but most restaurants tone it down for the American taste." Although ambivalent, I thought it sounded like it could be fun. Local food wasn't a particularly high priority for me; my stomach remembered what local food had done for me while vacationing in Mexico. But it would probably beat eating alone in the Officers' Club.

Unfortunately, this "relaxing" evening out to dramatically increased my terror quotient.

Chapter 3

THE SIGHTS AND SOUNDS OF OLONGAPO CITY

I met up with Chuck in the lobby of the BOQ just after 1800. He, his roommate Gordon, their friend Paul, and I shared a ten-minute cab ride to the main gate to Olongapo City. Paul was a supply officer from one of the destroyers in port; Gordon and Chuck were both marine captains who had just rotated out of Vietnam and were temporarily assigned to the marine contingent on the *Kitty Hawk*.

Gordon was to be the new commanding officer, or CO, of the marine detachment on board the *Kitty Hawk*. He and Chuck, as XO, looked forward to duty on the *Hawk* as R&R before going back in-country for what they called a little "huntin' and fishin'." They both looked very relaxed in civilian clothing with their untucked floral shirts and loose-fitting khaki slacks. But underneath the relaxed facade, they looked like they could handle themselves. In the pool at the Q that afternoon, they both appeared rock-solid without an ounce of flab—attributes that, to my complete astonishment, would come in very handy later that evening.

Chuck was about six feet tall and around 190 pounds; he had zero excess fat. Gordon was a little taller, approximately six feet one, and slim, almost wiry, at about 185 pounds. They were both very squared-away marines. Paul also had administrative duties as the XO on his tin can (destroyer) and was approximately five feet ten with a medium build. I was approximately five feet eleven and 165 pounds; we all looked bigger and stronger and at least a head taller than the local Philippine population.

*****

After a short cab ride we were dropped off at the main gate to Olongapo. Nothing in my relatively short life could have prepared me for Olongapo City. We went through the main gate, across the Olongapo River, and into the city. The total distance was only one hundred yards across a bridge, but it was light-years away from anything I had ever experienced. I felt as if I had left reality and crossed into pure fiction.

The river itself looked like a dark cauldron of sluggish molten iron. Some of the native population called it the Perfume River, but this could have been part of a sick joke. It was hardly moving; it was more of a drainage ditch than a flowing river. It smelled like a mixture of dead fish and raw sewage.

The atmosphere in "Po City" was electric, a combination of excitement and a premonition of foreboding. The main street was lined with nightspots: bars, restaurants, music halls, strip joints, and night markets. Every third or fourth establishment looked like a whorehouse or boom-boom joint. Women with heavy makeup patrolled out front. Some of the women were quite beautiful, although so heavily made-up that they almost looked like fake made-up dolls.

The central street in Olongapo resembled an old-fashioned western city in Colorado in the mid-1800s. The rooflines were all mismatched, and the buildings were all constructed of different materials: some stucco, some brick, but mostly wood. They were all connected with some narrow alleys in between. They looked almost like they had been thrown up as a prop for a western movie. Many of the buildings had saloon doors off a raised wooden sidewalk.

As we walked past each nightspot, I could see scantily clad waitresses serving the raucous sailors. The entire main street pulsed with excitement and a not-so-subtle hint of danger. It was a comfort to be with three other rather large men while out in this town. Although there were no streetlights and the night was completely dark, seeing wasn't difficult. The whole street was aglow with the light that radiated from the hundreds of open doors and windows.

The boats in the Olongapo River added to the glow with their kerosene lamps. Their diffuse lighting added to the excitement of the diverse sounds emanating from the multitude of Filipino bands. Music spilled out from the bars and music halls onto the street and drifted and blended with the crush of sailors, shoppers, and girls of the night who slowly strolled along the main street. No one seemed in a hurry to get anywhere.

We had all heard about the young sailor who had been mugged the week before. As the unsuspecting, somewhat naive sailor walked alone down the sidewalk in broad daylight, two Filipino gangsters had approached him from the rear. Once the muggers were on either side of him, they plunged ice picks into his kidneys. As he was falling to the ground, the muggers, on the pretext of helping the poor soul, stripped him of his watch, ring, and wallet. They left him in an alley to bleed to death. The whole tragic story heightened my concern and sharpened my senses. I kept glancing over my shoulder to see if anyone was close behind me.

The music, however, was very well done. One would swear that Chuck Berry, Elvis, the Kingston Trio, and the Supremes were booked and jamming together, spread out along the street. All of us were excited about going into these joints just to listen to the music and watch the unending theater.

There were hundreds of Jeepney taxis roaming the streets. Their traffic jammed the roads and competed with pedestrians for the right of way. The night was teeming with hawkers of every variety. Young Filipino men were selling everything imaginable: watches, pens, jewelry of all sorts, stereo radios, tape decks, and *even their sisters*. They'd say, "She for you sailor—guarantee she virgin!"

The girls, who hawked their wares all along the main street and from the doors and windows of nightspots, were admittedly very beautiful. It wasn't only their charm and beauty that was attractive, however. Every one of them was polite and courteous and never pressed us in any forcible way. Their beauty and personable approach were beguiling, and they showed kindness without a hint of hostility. Our objective that evening was some delicious local food, however, and not catching venereal trouble. At the time, I have to admit, most of us were on the cusp of which hunger to feed first.

Gordon and Chuck led the way as we picked our way down the crowded main thoroughfare. It was a hot, humid night, and the languid air smelled of rotting vegetation and exotic, spicy food. The dark, oily pool that was the Olongapo River still smelled like a mixture of dead fish, motor oil, and raw sewage, but the stench was partly overcome by the spicy food smell. After a few minutes of fighting pedestrian traffic, Paul hailed a passing Jeepney. The further we got from the river, the less malodorous our surroundings became. The stench lessened to the point where I could actually take a deep breath.

For some reason, the river spelled danger. The further away we got, the more relaxed we felt, and the easier it was to breathe.

The Jeepney vehicle looked like a modified World War II jeep with an elongated bed that provided bench seating for up to six passengers. Four metal poles at the corners held a makeshift canvas roof. The roof was bright orange with multicolored triangular flags flying from the edge of the canvas top, and this was one of the more conservative cabs on the street. The canvas roof looked like it might keep the sun off the passengers but would be totally ineffective in a driving rain.

These vehicles served as a mass-transit system in this teeming, throbbing, overcrowded city. Jeepneys were completely open, and the ride was bouncy and bone-jarring, forcing passengers to hang on for dear life as the vehicle tried to outmaneuver the ruts and gullies of the unevenly paved and unpaved streets. The Jeepney rides were always a little treacherous. Riding wasn't much faster than walking, but it was a little cooler.

In the evening the heat was less intense, but each building—indeed, each inanimate object—seemed to store and radiate the day's heat. Chuck asked if we had ever ridden in a Jeepney. "No," I said, "but the metal bench seating and lack of suspension seem familiar!" My thought was that this was more like riding a horse than riding in a taxi.

Paul asked if the odor could be identified. Gordon remarked, "It smells like a mixture of sewage, spicy exotic cooking, and traffic fumes." The pungent aroma somehow added to the pulsating excitement of Po City.

The atmosphere of unease was pervasive, and the intense feeling of foreboding was difficult to explain. The history of the Philippines during World War II augured a nervousness in me that prevailed even before we'd landed at Clark Air Force Base in Manila. Perhaps this feeling of unease and queasiness came from the history of the Japanese brutal treatment of American and Filipino soldiers, as well as the harsh treatment of the local civilian population, during World War II.

The Japanese soldiers felt vastly superior to any other racial group. Their culture emphasized the advantages of being "chosen" people.

If any Filipino residents came to the aid of an Allied soldier during the forced march from Corregidor, they were also beaten, shot, or beheaded by the Japanese invaders. The history of the Bataan Death March and the fighting on Corregidor was somewhat unnerving. The Japanese army knew where all our armaments were located, just as the chief had related to us on the bus ride to Subic Bay. The battle for Corregidor and the brutal treatment by the Japanese soldiers were still fresh for many Filipinos even in 1969, more than twenty-five years after the battle. My personal contact with local Filipinos was always cordial during our brief stay in the Philippines.

Gordon directed our driver to a quiet part of the city where he had discovered, courtesy of a Filipina friend, the Lazy Swan Restaurant. His command of the local language (Tagalog) was quite passable, and Chuck also spoke it a little. When I asked how he had learned it, Gordon replied, "After several visits to the Philippines and after you've gotten to know some of these girls well enough, you've got to learn some of the language for self-defense. The Filipina women are kind and bright, but they will talk your ear off if you can't talk back."

An Evening at the Lazy Swan

The Lazy Swan was a bar, nightclub, and dinner joint all rolled into one. If any of us had doubts about the establishment from its outward appearance, the minor doubts turned into outright concern once we were inside.

Gordon flashed us a toothy smile. "Don't panic yet." Gordon assured us he had eaten there a few times and said it was clean with terrific food that wasn't too spicy.

It took me a few minutes to get accustomed to the gloom. It was early evening, and the restaurant was sparsely populated. The walls were a dark pink decorated with World War II campaign posters. None of the posters were very complimentary toward the Japanese. I passed my hand over a couple of the tables as we were escorted to our seats. Although the tables were not well lit, they didn't feel greasy.

As we sat at a circular table near the far wall, a young waitress immediately appeared at our side. Instead of taking our order for a beer, she began stroking the back of Paul's neck! She looked about fourteen or fifteen years old and flat-chested, but she was very pretty, with sparkling dark eyes and shoulder-length, silky black hair. Three other girls who could have been her sisters materialized out of nowhere. They seemed to want to involve themselves with the rest of us. Gordon remarked, "My waitress has quite perky tits."

It didn't seem necessary to have four waitresses for one table until one of them whispered in my ear, "You numba one sailor! Short time, five dollar; long time fucky-fucky all night, fifteen dollar."

When I rasped, "No, thank you," she replied, "You numba one sailor. For you, you special sailor, ten dollar—fa all night!"

I leaned across the table and loudly whispered, "Hey, guys, what the devil is going on here?"

Gordon's waitress, who had now climbed into his lap, was facing him and groping his not-altogether-quiescent privates (making it difficult, I'm sure, for him to read the menu). As Gordon attempted to slide his supposed waitress off his lap, he discovered she had forgotten to wear any undergarments that evening.

He clapped his hands twice behind her back. An older woman instantly materialized, and Gordon warned her, "Mamasan, we are here to sample your delicious food and have a few beers; please respect our wishes."

The mamasan barked an order in Tagalog, and the young "waitresses" were gone in an instant. Paul said something about saving us from standing in line at the "short-arm" inspection at the base clinic the next morning. We were normal twenty-somethings with needs; our needs, however, didn't include grade-school girls. Chuck added a seemingly unnecessary comment: "It is easy to fall in love with these girls; look, but don't touch. They could be hazardous to your health!"

Paul retorted, "If you care for that sort of sex, the young whores would park themselves between your legs under the table and give you pretty good head while you enjoy your meal." That was a difficult scene for any of us to conjure up.

*****

On reflection, the way young Filipina women were treated by some of the American soldiers should have been no surprise. Fifteen years later, in 1984, it was my honor and pleasure to lecture at three of the dental schools in Thailand. A fellow faculty member and one of my Thai students at Tufts University's School of Dental Medicine set up the trip. My brother Jon also accompanied me. He was the captain of a large oil tanker at the time and had been to Bangkok on other occasions. We stayed at a beautiful hotel in downtown Bangkok, the Dusit Thani.

The series of lectures that I was giving came from a book I had completed with a couple of professors at Tufts and one of my students at Harvard on maxillofacial orthopedic techniques. The first three-hour lecture was the morning after our arrival, at the Chulalongkorn University Dental School. Although I was slightly nervous to lecture to students who might not understand English too well, it was nothing compared to the stomach-grinding apprehension I had experienced while in the Philippines.

We had arrived at the hotel in Bangkok after a long flight on Singapore Airlines and had registered at the hotel close to midnight. As we walked to the elevator that would take us to our room, we noticed a large glass-enclosed section of the hotel lobby where five rows of bleacher-like seating were occupied by several young, very beautiful teen age looking girls. They were all dressed in the same skimpy uniform: miniskirt and tight blue top. Some of the young girls had red numbers on their shirts, and some had light blue numbers. They appeared to be around fourteen to sixteen years old.

I asked our porter, "Sir, what is going on here?"

Our young but knowledgeable porter explained that the blue numbers were for "short time," and the red numbers were for "long time, all night." Selling women as prostitutes out of a hotel lobby might have been standard practice in all the hotels in Bangkok, but it made me realize that Asian views toward women could be very different from American views. The porter gave us several hints about what to see in and around Bangkok. He mentioned a Buddhist temple, exotic Thai dancers, and several places in an area of Bangkok called Pat Pong where he said, "Sirs, you get free blow job with first drink, thank you bery much!"

*****

Back in the Philippines, we all followed Gordon's lead at the Lazy Swan and ordered the roast duck. Although small and scrawny, it was absolutely delicious. The delicate spicy flavor was perfect. Paul commented that it looked more like roast pigeon, but he ate everything except the bones and the webbed feet. The restaurant was undoubtedly used to feeding the local population; I'm sure we all could have eaten at least two servings.

One lasting memory from the restaurant involved some Filipino sailors at the bar eating *balut*. This is a Philippine delicacy that consists of unhatched duck eggs that people "season" by incubating them until the birds are almost ready to hatch and then boiling the eggs.

The men at the bar would make a small hole in the top of a shell with a knife, suck out the liquid, and then crack open the shell and eat the unborn duck body with gusto. It sounded almost like peanuts crunching in the sailors' mouths. The lucky fellows would then pick their teeth with the little webbed duck feet. There were many customs to learn about in this beautiful tropical country, but the food was delicious, and the people were fun-loving and kind.

Gordon asked us, "Would you men like to stick around and see the show?"

"What show?" I foolishly asked.

"Basically, it is Olongapo's answer to the Boston Ballet," said Paul, grinning. "There is music and dancing, and the entertainers are energetic. However, any further similarities to anything you're accustomed to seeing would be purely accidental."

"You mean it's a strip show?" I asked, demonstrating my ignorance.

"That and a whole lot more," growled Gordon with a satirical smile. "Why don't we get out of here and try to find a Jeepney?"

The show began before we had a chance to leave. The restaurant was getting busy, and the crowd seemed to be in a celebratory mood. Paul was right: there was music and dancing. The waitresses were bobbing and grinding their way across the stage while smoking cigars and opening Coke bottles with certain parts of their anatomy. The performance was denigrating and disgusting and treated the women like pure objects. The Filipino band was quite loud, the atmosphere was hazy with smoke, and the bar section was packed with jovial patrons. Paul and I followed Chuck and Gordon as they threaded their way through the throng of hooting sailors and Filipinos, making a break for the nearest exit.

Our Memorable Trip Back to Subic Bay

Our ride back to Subic Bay was almost uneventful. We walked about a mile before we could find a Jeepney with enough empty seats. Chuck and I were headed for the BOQ, and Gordon and Paul said they were just off to listen to some terrific Filipino tunes in one of the many nightclubs or music halls. They promised to stay out of trouble with the local beauties.

When asked whether they would ever bring their wives out here to Asia, Paul remarked, "Why would anyone ever want to bring a ham sandwich to a banquet?" It seemed that he was picking up some of the local attitude toward women. At first blush, this attitude seemed unhealthy, but none of us were in a position to pass judgment.

On the trip back to the main street in Olongapo City, people were getting on and off our Jeepney all the time while chatting in Tagalog. To this day, over forty years later, it still isn't clear to me whether it was the young schoolgirl prostitutes who approached us in the restaurant, the depressing, squalid housing conditions, or the open-sewer smell of the Olongapo River that gave me a feeling of unease and queasiness. The sense of foreboding that had begun on the flight to the Philippines increased as our departure time for the *Kitty Hawk* drew nearer.

As we approached the main street in Olongapo, the surroundings helped me feel a little more comfortable. Paul and Gordon got off the Jeepney to go listen to some of the scintillating music. The area was starting to look more familiar, and the music from the bars and nightclubs sounded almost exactly like American or British artists. Through the open doors of the establishments, you could see performers dressed like and adroitly mimicking the styles and voices of well-known performers.

Chuck tried to explain about the young girls in the restaurant by saying, "This is their way of life." He referred to them as "LBFMs": little brown fucking machines. Jeez, was that depressing! Chuck added, "The sailors probably look like money magnets that offer opportunities for the women to better themselves."

He continued, "Although it's really quite sad, many of these bar girls are fighting their own war: venereal disease, malnutrition, and physical and mental abuse in order to make life a little easier for themselves and their families. More than a few of these women have married US naval personnel, and they usually make excellent wives for the servicemen."

As we slowly traveled down the main street, Gordon and Paul hopped off the Jeepney and headed for a well-known dance hall in the heart of Olongapo City's music center.

While we continued riding down the main street of Po City in the back of the Jeepney, Chuck tapped me on the side of my knee to get my attention. At first I thought he wanted me to move over a little. There were several young men getting on and off the vehicle, all chatting animatedly in Tagalog. "What's happening, Chuck?" I asked, but he put his finger to his lips to silence me and gave me a hard look.

As I studied Chuck's face, trying to get some idea of what he was trying to tell me, he furtively reached under his right pant leg and quickly unsheathed a six-inch knife with a flat handle. The knife was mostly covered and hidden by his sock. He concealed it under his palm and wrist. Although I could only glimpse the knife out of the corner of my eye, it appeared to be a Fairbairn blade, which had been developed by a British soldier while he served on the Shanghai Municipal Police Force in China before World War II.

The blade was small and swordlike in appearance, sharpened on both edges. Chuck could see the panic in my eyes. Since we were slowly traversing the main street in barely moving traffic, my initial reaction was to leap out of the Jeepney and make a dash for the main gate to the base. I actually repositioned myself, at the ready to bail out. Chuck held up his index finger, signaling me to wait. I didn't realize that Chuck was able to understand a little of the Tagalog that the Filipino men were speaking. It just sounded like gibberish to me.

The city lights glinting off the steel blade were all my brain needed to go into overdrive. The idea that this marine officer was walking around with a swordlike knife in his sock gave me the shivers. The entire evening had been a bit of a shock to my system—and now this! I stiffened up, and the adrenaline pumped hard through my body. I could feel my heart beating through my fingers as I gripped the seat. It was difficult for me to get a full breath. I must have been hyperventilating.

As we got closer to the gate, with the intimidating MPs plainly visible, my body began to relax; my breathing got so that I could take a deep breath.

At that moment, our Jeepney driver suddenly hit the gas, took a sharp right turn, and sped down a darkened alley that paralleled the Olongapo River. The acceleration and sharp turn almost threw me out of the vehicle. Immediately, the three Filipino male passengers all pulled out knives that looked much too large to have been concealed.

"Watch out, Chuck," I warned, but he was busy. In one swift motion, he had grabbed the Jeepney driver from behind, put his forearm around his neck, and pulled him over the front seat so hard that if his back weren't broken by the force, something had to be dislocated at least. The driver's feet wound up flailing on the dashboard of the vehicle. Chuck's knife began to draw more than a trickle of blood on the poor devil's neck. Since the driver couldn't reach the foot pedals, the Jeepney rolled to a stop as Chuck screamed in his ear, "Main gate, main gate!"

The sight of the blood pulsating and flowing from the driver's neck was too much for his three knife-wielding riding companions. They jumped from the vehicle and vanished into the gloom of the night. In retrospect, we probably should have bolted from the Jeepney and left the driver covered in his own blood. Their plan had evidently been to rob us, use our bodies for knife practice, and toss us into the Po River.

My entire body was shaking so badly that it was difficult to stay seated. I took a deep breath and noticed that we were almost completely enveloped in the dim light of low fog and mist along the edges of the dark, hardly moving, foreboding tidal estuary. Oddly enough, I couldn't even discern the overpowering odor of the river.

Chuck had been able to decipher their wicked plans from his limited Tagalog and thwart their ambitions. As the terrified driver grudgingly turned the Jeepney around toward the main gate, Chuck suggested we omit the peso or two that was the customary fare. Screaming profanities in the driver's ear and commenting on his mother probably wasn't the most effective protest, but it made me feel somewhat better.

The driver needed immediate medical care for his spurting neck wound, which was rapidly covering his shirt and shorts with blood. It was difficult to feel sorry for him, but I placed my handkerchief in his hand and clasped his hand over his neck wound. As he dropped us off, blood was pulsating around my reddened handkerchief. With one hand over his neck wound, the blood oozing out from around his fingers, the driver sped off into the fog and dreariness that hung close to the Po River.

The marine guards at the main gate paid us little attention after we showed them our ID cards. They saluted and went about their business. Only my laundry lady would know of the indignities I suffered that night. Chuck seemed to take the attempted assault in stride and to not give it much thought. He did suggest that we stop by the Officers' Club for a nightcap.

"You may need it to calm your nerves, and you'll probably sleep better." He also needed to wash his hand, his arm, and the right sleeve of his shirt. He was covered in blood.

The whole episode seemed almost routine to him. Events later that year would give me some additional insight into the thought processes of marines. From outward appearances all that could be done in that moment was shake; it took me several hours to stop trembling.

*****

Entering the O. Club, we washed up in the men's room and then headed straight for the bar. The place wasn't crowded, and there was soft music playing throughout the dining room and lounge. The darkly paneled bar was welcoming. My reflection in the mirror behind the bar looked surprisingly normal. The entire club was tastefully furnished in somber wood hues and leather. The contrast from our earlier dining experience was mind-numbing.

We ordered a couple of scotches on the rocks, and as we rested on barstools with comfortable backs and black leather armrests, Chuck started telling me about his unit in the central highlands the previous fall. Perhaps he thought telling me a bit of his history might relax me.

On Patrol

"We responded to an emergency call from a downed marine helicopter," said Chuck. "The aircraft had been brought down by triple-A fire near the Laotian border just south of Khe Sanh. My radio operator said they had injuries and were in an exposed location out in an open area of rice paddies. They were about twelve klicks from our location.

"It was twilight—almost dark—so our unit proceeded with caution to a ridgeline within three or four kilometers of the crash site, which bordered a grassy field and rice paddies below the ridge. The North Vietnamese Army often use downed aircraft as bait to lure in other aircraft or rescue patrols, so we proceeded very cautiously. By the time our patrol arrived, it was totally dark, but we were in radio contact with the helicopter. The helicopter pilot related that they had one KIA—killed in action—from the triple-A fire, and the rest had injuries from the forced crash landing.

"While watching over the crash site, we noticed some movement near a small stream running down from the base of the ridge about three hundred meters away. The corporal in the unit whispered to me, 'Captain, take a look through the Starlight scope; the safety is on.' The scope made everything magnified and reasonably bright, but only in shades of green and black. It was mounted on the top of an M-16 assault rifle.

"As I panned the stream, a monster tiger came into view. It looked like it had green and black stripes. The animal filled the viewfinder of the scope, and he must have smelled us: at that moment the large, fierce tiger turned toward us and looked directly at me. The animal's eyes burned with a yellowish-green glow that seemed to radiate evil.

"That's when I noticed that the tiger seemed to have another interest. As I panned another hundred meters or so further on, there was additional movement beyond some rocks in the middle of the stream. It was a patrol of five gomers heading toward the helicopter and its exposed crew. The tiger was shadowing the patrol, perhaps looking for a bite to eat.

"We had to be very cautious. We had no idea whether this was the patrol of Vietcong that had brought down the helicopter or whether there were additional enemy in the area. As I watched through the Starlight scope, one of the VC lagged a few meters behind the others in the patrol. That was all it took for the tiger to lunge for his prey and lope off into the jungle. The VC victim had no chance to warn his companions. The rest of his patrol kept quietly moving toward the downed helicopter without realizing the immediate danger. One gomer down, four to go.

"We eliminated two more of the VC patrol using the Starlight scope that we remounted on our M-40 sniper rifle. This weapon is extremely accurate up to one thousand meters. The corporal was usually deadly accurate. He might have wounded or killed off the remaining two VC, starting from the last in line as he worked his way forward. The last two were probably not killed because we never found any of the enemy bodies.

"The helicopter crew was rescued after we secured the area. One of the crew died from the crash and antiaircraft fire, and the others all sustained injuries, but that was one grateful crew—especially after we told them about the giant hungry tiger.

"It was time to 'Dixie.' We called in a medevac helicopter to take out the injured as well as the deceased crew member and made our way back to our base. It was in the back of our mind that the monster tiger that had grabbed one of the VC might have a friend or might have developed a taste for human flesh."

"Hey, Chuck," I interjected, "if you're going to regale me with any more bedtime stories, I'm going to need another sixty-five-cent scotch."

"Relax, we need some sleep tonight. Sorry about the war stories, but those hoodlum creeps in the Jeepney this evening had no idea who they were dealing with."

Chapter 4

ON OUR WAY—FLIGHT OF THE COD

The flight out to the carrier deck on the carrier onboard delivery (COD) aircraft the next day was unnerving, terrifying, and thrilling at the same time. It was a relief to put some distance between us and Olongapo City. The flight itself was probably routine for the other sixteen officers and enlisted men; to me it was a nerve-racking, bone-jarring adventure.

After a thirty-five-minute flight in the extremely loud turbojet COD, we touched down on the flight deck of the *Kitty Hawk* at a speed of approximately 90–110 knots and came to a dead stop in less than three seconds. The copilot had given us explicit instructions: "Once the aircraft touches the flight deck and the tail hook engages a wire, you will be hanging in your straps. Your webbed belts and shoulder harnesses should be as tight as possible; if you are not tightly belted, the abrupt stop could snap your neck or scramble your insides." The landing felt like a controlled crash right onto the two-inch-steel flight deck of the *Kitty Hawk*.

It was difficult to believe that our landing on the deck of *Kitty Hawk* on a turboprop aircraft at this speed was taking place approximately fifty-eight years after the first pilot ever landed on a ship. Twenty-four-year-old Eugene Ely had landed on a ship in San Francisco harbor on January 18, 1911. His historic landing was only eight years after the Wright brothers' first flight on December 17, 1903, at Kitty Hawk, North Carolina. The Wright brothers' historic flight lasted all of 120 feet!

Ely landed on a 133-foot wooden landing strip built as part of an experiment on the cruiser USS *Pennsylvania*. The tail hook, affixed to the wheel axle, grabbed one or two of the twenty-two ropes strung across the flight deck. Each end of each rope was weighted with fifty-pound sandbags. He made a perfect landing and, after lunch in the officers' mess, accomplished a perfect takeoff.

Officer Country

Chuck became my first cabin mate in "officer country" aboard the *Kitty Hawk*. Our room was small and crammed with bunk beds, two pull-down desks with two swivel chairs and storage above and below, and two small closets. Chuck was a great person to room with; he taught me a lot about shipboard protocol and uniform etiquette. Although crammed, the room was quite comfortable.

The noise from the steam catapults was almost deafening and quite startling the first time I heard it. The firing of the catapults resulted in a loud hissing sound from the compression of the pistons. In addition, the hydraulic arresting gear and the snap of the arresting wire made a high-pitched screeching noise that caused a person to break out in a cold sweat the first time he heard it. All that equipment seemed to be directly over our heads. It was amazing how fast we got used to the tumult, the confused cacophony of banging sounds, and the roar of jet aircraft taking off and landing on the "roof" of our new home. After the first night, getting to sleep was never a problem. We worked long hours and were usually dog-tired at the end of the day.

Chuck was one dedicated, smart, and tough marine. His quick, violent reflexes on the Jeepney after the attempted assault contrasted remarkably with his calm, poised, and polite manner on the ship. Although confident, he seemed completely devoid of arrogance. Perhaps marine officers get special training in how to handle perplexing situations in periods of extreme duress.

This characteristic coolness under fire would be demonstrated in spades by other marines in just a few short months. It took a few days for me to completely recover from the trip to Olongapo City. The experience had done nothing to ease the pervasive feeling of foreboding that was gnawing at the pit of my stomach. The only other time Chuck ever raised his voice in my presence occurred when he was giving a guided tour of the ship's brig.

Brig Tour

The brig was a small complex that consisted of an office and two cells, located deep in the bowels of the *Kitty Hawk*. On the day Chuck showed me around, there was one sinewy, tough-looking, muscular prisoner in the cell who had been caught stealing from another sailor. Chuck ordered the marine corporal guarding the brig to open the cell door so that he could "inspect" the cell.

The prisoner was a mean-looking bastard with a protruding lower jaw and gnarled teeth. The marine corporal guarding the brig was a rather large African American marine whom no one would consider messing with. The guard must have been six feet four and wore a uniform that seemed almost one or two sizes too small for his frame. He looked much too large for his small office and even too large to get through some of the passageways on the *Kitty Hawk*.

My first thought was that unlocking the cell might prove extremely unwise. "Captain, are you sure you want to do that?" I asked. The prospect of his unlocking the cell with the scary-looking prisoner inside was a little unsettling.

With a quick nod to me, Chuck ordered, "You, Puke! Up against the back wall!" He delivered the order in a loud, commanding voice within a couple inches of the prisoner's ear. The tone of his voice scared me, and I was six feet behind him. The corporal simultaneously chambered a round in his rifle.

This so-called tour was pretty unnerving. Chuck assured me, "If a prisoner tries to escape, the corporal has authorization to shoot him." He also mentioned, "It's a long swim in shark-infested waters for any prisoner to get to some very hostile territory, the coast of North Vietnam."

*****

Maintaining very tight security on a ship the size of the *Kitty Hawk* was crucial for its smooth operation. The sixty-five enlisted marines and two officers were always busy with various aspects of the ship's security. This marine detachment (or MARDET) stood watch in all parts of the ship, from the bilge area to the bridge. In addition, they had various specialized teams such as the Reactionary Force for internal security, the Flight Deck Alert Force to deter unwanted aircraft from our flight deck, and the Operation Gunsmoke Force to discourage unauthorized boarding, especially while we were in port.

On two occasions, Operation Gunsmoke quickly foiled the plans of intruders who wanted to gain access to the *Hawk* while the ship was in Hong Kong. In addition, it was rumored that the MARDET also guarded the nuclear weapons. Since weapons were not the dental department's area of expertise, we never knew for sure whether the ship carried nuclear weapons, though we had our suspicions.

Chapter 5

HONG KONG LIBERTY WITH THE YANKEE AIR PIRATES MUSIC SOCIETY, AUGUST 1969

After I had been on the ship for a couple of months, one of the flight deck officers heard about my banjo and invited me to come to a *Kitty Hawk* Band rehearsal. It was an honor to play music with these men, many of whom were semiprofessional or professional musicians. The trumpet player could play hundreds of tunes by ear and had played in a professional band.

My only previous experience playing professionally had been with the Red Garter Corporation on 2222 Market Street in Philadelphia. My position as third banjo player in a beer-and-peanuts joint had been a pleasant diversion on the weekends during my third and fourth years of dental school.

The Red Garter was a small, dark, packed nightspot near Center City, Philadelphia. The floor was usually carpeted with peanut shells, damp with beer, and populated by enthusiastic, somewhat inebriated college coeds. All of us in the band encouraged the audience to indulge in beer by gulping our own beer out of a full pitcher by our side. Our pitchers were considerably watered down, and I was never able to build enough confidence to meet a lot of women. Life as a single dental student carried a lot of stress. I was grateful to be able to mitigate a little of that stress by making fun music with this banjo band on weekends.

Although I was terrified to play in front of a large audience, it was delightfully fun to learn all the music. Playing at the Garter in front of an audience in Philadelphia did help build my confidence in some music ability. We played mostly old-time favorites, show hits, and Dixieland, and the shipboard band concentrated on many of these same tunes.

*****

The shipboard band was my first encounter with a fabulous trombone player and pilot from the air wing, who later became a friend on the ship—Lt. Daniel Kirk. The trombone really added breadth and depth to the music. He could ad-lib almost any of the music the rest of us could play. His confidence was contagious.

Our next port of call was the liberty port of Hong Kong. The public relations department had arranged for many of the wives of the ship's company to come out for a visit coinciding with our time at this exotic port. Daniel's family included three young children, so his wife wasn't able to travel to the Orient; it was wonderful, however, to hear all about his family. He was totally devoted and loved to tell everyone about them.

Daniel had lots of humorous anecdotes about his wife and each of his children. What impressed me was his dedication and devotion to his young family. You could tell his love of flying didn't compensate adequately for how much he missed his loved ones. Although I was single at the time and didn't have to worry about children to raise or a family to support, his dedication made me think about how incredibly wasteful this war in Southeast Asia was to American interests.

*****

The war had degemerated into "Johnson's War." Lyndon Johnson was president for most of the Vietnam War buildup, and he and his general in charge, "Westy" Westmoreland, were prosecuting the war on a political footing instead of a solid military plan. When General Curtis LeMay retired from the US Air Force in January 1965, he made clear the strategy that he would implement to end the war quickly. It wasn't until December 1972 that his plan, Operation Linebacker and B-52s from the Eighth Air Force, brought the North Vietnamese to the bargaining table.

In 1985 LeMay commented to a news reporter, "In Japan we dropped 502,000 tons of bombs and we won the war. In Vietnam we dropped 6,162,000 tons of bombs and we lost the war. The difference was that McNamara (JFK's controversial secretary of defense) chose the targets in Vietnam and I chose the targets in Japan."

The Tet Offensive in the winter of 1968 seemed to catch many of the generals, including Westmoreland, literally with their pants down. The Tet Offensive did not bring the North Vietnamese generals the hoped for outpouring of popular support from the South Vietnamese people. However, there was enough backlash from the American public and from well-placed politicians in the United States to cause President Johnson to rethink his political ambitions for a second term.

Both Eugene McCarthy and Robert Kennedy made statements after the Tet Offensive indicating that they would be in favor of a negotiated settlement and a military withdrawal from Vietnam. President Johnson saw the writing on the political wall and stated in a television appearance on March 31, 1968, "I shall not seek, nor will I accept, the nomination of my party for another term as your president."

******

The Tet Offensive, seemed like a total impossibility to most American politicians, generals, and highly placed political "thinkers" at the Pentagon. It was an exceptionly well planned and coordinated attack on all the major cities and provincial capitals in South Vietnam.

The main architect of the plan was North Vietnamese General Vo Nguyen Giap. He was the same general who was victorious in the Vietminh battle against the French in May, 1954 at Dien Bien Phu. It was his plan to take the war to the cities of South Vietnam with the two cardinal principles of the art of war: secrecy and surprise. He wanted to make the population of South Vietnam insecure in their cities; and he hoped the American population would grow weary of a protracted struggle in a country so far from their home.

******

After easily winning the California primary in early June 1968, Robert Kennedy left a congratulatory reception *via* a shortcut through the kitchen of the Ambassador Hotel in Los Angeles. He was trying to avoid the crush of reporters and well-wishers. But evil was lurking in the kitchen. Sirhan Sirhan, a disgruntled Palestinian, fired one shot from a small-caliber handgun. It caught Kennedy right behind the ear, and the promising presidential candidate died the next morning without regaining consciousness.

*****

On the *Kitty Hawk* our public relations department had set up a buffet and dance in the grand ballroom of the Peninsula Hotel in Hong Kong for the officers and their wives or girlfriends. Our band was part of the entertainment for the party. Although we were all pretty nervous about playing in front of a large crowd, Daniel assured everyone that it would go well.

To warm up for the Peninsula Hotel gig, we practiced on the Star Ferry that went between Hong Kong and Kowloon. Fifteen American band members played Dixieland music for a boatload of Chinese businessmen and tourists—and they loved it! None of us had a clue that the Chinese were so fond of old-time American favorites. It was an excellent warm-up for the Peninsula performance and really boosted our confidence. Most of the band members were pilots; that's why the band was appropriately called the Yankee Air Pirates Tonkin Gulf Music Society. The name could well have come from the North Vietnamese.

Hong Kong was a terrific liberty port. Our reception at the Peninsula Hotel was cheered with much passion and enthusiasm. We played in front of several hundred people, and it seemed like the entire kitchen and waitstaff from the hotel as well as our honored guests cheered us on.

The next night we debuted at the Hong Kong Hilton. At the Hilton we started off with a medley of show hits: "Hello, Dolly," "Cabaret," and "Lara's Theme" from *Dr. Zhivago.* We played for about forty-five minutes before taking a break. The crowd's wild cheering demanded that we keep playing. After about a ten-minute break we continued with "Up a Lazy River," "Dixie," "Bye Bye Blues," and the theme from *Thoroughly Modern*

Millie. It seemed like we were hogging the show, and I felt a little bad for the dance band that had been hired, but the crowd seemed to enjoy our music.

After our enthusiastic and almost inspiring reception at the Hilton, I had packed up the banjo, and it was about time for one last pass at the buffet. As I was headed for some desserts on the buffet tables, a young woman approached me and started a casual conversation about the ship and our pilots. She seemed to want to know about our schedule. Perhaps she had an interest in our next ship visit to Hong Kong, I thought.

She was an absolute stunner and said her name was Jinju. Her scent was pure delight. She smelled like a field of flowers. She also was dressed in a rather revealing, almost provocative outfit that left very little to the imagination. She was so beautiful that my brain flashed a signal: look, but don't touch.

"You should talk to one of the other band members about our schedule," I replied. "Most of them are pilots or flight deck officers and would be able to tell you much more about what they are involved in on the *Hawk.*"

Almost immediately, we were joined by her equally beautiful and curvaceous friend Suzie. I was in the middle of the Hong Kong Hilton's grand ballroom. Two of the most beautiful women on the planet were actually talking to a lowly lieutenant from Massachusetts. Their ardent passion about our conversation was surprising. Unfortunately, by this time, many of the band members had left the ballroom. Still, it certainly couldn't hurt for my remaining shipmates to see me mingling with these two absolutely stunning goddesses.

Something should have occurred to me when Jinju kept touching my arm and chest. My first thought was that she was pointing out food stains on my elegant Filipino-style shirt. I kept looking down at what she was touching. Finally, in a very sexy voice, she invited us—Suzie and me—up to her room for a sandwich.

Looking back on this incident, it is hard to believe the stupidity of my reply: "Oh, thanks so much, but we had a wonderful buffet right here in the ballroom. You ladies could probably still get something to eat even now."

Oddly enough, the beautiful women seemed to lose their appetite and simply vanished, leaving me wondering what had gone wrong.

On the launch back to the *Hawk* that night, one of the medical officers from the ship explained to me that in Hong Kong, a sandwich had nothing to do with food. He claimed that they might have been looking for information on the ship's operation or future schedule. "You were smart to graciously decline their invitation."

"I guess it was just my luck."

*****

Another interesting incident occurred the next evening. David, an engineering officer on the *Hawk*, worked somewhere in the bowels of the ship. He continually complained to anyone who would listen that it was always hot where he worked. He was from the Bradenton area in Florida and said he was used to working in pretty warm environments, but the engineering spaces on the *Hawk* were ridiculously hot. We used to eat together a lot because we had similar schedules and were both single at the time; also, he would use any excuse to get out of the sweltering engineering spaces.

At lunch in the air-conditioned wardroom the day after the Hilton performance, I was sharing a casual meal of a sandwich and chips with my pilot friend and fellow band member Daniel. David came over to our table and joined us for lunch. He excitedly remarked, "Hey, guys, I found out about a little supper club called 'Sing for Your Supper' in Kowloon that includes a show with your meal."

A friend of David's had been there and insisted that the food was terrific and very reasonable and that the show was even better. David had a healthy appetite and a medium build that looked like it might expand into a more corpulent build if he wasn't careful.

David intoned, "It's only a short rickshaw ride from the Star Ferry landing, and you eat during the show, so it won't be a late evening." It sounded like it might be fun and worth a try, so Daniel and I agreed to join him.

The next evening the rickshaw driver knew exactly where we wanted to go and expertly wound his way around traffic and down narrow streets and alleys to our destination. We got there early, around 1930, but the place was already packed. Indirect lighting was designed to highlight the

43

bordello-red wall covering. With the ambience, the hall seemed to overflow with the one hundred or so patrons. This place was way too small for all these people. I was glad I wasn't claustrophobic.

The hostess said there was only one small table left, and it was right next to the stage. With an aversion to loud music, I though it prudent to beg off, but David said something like "Good seats are hard to find." The "stage" was only a foot or so off the floor, and if the music were loud, it could blow us off our chairs. The comely hostess assured us that the music and floor show were not loud and that normal conversation was allowed during the performance. We all threaded our way behind her and followed her to the table.

The meal was very much in the Chinese tradition and consisted of several small courses. Although it was delicious, my friends from the ship and I always felt like we could eat more. We kept expecting the next course to fill us up. It almost never did.

The "band" was an electric guitarist with the volume turned down and a "soft-handed" drummer who played something that looked like large bongo drums. About halfway through our meal, four beautiful young Asian women, who really looked like teenage models, came out onto the stage and started swaying and dancing to the beat of the music.

"For a snipe, you picked a pretty great spot for dinner," I said to David. "The music isn't too loud, and the dancers are real lookers." (A snipe was anyone who worked in the engineering spaces below deck on a ship).

It didn't seem too odd when the beautiful, graceful ladies paired up and started swing-dancing with each other. In high school, the girls would often pair up and swing-dance with each other. The music gradually slowed, and the performers on the stage started slow-dancing with each other. Although this seemed a little odd, perhaps it was an Asian cultural custom that was unfamiliar to Americans.

The music slowed some more, and the dancers started kissing and fondling each other while grinding their bodies into each other in time with the bongo drum and music. When they started doing a slow, sultry striptease with each other, it became evident that this was no regular supper club. They very slowly removed each other's clothing, one piece at a time. The young women, eventually totally naked, started making mad, passionate love to each other at our feet. Some of the things they were doing, although possibly titillating, looked almost dangerous. Daniel said, "I hope we don't lose the delicious dinner we just finished."

David stood up and suggested we skip dessert and take off. As we wound our way out of the building, the rest of the patrons seemed to be continuing unabashedly with their meal. Daniel said, "How can these folks eat with that sort of show going on?"

I remarked, "What the hell do they do for dessert?"

The next day, my physician friend from medical who had explained the "sandwich" said, "Oh yes. You get that sort of thing all over the Orient."

David apologized but quipped, "You didn't have any complaints about the food, did you?"

*****

The next day was our preparation-for-departure day from the liberty port of Hong Kong. In port, a good portion (approximately two-thirds) of a ship's company is on liberty. Once we were on our way back out to Yankee Station, our air wing began flight operations, and we all immediately fell into our shipboard routine.

For the pilots, the Yankee Air Pirates' band was a welcome break from the reality of flying dangerous combat sorties off the deck of the *Kitty Hawk*. Although the ship was their home away from home, it was a perilous and sometimes deadly environment. All the incidents and accidents that occurred on the flight deck were instantly known throughout the ship by way of the closed-circuit television news. As I learned what these naval aviators faced over enemy territory in Vietnam, my appreciation for them grew exponentially. So did my own nervous apprehension.

The entire Hong Kong liberty visit, although relaxing and very different from our normal shipboard routine in the dental department, was at the same time a little unnerving. There was another incident in Hong Kong that was related to me after we were on our way back to the Gulf of Tonkin. One of our enlisted men in the supply department got in with the wrong crowd and took an overdose of a controlled substance, probably heroin. His death in a seedy hotel room was described in the ship's newsletter: "the sailor choked to death on his own vomit." Everyone on the ship felt horrible about that news.

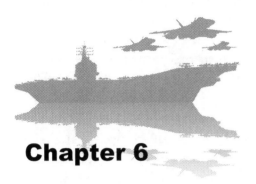

Chapter 6

DANGER ON THE FLIGHT DECK—FLY THE BALL, SEPTEMBER 1969

Over lunch the next day, Daniel explained to me that flight operations on an aircraft carrier in a combat zone could go pretty much around the clock. Our area of operations in the Gulf of Tonkin was called Yankee Station. It ranged from the southernmost tip of South Vietnam north to the Chinese waters off the island of Hainan. It extended approximately twenty miles west off the coast of South Vietnam and out about one hundred miles to the east toward the Philippine islands. There were often two or three carriers operating on Yankee Station.

The southernmost area of operation was called Dixie Station. This operating station in the South China Sea was for one carrier off the Mekong Delta.

During the period of sustained air operations against North Vietnam (March 1965–December 1972), there were normally three aircraft carriers on line that made up part of Task Force 77. Each carrier would conduct air operations for twelve hours on a rotating schedule.

The *Kitty Hawk* was the first aircraft carrier ordered to the Tonkin Gulf in April 1964. The second carrier to join the USS *Kitty Hawk*, the USS *Ticonderoga*, came out to Yankee Station in May 1964. The third big deck carrier, the USS *Constellation*, came out to Yankee Station in June 1964. All three carriers were on station two months before the Gulf of Tonkin Resolution, which was passed by the US Congress on August 7,

1964. The *Ticonderoga* and the *Constellation* conducted their first air strikes on August 5, 1964.

Since all three aircraft carriers were on Yankee Station before the Gulf of Tonkin "incident," some congressmen raised the issue of a possible false flag or provocative incident in order to take the air war to the North Vietnamese.

The *Kitty Hawk* was always protected by at least one destroyer that we could see and probably other ships beyond our horizon and field of vision. One "tin can," or destroyer, usually trailed us by one to three miles. In addition to providing carrier protection, the destroyer would also pick up any less-than-careful sailors blown off the flight deck from the thrust of the powerful jet aircraft engines or any pilots who had to ditch at sea near the carrier.

There was probably at least one submarine accompanying our small armada. And during flight operations there was always a helicopter flying "plane guard" about a mile or two off the port bow to help pick up pilots that might have an accident on takeoff or landing. An accident in the middle of the ocean often meant landing in the water. Military aircraft did not float too well or for too long on the surface, so the pilots had to exit or eject rather quickly if their aircraft was headed for a wet landing.

A naval aviator is very different from any other type of pilot. These highly trained men and women are the best of the best. The men and women who excel in carrier operations are an elite and select few: these aviators have to land on a moving runway that is about as long as a standard runway is wide.

Some of the dangers facing these aviators include catapult launches that go wrong and arresting gear landings or traps during inclement weather. Four thin wires are stretched across the flight deck. The pilot needs to catch one of the wires with a tail hook mounted on the rear of the aircraft as it lands on the deck of a moving, rolling, sometimes-pitching, always-short runway.

Even during clear weather and calm seas, landing on a carrier is basically akin to a high-speed controlled crash. It is a nerve-racking, gut-wrenching, high-speed crash landing. The pilot must land under full power. If he or she misses the arresting wires, the aircraft needs enough speed to take off again for another attempt at landing. If all four wires are missed with the tail hook, it is called a bolter.

When a pilot is out in the middle of the ocean with nothing but blue water surrounding the ship's flight deck, the options are a bit limited for landing. This piloting operation takes a highly trained aviator with nerves of steel. I would often break out in a nervous sweat just watching what the pilots went through to bring their aircraft in for a safe landing on the flight deck.

The catapult launch presents an entirely different set of problems. The aircraft is basically flung off the ship while the pilot maintains full power. The pilot grips a fixed T-shaped throttle brace while he brings the engines to full power during the launch. If his hand slips off the throttle brace due to the G- forces from the catapult launch, the plane will lose power and crash into the sea in front of the ship.

Once the steam-driven catapult is attached to the aircraft by way of a shuttle connection and the hold-back bar is in place, the catapult officer, or cat officer, raises the jet blast deflector. Now the pilot can bring the jet engines up to full power without affecting the aircraft or personnel directly behind him. The hold-back bar prevents the aircraft from moving. On the pilot's salute, the cat officer fires the steam piston that throws the aircraft off the ship. The powerful steam catapult can accelerate a 45,000-pound aircraft up to 165 miles per hour in two seconds. The cat shot gives the pilots an amazing thrill ride. However, there are numerous difficulties that can arise with the launch: mechanical issues with the aircraft or catapult or errors from the deck crew or pilot.

Flight Deck Dangers

The worst accident on the ship in 1969 was a disastrous COD launch. The COD aircraft was a turboprop that could seat up to twenty people. This was the same type of aircraft that had flown us onto the *Hawk* earlier in the summer. On this particular day, the COD carried six passengers and a strapped-down jet engine in need of repair. There was a complete avionics or engine machine shop at the Subic Bay Naval Station at Cubi Point that could repair almost any part of our aircraft. This particular accident still causes me nightmares. Even retelling the incident causes nausea. It was an ill omen for what was to come.

After work, it was common practice to go up to the tower, the highest point on the ship, to unwind and watch flight operations in order to wrap up the day. After a day mostly spent removing wisdom teeth from eighteen- to twenty-five-year-old sailors, it was exciting yet relaxing to watch routine flight operations. My roommate at the time was a fellow dentist from California. Jim and I climbed up several flights of stairs and ladders to an open space at the top of the *Kitty Hawk*'s tower. Since we were both dentists, watching the flight ops was a totally new and amazing experience for us. The smell of the jet fuel (JP-5) and the exhaust from the *Kitty Hawk* bunkers assaulted our senses and often caused dizziness. After a couple of weeks, it didn't bother us anymore.

This particular evening, the catapult officers were launching F-4s, A-6s, and A-7s heavily loaded with ordnance (bombs, rockets, antiaircraft missiles, machine-gun ammunition, and fuel), to send them on their way to their targets. Daniel insisted that landing on the flight deck was more challenging than taking off. He mentioned that landing on the flight deck at night during a storm was particularly hazardous, "like trying to land on a bobbing toothpick."

It was always a wonder to me how the cat officers and deck crew got the planes, loaded with ordnance, up to the catapults and fired them off the deck so smoothly. One false positioning of the flight deck crew could blow them off the flight deck and ten stories down into the Gulf of Tonkin. The backwash of the jet engines was somewhat unpredictable and always dangerous. That particular evening was clear and calm, though there was heavy humidity in the Gulf of Tonkin. The ever-present stench of jet fuel fouled the air, but the ocean sparkled with the glint of flying fish coursing through our bow wake.

The roar of the multiple jet aircraft engines and the sour, pungent smell of the JP-5 jet fuel were truly nauseating. The professionalism and efficiency of the flight deck personnel were exemplary. They literally ran an airport, with hundreds of takeoffs and landings each week, on a very limited amount of runway space surrounded by stacks of bombs and jet fuel. Indeed, Lloyds of London considers flight deck officer one of the most dangerous jobs in the world.

It was the last catapult launch of the day. I decided to return to the officers' wardroom and see what was on the menue for dinner. There was only one aircraft, the COD, left for takeoff on the catapult. It was carrying six passengers and a jet engine in need of repairs back to Subic Bay. After a picture-perfect cat shot, it was time to head down the ladder and get cleaned up for the junior officer first seating in the wardroom. After the second seating (for the senior officer's dinner), each evening there was a movie played for all the officers.

All of a sudden, a strange screeching sound came from the departing COD. Both turboprop engines sounded very strange, almost like a high-pitched whine—actually more like a scream. Turning back to look at the aircraft, we saw that it had assumed an almost perpendicular angle to the bow of the flight deck. It was pointing almost straight up! The only aircraft I had ever seen take off at such an extreme angle was the spy plane SR-71, nicknamed "Black Bird." That aircraft, shaped like a rocket with wings, seemed to climb effortlessly up to seventy or eighty thousand feet at what seemed like close to a ninety-degree angle from the flight deck.

Something had gone terribly wrong with the COD. It seemed to be struggling in this perpendicular attitude with the turboprops fighting, screaming, and thrashing to claw back to a proper glide angle. The aircraft hovered with an earsplitting shriek for almost three seconds before it lost its struggle with gravity and slowly sank out of sight below the flight deck. All we heard was a loud, sickening crunch of metal on metal, confirming that the COD was completely squashed under the weight of the bow section of the *Kitty Hawk* as it proceded at flank speed required for catapult launches.

It was theorized later that the jet engine aboard the COD for repair could not have been strapped down sufficiently to counter the powerful catapult surge. It had probably killed all the passengers as it shot to the back of the aircraft, even before the plane sank in front of our ship. There was nothing the captain or crew of the *Kitty Hawk* could have done to avert this horrible tragedy. It was an extremely unnerving and unsettling accident; those men had been our friends and coworkers.

The COD almost crashed tail first on the bow section of the flight deck. The *Hawk* was under full power for flight ops and traveling over 30 knots. Had the COD crashed and exploded on the bow of our flight deck, there is no telling what the consequences could have been. There were some aircraft still loaded with fuel, bombs, and rockets sitting on the flight deck and on the hangar deck one deck below.

*****

The second-worst accident witnessed by our ship's dental technicians had a far different ending. One early evening, two techs from our dental department were up on the tower watching flight operations. Our ship had turned into the wind, and we were getting ready to commence flight ops. A few of the A-6s and A-7s had been launched, and it was time to launch a pair of F-4s. The catapult crew had fastened the barbell-like yoke to the first F-4 and was getting ready to fire the catapult. The cat officer had his hand up, waiting for the pilot to first nod or salute that he was set at full power: when the cat officer swings his arm down and points it toward the bow and touches the deck, there is a slight delay of a second or so, but there is no stopping the steam catapult as it fires the aircraft off the ship.

The pilot gave the salute, and the cat officer swung his arm in a wide arc and touched the deck as he pointed to the bow of the ship, signaling to the pilots that the catapult had been fired. In that split-second, the entire rear of the aircraft burst into flames. But there was no stopping the F-4 aircraft. It roared down the flight deck trailing a huge ball of smoke and flames behind it—a spectacular sight in the early evening twilight.

The aircraft had made it about a quarter mile off the ship when the ship's captain ordered over the speakers, "Just-launched F-4, squadron VF-114, both pilots punch out!" There was a puff of smoke as both pilots blew through their canopy. Their chutes hadn't even opened before there was a tremendous explosion as the plane blew apart. Some of the aircraft parts blew back down onto the *Kitty Hawk*'s flight deck.

Both pilots were rescued by the helicopter that flew plane guard for the ship. One of the pilots told me a few nights later, "We never even thought about questioning the old man's order to eject from the aircraft." That was an impressive display of leadership and training, particularly since neither pilot realized their aircraft was on fire. The pilot explained to me that following the old man's orders was the surest way of staying alive on perhaps the most dangerous piece of real estate in the world: the flight deck of a US Navy aircraft carrier during flight operations.

*****

The same pilot remembered one other incident while the ship was moored at the dock on Coronado Island, San Diego, California. A high-ranking supply admiral had come aboard for an inspection and visitation. As he toured the flight deck, he lit up a cigar.

The chief bosun's mate accompanying the group quickly knocked the cigar out of the admiral's hand and stomped it out in front of all the dignitaries. In addition, he admonished the admiral in front of everyone. "Sir, you cannot have any open flames or smoking materials on this flight deck at any time."

Later, the ship's captain put a letter in the chief's record, complimenting him on his quick thinking and politeness to the admiral during an exceedingly dangerous and politically ticklish situation.

*****

Landing on the flight deck of an aircraft carrier at night is not easy; during stormy weather at night, it can be absolutely terrifying. It is a very short landing strip that rolls from side to side, pitches in heavy surf, and moves forward at twenty to thirty knots while rain beats on the pilot's windscreen. Pilots are usually dog-tired from flying around unfamiliar landscapes and dropping their ordnance in the dark while trying to avoid antiaircraft fire, a plethora of surface-to-air missiles, tons of flak, and the peaks of fog-shrouded mountains.

In addition to inclement weather, there are often wide-ranging temperature differences that affect the performance of the aircraft and the ordnance that is delivered. A pilot can go from cool, dry, mountainous conditions to torrential rain with humid and very hot conditions in a matter of seconds, flying at four to five hundred miles per hour. Flying under these conditions is difficult at best.

The men in Daniel's squadron looked up to him and referred to him as "The Magnet" because his expert, aggressive flying almost always made him the one to draw the surface-to-air missiles out of the bushes. When I first met Daniel, he seemed very relaxed, almost a "happy-go-lucky" type with very few worries. Just meeting him, one would never know what nerves of hardened steel and fearlessness in combat were locked up inside him. He would always temper remarks about his flying ability by saying, "Our main goal is to get the job done safely."

*****

On one stormy night, I found that watching flight ops on a monitor was easier and much more comfortable than watching out in the open observation deck of the tower. Since this was monsoon season, it was an absolutely horrible night for flying.

A lot of the squadron pilots had decided to fly back to the airfield at Da Nang or Cubi Point Naval Air Station, adjacent to Subic Bay, rather than chance a night landing during this particularly dark and stormy evening. Unfortunately, the weather at Da Nang was rapidly deteriorating and finally forced the closing of the airport. One unlucky A-6 pilot had used up most of his fuel and all his luck over the Ho Chi Minh Trail. He had insufficient fuel to reach the airport at Cubi Point in the Philippines, and the weather had socked in all available airports in South Vietnam. His wingman had enough fuel to make it to Cubi Point. It was so stormy that the tanker pilots who frequently refueled the aircraft found it too nasty for a launch.

The pilot, Lieutenant Henderson, knew he was safe in the air. It was trying to land on that bobbing toothpick where things might get a little dicey. His first landing attempt onto the flight deck was a little high.

*****

There were four parallel arresting wires spaced about fifty feet apart on the flight deck of the *Kitty Hawk*. The newer aircraft carriers need only three wires. The very latest aircraft carriers on the drawing boards have done away with much of the arresting gear and catapults altogether. In the future, aircraft will hover and just plunk themselves down or lift themselves off the flight deck.

The new F-35 being tested now in Florida will replace at least three different aircraft and provide an attack fighter-bomber for use by the US Navy, Marines, and Air Force. Although the cost of this aircraft may sink it in its final version, approximately two thousand of these stealthy, sleek aircraft are on tentative order. One of the problems interfering with its stealth characteristics is the large hump behind the pilots. The hump is for a large turbofan jet that allows for vertical takeoff and landings. The short landing feature is excellent for the newer carriers and for the marines who may need short takeoff and landing capabilities.

Everything on the F-35 is sleek. There are no external fuel tanks or armaments. The aircraft is stealthy and streamlined. There is even consideration of eliminating the tail hook. That, however, would restrict the plane from traditional landings on older carriers; the plane would need to depend on vertical landing capabilities for all aircraft carriers.

On future carriers, the aircraft could be pilotless! The pilot could sit in a comfortable office on the ship and fly the aircraft with computer-aided controls.

*****

Each end of the arresting wires on the older carriers is attached to a hydraulic cylinder below the deck. This cylinder absorbs the energy from the pull of the wire as the plane's tail hook snags the arresting gear wire. These wires are high-tensile, woven steel cables, up to one-and-three-eighths inches thick, with an oiled hemp core. This core provides a cushion and lubrication for the abrupt tension on the wire as the landing aircraft tail hook snags it. This arresting gear mechanism can stop a 54,000-pound aircraft traveling at 150 miles per hour in 3 seconds on a landing strip only 300 feet long.

Although the pilot's objective was to catch any one of the four wires, the third wire was the most desirable. The first wire was closest to the stern of the ship; coming in at too low an angle could cause the pilot to crash into the stern of the ship. The fourth wire was a little chancy because a missed wire trap would entail a full-power takeoff from what was left of the angled flight deck. Misses or bolters were uncommon—except in stormy weather. During the A-6's first landing attempt, the tail hook hit the deck about thirty feet beyond the fourth wire. The pilot had no choice but to maintain full power and take off from what little was left of the flight deck.

*****

Landing signal officers, or LSOs, guide the planes in. This is a very tricky task during stormy nights. The LSO has direct contact with the pilot and is continually encouraging him to "fly the ball." The ball, or meatball, is a series of light beams set at different angles in the sky, mounted on a gyroscopically stabilized platform. If the pilot's angle of approach is correct, the ball will glow amber in line with a series of green lights. If the pilot comes in too high, the amber light shows above the green lights; if too low, the amber light is below the green row of lights. If the angle is dangerously low, then the pilot sees red lights.

On this particular night, under the most difficult and squalid weather conditions imaginable, Lieutenant Henderson was tired, nervous, probably extremely apprehensive, and about out of fuel. Sweat was trickling down his back, and his hands were soaked inside his gloves. His second approach looked very shaky on the in-house television screen. As he approached the stern of the ship, it looked like he was trying to gauge his wing angle and keep it parallel to the roll of the ship. The LSO later stated that he could tell the pilot was extremely apprehensive, even though his voice was calm and professional.

To this day it isn't clear exactly what happened, even though the entire landing sequence was clearly visible and recorded on the television monitor. It looked like the lieutenant tried to set his aircraft on the deck to catch the third wire. He missed. However, his left wingtip edge caught the fourth wire as the ship rolled in the storm. This flipped his aircraft. An explosion followed, and sparks, flames, and smoke careened down the angled flight deck as the inverted aircraft then went over the side and down ten stories into a very stormy sea.

*****

Lieutenant Henderson now had a predicament. Stuck inside his aircraft in the stormy Gulf of Tonkin, he was strapped to his seat, completely disoriented, and scared out of his mind. Here is where training and experience kicked in. Reacting immediately, he reached down between his legs and pulled hard on his ejection handle.

There was only one problem: his aircraft was inverted in the water. The explosive charge under his seat drove him through his shattered canopy and straight down into the gulf; the worst scenario possible. Now the pilot was underwater and entangled in his parachute lines. He probably said his prayers, knowing his aircraft would not float at all and was about to sink like a rock.

As the ship sped past his sinking aircraft, the wake of the *Kitty Hawk* and the turbulence from its powerful 280,000-horsepower-engine backwash tossed the aircraft around as if it were made of cork. Underwater, almost completely out of air and out of options, Lieutenant Henderson frantically struggled with his parachute lines, helmet, and other gear. Suddenly, he felt something firm under his feet. He tried standing. The wing of the aircraft had actually come up to meet his feet and propelled him to the surface.

Watching this horrific accident unfold on the television monitor, I was sure he was a goner. But there he was one hour later on the television, telling us of his miraculous survival. Apparently, the backwash had been so powerful that it flipped the plane over, allowing a wing to catch his feet as it turned over, lifting him out of the water. This allowed him to take a breath, inflate his emergency life jacket, and cut his way free of the parachute shrouds. The destroyer guard trailing us immediately plucked him out of the South China Sea.

The aircraft had to be completely destroyed after roaring down the flight deck inverted. I was positive the pilot had been crushed, burned, asphyxiated, or all three, on his way to a watery grave.

It was this miraculous outcome that decades later gave me hope for Daniel's survival after his plane went down in Laos.

*****

Since the location of Daniel's aircraft crash in the Laotian jungle could be pretty well determined with some precision and accuracy, why is it that only a helmet can be found after all these years? Does the government of the United States know anything more about the fate of this pilot and scores of other pilots and servicemen listed as MIA/BNR (missing in action/body not recovered)? Is it possible that any of these men could be prisoners of war to this day?

Joseph D. Douglass Jr. has written about the possibility of American prisoners of war being held by the Soviet Union, China, and Czechoslovakia since the end of the Korean and Vietnam Wars. His book *Betrayed* includes information from a Czechoslovakian general major, Jan Sejna, who sought asylum in the United States in 1968.

General Sejna fled Czechoslovakia in February 1968 after he learned of his imminent arrest. He appeared before the Senate Select Committee on POW/MIA Affairs on November 5, 1992. At this meeting he discussed what he knew of the prisoners of war in Vietnam and Laos. He claimed he was in a position to know about many POWs because he had held an official position that brought him into "direct contact" with various Soviet operations involving POWs from the Korean and Vietnam Wars.

The general claimed to have been present at many of the meetings in the Soviet Union and Czechoslovakia where the fate and disposition of many of these prisoners was discussed among Czechoslovak, Soviet, Korean, and North Vietnamese officials. Part of his testimony was especially chilling: "Special experiments were devised and run to test the psychological and physiologic endurance limits of US servicemen. POWs were also used as guinea pigs to test a variety of chemical and biological warfare agents and drugs that were being developed for military and military intelligence use."(From Douglass, Joseph D. Jr., "Betrayed" 2002. p 275)..

In addition to studying the effectiveness of different "mind control" drugs, Sejna was also directly involved with international narcotic trafficking designed to bring a flood of drugs into the United States, directly targeting US youth. According to the general, the Soviets believed that this narcotic trafficking into the United States was one of their "most important and successful" military intelligence operations.

The question is still in the minds and thoughts of many people in the United States: what has happened to the scores of military personnel who have never been recovered from the Vietnam War?

Chapter 7

In-Country Vietnam, November 1, 1969

It had always been a mystery to me why some of my friends and dental colleagues who were stationed in Vietnam would try to get out to the *Kitty Hawk* in order to go on leave and R&R. One might think that a more exotic or friendly location would be a higher priority and much more exciting. Bangkok, Okinawa, Singapore, and Hawaii all came to mind. There were no women on the *Kitty Hawk*.

A friend I had met while in dental school, JB, worked as a nurse at a hospital in Philadelphia and had also joined the navy. He played the trumpet and was a frequent stand-in when we both played at the Red Garter on Market Street in Philadelphia. He was very talented and could improvise and play almost any music included in our repertory of old-time favorites, show hits, and Dixieland.

He came out to our ship for a week's leave from the hospital at the Tan Son Nhut Air Base and explained it this way: "Even though you work a full day every day, including weekends and holidays, and see emergencies twenty-four hours a day, you have terrific food, clean sheets and towels, and air conditioning that is reliable, and no one is shooting or lobbing rockets at you." A series of events on the *Hawk* helped me understand his logic. JB shared some terrifying experiences with me in Quang Tri Provence near the seventeenth parallel in northern South Vietnam.

*****

When I was on duty one evening in the dental clinic, there was an emergency call from the flight deck. One of the starters had suffered an accident. A starter is a member of the flight deck crew who ensures the smooth ignition of the jet aircraft that are being warmed up to fly their missions. In order to start a cold jet engine on the flight deck, ambient air is forced into the engine under extreme pressure and mixed with the JP-5 fuel, which, when the pilot fires the igniters, causes the engine to roar to life. The starting air compressor is called a huffer.

The air mixture is delivered directly into the engine from a compressor on a cart with a high-pressure (eight hundred pounds per square inch) air hose. The hose is secured to the engine with a high-pressure coupling. The compressed air starts the jet turbine spinning so that the pilot can mix in the vaporized kerosene (JP-5 fuel) and ignite the fuel mix to start the engine. The JP-5 fuel has a higher flash point than commercial fuels, which makes it somewhat safer for storage on aircraft carriers.

Evidently, the poor fellow who attached the high-pressure air hose coupling to the jet engine, Hank, hadn't secured it quite properly. As soon as the air pressure hit the metal coupling, the coupling flew off with a loud bang and broke several bones and teeth in Hank's mouth and face. The starter was brought down to sick bay on a stretcher, moaning incoherently and struggling to speak.

As soon as the medical officer had gone over the patient's record, he had a corpsman administer one hundred milligrams of intramuscular Demerol. Since I had the duty that evening, I was called over to the medical clinic for consultation. His face was covered with blood, and his lips, nose, and cheeks were so swollen that it was difficult to determine exactly what had been broken. The patient was stabilized with a head frame splint. The docs did what they could to clean and patch him up and make him comfortable, but it was obvious that Hank would need much more extensive medical and dental attention than we could render aboard the ship.

The lateral skull radiograph displayed multiple facial fractures, including the body of the mandible, the right condyle, the maxilla, the zygomatic arch on the right side, and the floor of the right orbit. Basically, his entire facial skeleton was involved, and he had lost or broken at least four maxillary teeth. His mouth was a bloody mess. One of the corpsmen, Conklin, attempted to place an intravenous line, but the patient, now completely irrational, thrashed about, and after three attempts to find a compatible vein, the corpsman decided that the ride to the closest large medical facility (a hospital ship) was short enough to avoid an IV line. The Hank was a large man and the Demerol that had been given hadn't measurably lessened his anxiety.

The department head, a navy captain, came in while I was cleaning out the patient's mouth and airway. Looking at the naval corpsman and me, he ordered, "You two get him to the hospital ship right now."

The corpsman replied with an ardent "Yes, sir!"

I nodded and answered, "Yes, Captain."

If we'd had any idea of the nightmare that was about to unfold, it is doubtful that the corpsman's confirmation would have been quite so enthusiastic.

No Joy Ride

The trip from the *Kitty Hawk* on Yankee Station to the hospital ship, the USS *Repose*, normally would have taken under one hour. Two problems made this estimate a little sticky. First, our ship was quite far north on Yankee Station. Earlier in the day, we could spot the Chinese island of Hainan, on the northern perimeter of the Gulf of Tonkin. Second, the weather was less than ideal. The ten-foot swells were of no consequence to a ship more than three football fields long, but the skies were threatening and dark with wind-whipped clouds. Light rain and salt spray peppered the flight deck. An ominous and persistent sense of foreboding washed over the ship.

The gray ship, the slate-gray sky, and the never-ending grayness of the Gulf of Tonkin put me in a less than exuberant mood for this quick trip.

Hank, strapped to a stretcher, was loaded onto the helicopter. Although it was late in the day, there was enough light left for a daylight takeoff. Since it was my turn for duty in the dental department, my commanding officer, Commander Hyde, approved my leaving the ship on an emergency mission. I made a quick call to Daniel to let him know I would miss band rehearsal that evening. He teased me by saying, "Don't worry, Doc. Our squadron has your back!" I didn't know at the time how prophetic his words would be.

It was urgent that we get Hank to an operating room where he could receive the necessary maxillofacial surgery and dental care. The medical corpsman, Second Class Petty Officer Conklin, had worked with the dental department before and was extremely competent and had a lot of common sense. We figured we'd return with the helicopter, so neither of us packed anything, not even a change of clothes.

The helicopter pilots for our trip were some of the most experienced and fearless in the world. Although these pilots were young, they constantly flew rescue missions in and out of Vietnam under the most challenging weather conditions. They were certainly not at fault for what was about to happen.

We had barely taken off from the *Hawk* when our patient started moaning and tossing about. The Demerol shouldn't have worn off so soon, but because of his size, weighing over two hundred pounds the narcotic analgesic wasn't totally effective. The corpsman tried to make the patient feel more comfortable by propping towels around his head, and I gave him another hundred milligrams of intramuscular Demerol. Hank seemed to calm down a bit, with less thrashing and moaning.

On a clear and calm day, a helicopter ride is not exactly as smooth as silk. On this particular stormy night, even strapped in, it felt like we were on some sort of carnival ride. The wild up-and-down and sideways tilt of the aircraft was making me nauseous and dizzy, but we tried to hang on and concentrate on our patient's comfort. Air sickness wasn't something I wanted to demonstrate in front of the pilots or the corpsman. We hadn't been in the air more than ten minutes when old Hank started vomiting great quantities of blood.

Whatever the general population thinks most dentists learn in dental school, this was rather new territory for me. We hadn't had time to assess Hank's internal injuries; we had just gone on the assumption that he had swallowed a lot of blood. His breathing was becoming labored, with rasping, wheezing, and coughing between fits of vomiting. It was obvious that without immediate intubation, he could not maintain a patent airway, and he could aspirate blood and stomach contents into his lungs and drown in his own blood and vomit.

However, Hank had stubborn caregivers, and we were dammed if we were going to lose him. Supplies were located for endotracheal intubation, and Conklin began to set up for that procedure or an emergency tracheotomy. While getting out the emergency supplies, we turned our patient on his side, but his breathing didn't improve even marginally.

My previous intubation experience had been under ideal operating-room conditions, with a seasoned anesthesiologist guiding every move, and that was two years earlier during an anesthesia rotation as part of postgraduate training at University Hospital in Boston. The tutor, Dr. Benjamin Kripke, was head of anesthesiology and had lobbied hard to make this a five-month instead of two-month training rotation. Little did I know during my training that someday all those techniques I learned that summer would come in handy and might save a life.

Still, applying the anesthesia training while riding a bucking helicopter on a very dark and stormy night proved extremely challenging. "Corpsman, are you up for this procedure?" I asked.

"Okay, Doc, let's give it a go. What's the worst that could happen?"

Conklin's confidence certainly surpassed my own. The helicopter kept swaying from side to side while rising and falling. I didn't want the endotracheal tube to injure his windpipe. The emergency scope had a weak light, and at first all I could see was blood and vomitus. His throat looked like it was choked up with mashed-up tomatoes. After clearing his mouth and airway, we were finally able to get Hank intubated and breathing more comfortably.

It was luck that Hank had enough Demerol on board to prevent him from going into laryngospasm. Spasm of the larynx could compromise his airway and necessitate an emergency tracheotomy, or an opening into his windpipe through his throat. Although we briefly discussed performing an emergency tracheotomy, we decided the helicopter turbulence would turn that procedure into a bloody mess. Someone upstairs was helping us. Hank started to breathe more easily—and so did the corpsman and I. Unfortunately, our troubles that night were only just beginning.

*****

One could surmise that a five-hundred-foot hospital ship painted white with a huge red cross on it, anchored in a major river in South Vietnam, would be fairly easy to find. However, the dark, moonless night, the howling wind, and the low, thick cloud cover continued to challenge our pilots. Fog had encompassed us like a cocoon, and heavy monsoon rain was beating down on the helicopter. The pilot flew lower and lower to get a visual bearing for the trip up the Mekong River to the hospital ship, USS *Repose*.

Commissioned in 1945, the *Repose* had enough beds for 750 patients. Her medical component included 25 physicians and 3 dentists in addition to 29 nurses assisted by over 300 chief petty officers and corpsmen. The ship's crew included 315 enlisted men and 25 line and staff officers. This floating city of a hospital would have been the ideal place for Hank to receive the medical and dental care he urgently needed.

Conklin glanced out the open bay of the helicopter and immediately yelled, "Captain, watch out!" We were flying low, level with the treetops in the jungle. The jungle rose up to meet us as the copter blades tipped toward the treetops. Below it looked like Fourth of July sparklers going off. Suddenly, above the noise of the aircraft and storm, we heard an unfamiliar sound, like someone throwing rocks at the bottom of the helicopter: *Bang-bang! Bang! Bang-bang! Bang!*

*****

The South Vietnamese called this area of the Mekong River that lay forty kilometers north of Saigon the Iron Triangle. The Vietcong called it home. This group of Vietnamese and their philosophy had evolved from a group founded by Ho Chi Minh in May 1941 called the Vietminh. These Vietnamese patriots had formed a government called the Democratic Republic of Vietnam on September 2, 1945.

The Geneva Accords of 1954 initially confined Ho Chi Minh's government to the northern part of Vietnam. The National Front for the Liberation of the South, or the NLF, was formed on December 20, 1960. Its stated goal was to overthrow the government of South Vietnam and reunite the north with the south. At the time of its formation, the NLF included communist and noncommunist sympathizers from both the north and the south. The term Vietcong had been used since 1956 as a derogatory reference to the NLF. The name Vietcong comes from a contraction of Vietnam Cong San, meaning Vietnamese communist.

*****

Luckily, our helicopter pilots knew exactly what was happening. We had disturbed someone's peace and quiet in the jungle and were receiving small-arms fire from some unfriendly locals, probably the Vietcong. Fortunately, on this night they didn't have heavier weapons. A rocket-propelled grenade easily could have crippled our aircraft and brought it down.

It was no accident that there was a hardened steel plate in the floor of these helicopters. If pressed, a helicopter could climb quite quickly. We shot out of there like a cork from a freshly shaken bottle of champagne. Conklin blew his lunch all over the bulkhead of the helicopter, and the bile was certainly rising in my stomach.

"Captain," I said, "we need to get Hank to a medical facility as soon as possible if we hope to save his ass."

The pilot set a course for the next nearest medical facility: Tan Son Nhut Air Base outside Saigon. As we descended through the murk and rain, a brilliantly lit runway and city emerged below us. At this time many considered Tan Son Nhut the world's busiest airport. With the mix of civilian and military air traffic, it was certainly the most chaotic. It was disconcerting to see all the sandbagged bunkers ringing the giant air base; all the defensive armaments made me uneasy. Would the Vietcong and NVA actually attack such a large, well-fortified base? Yes!

*****

The year before, on the night of January 30, 1968, the Vietcong and the North Vietnamese Army (NVA) had begun the Tet Offensive, and the giant air base at Tan Son Nhut was on their list of objectives. In addition, the Vietcong and the NVA attacked every major city and province capital in South Vietnam. General Westmoreland and many of the other high-ranking officers had no idea that the communist forces could plan and execute such a widespread attack. Westmoreland and much of the Army of South Vietnam (ARVN) had been concentrating their efforts and fortifying the border areas near Laos and Cambodia, near the seventeenth parallel, and around the firebase in the Khe Sanh area.

The Vietcong and the North Vietnamese Army were successful in their initial attacks for three reasons. First, the offensive was launched on the most important holiday in Vietnam, the Tet Nguyen Dan holiday, which marked the lunar new year. Second, the Vietcong had been completely re-equipped with new Russian high-quality AK-47 assault rifles and lethal B-41RPG launchers. These rocket-propelled grenades were capable of destroying well-fortified bunkers and armored vehicles, including main battle tanks. And third, fully 50 percent of the ARVN forces were off duty for the holiday celebrations. For the attack, the North Vietnamese had brought seven infantry regiments and twenty separate battalions into the south, via Laos down the highway known as the Ho Chi Minh Trail.

The NVA objective was to provide overpowering force in order to convince the local populations to rise up and join them. This did not happen, and after weeks of bloody fighting, the US Army, the US Marines, and the Army of South Vietnam prevailed and drove off the attackers.

*****

January 31, 1968, 0200

Just after 2:00 a.m. on the morning of January 31, a bus rolled up to the gate leading to the Joint General Staff compound next to the huge Tan Son Nhut Air Base. More than a dozen VC sappers carrying explosive charges ran up to the gate in order to open a breach into the air base. After a furious firefight these enemy soldiers were turned back. However, on the other side of the base, the VC from three separate battalions took over the Vinatexco textile mill complex. From this vantage point they were able to rake the air force base with concentrated fire from machine guns and recoilless rifles. Rockets from the mill buildings destroyed Gate 51 at the air base, and swarms of VC fighters headed toward the runway in order to destroy aircraft and ancillary buildings.

Fortunately for the South Vietnamese, there were two companies from the Eighth ARVN Airborne Battalion waiting for transport north to I Corps. They immediately joined the airport security forces to halt the initial attack of the Vietcong. It took a squadron commander from the reconnaissance unit of the Twenty-Fifth Division of the Tropic Lightning Infantry, Lieutenant Colonel Glenn Otis, who was stationed nearby at Chu

Chi, joining the fight at Gate 51 to completely defeat and secure the base by early afternoon on January 31,1968.

*****

November 1969

As we landed, corpsmen from the hospital rushed out to our aircraft and immediately grabbed the stretcher to transfer Hank to the emergency room. Conklin and I both wanted to fill in the medics regarding Hank's condition. It was this bit of conscientiousness that caused us to lose our ride back to the ship. The pilots had other missions to fly, and taking us back to the *Kitty Hawk* was pretty low on their priority list. We had no idea what kind of a nightmare would follow.

After checking our patient in, we found bunks in adjacent rooms at the base hospital. It was now around 11:30 p.m., 2330 hours in military time, past my usual bedtime on the ship. Suddenly, there was a sharp knock on the door. I cracked the door.

"Very sorry to disturb you, sir," a hospital corpsman said, "but we have orders for you and your corpsman."

This had to be a mistake. How could we get a set of orders in the middle of the night? Surely nobody knew where we were. In retrospect, while serving as a reserve dental officer several years later, I realized that immediate orders weren't so hard to understand. If the chain of command wants you to do something badly enough, they can get you a set of orders pretty quickly.

A Call to Duty: 1991

Our dental practice was about eighteen years old and going relatively smoothly when the Iraq military and Saddam Hussein decided it was a good time to take over the oil fields in Kuwait. The date was August 1, 1990. Hussein's announcement that Iraq had annexed Kuwait and had moved much of Iraq's army to the Saudi Arabian border didn't sit well with those in power in America, Kuwait, or Saudi Arabia. The army of

Iraq quickly overran the country of Kuwait and the Kuwait political leaders fled to Saudi Arabia.

Operation Desert Shield commenced on August 7, 1990. President Bush sent American paratroopers, an armored brigade, and fighter aircraft to protect the kingdom of Saudi Arabia. The 116 F-15 fighter/bomber aircraft were sent to counter Saddam Hussein's air force of over 550 warplanes. The ensuing air battle wasn't even a close fight: the F-15s swept the skies free of all Iraqi aircraft. Iraq's highly prized Mig-29 Fulcrum aircraft proved quite vulnerable to the US Air Force's F-15s.

A call came the following Tuesday from my US Navy detailer, informing me of a recall to active duty. The navy chief gave me a choice: "Where would you like to go, Doc: Marine Base Camp Fort Lejeune or Marine Base Camp Pendleton? There is an urgent need for dental officers at both facilities."

The call came in the middle of my workday, and a recall to active duty was not one of my top priorities at that moment. Without thinking too hard or really listening carefully to the detailer, I decided to choose the duty station closest to my home in Gloucester. "Chief, Camp Pendleton will be fine. When do they need me there?" For some reason, I was thinking that Pendleton was in Pennsylvania.

"Sir, your orders are in the works."

I wasn't too concerned about leaving my practice because it usually took several weeks to get a set of orders. There would normally be plenty of time to make arrangements for coverage and explain everything to my wife and new son. Two days later, a sailor came into my office in Gloucester with orders for me to report no later than 0800 hours to the commanding officer at the dental clinic at Camp Pendleton, *California*, on Saturday—just two days away!

Uncharted Territory: November 1969

On receiving my orders at the Tan Son Nhut Base hospital, I immediately picked up the phone and called the hospital base CO's office to make sure I completely understood the orders. I learned that I, along with the corpsman who was with me and two of the base personnel—a medical service officer and my friend JB from Philadelphia—had been ordered to be included in two squads of marines that were leaving the base at 0230 hours. They needed us to relieve and treat the wounded in a badly shot-up battalion of US marines and ARVN (Army of Vietnam) soldiers approximately sixty-five kilometers northwest of Base Delta (Da Nang).

Conklin yelled into my room, "Hey, Doc, what is all this crap about Firebase 14? I can't pack anything up—I don't have anything to pack. And the exchange is closed. Cripes, I don't even have a toothbrush!"

"Don't worry, Conk. I'm sure there will be some facilities at the firebase. The night-duty sailor at the hospital CO's office filled me in a little on our destination."

Firebase 14 was a 450-acre raised-hill site approximately sixty-minutes by helicopter from Da Nang. It had only a number because it hadn't yet received its heavy howitzer firepower. This area was under the control of the Third Marine Division stationed near Dong Ha. The orders probably came under the heading "needs of the fleet." It is hard to even begin to describe what was going through my mind. My temporary additional duty, or TAD, orders were open-ended: they came with a start date—early the next morning—but no ending date or time limit.

The first thought that occurred to me was that this was impossible: patients were scheduled all week back on the *Kitty Hawk*. What purpose would a dentist serve at a firebase? However, after a moment or two of reflection, it seemed best to get a message to Commander Hayne, my dental CO on the ship, to explain the circumstances.

I also sent off a message to Lt. Daniel Kirk, VA-192 of the Golden Dragons, to let him know that I might miss a few more band rehearsals and, more importantly, to let his squadron know exactly where my corpsman and I were headed in case the marine battalion encountered, shall we say, additional difficulties. It was somewhat comforting to have JB along; he was a competent nurse anesthetist.

Several thoughts flashed at once. Fear of the unknown and excitement caused me to think that at least Conklin and I were single, so there was no immediate family to worry about. Many of my friends were married and had children, like Daniel. Past relationships with teachers, and professors in college and dental school floated through my mind. I remembered one high school girlfriend, Lorna, whom I had inadvertently insulted. I remembered the high school event like it was yesterday—and had regretted it ever since. She never spoke to me again.

My whole life had seemed to consist of a series of diverse and unrelated events. My best teacher at Reading Memorial High School, Mr. Spence, had motivated me to study science and math. My favorite college course was organic chemistry, taught by the professor who developed Halo Shampoo. Curiously, not even one of my dental school professors came to mind—even though it had been less than five months since graduation. The dental school professors had all seemed hell-bent on getting us all to flunk out or quit. It is amazing what a little stress will cause one to think about. Needless to say, there was no thought of sleep that night.

*****

It was a bit of a hurried send-off; we barely had time to check our patient. Hank was stable and seemed comfortable. He would be assigned to the base hospital for several days. He would then be medevacked to Hawaii for more extensive rehabilitation before being reassigned to light duty in the continental United States. His jaws would be wired together for at least six weeks. He would then be fitted with a dental prosthesis to replace his fractured teeth.

We didn't know it at the time, but compared to the injuries suffered by the marines up at the firebase, Hank was one of the lucky patients in the Vietnam Conflict.

Four Bell HU-1 helicopters, known as Hueys, were to lift off at precisely 0230 hours. The Hueys were the workhorses in this war; over seven thousands of them were used in Vietnam. Our helicopters were loaded with food rations (known as C-rats); medical supplies, including crates of IV solutions; and interestingly enough, ten cases of Anheuser-Busch beer! In addition, there were crates of mortar shells and ammunition. As we bent low and ran out to board, the whirlwind from the rotors created hurricane-like conditions around the aircraft. We held on to our covers (hats) as we scuttled aboard.

There was a full moon partially covered by a thin layer of clouds. Visibility was excellent. The high humidity and dampness weren't unusual, but the stress and the noise of the helicopters caused an excessive outpouring of sweat, soaking our uniforms. There was a persistent ache and soreness from muscle tension in my neck and shoulders working its way up to a pounding headache. As we ascended to flight altitude, the cool early-morning air was comfortable and refreshing. However, after about five minutes everyone was shivering from the wind and cold.

Each aircraft had two waist gunners with large-caliber machine guns poking out the sides. The machine guns were M-60s, which fired a 7.62mm deadly shell. The marines were eager, even enthusiastic, to get out and relieve their fellow marines. Conklin yelled, "The phrase 'gung-ho' comes to mind."

They seemed confident and in excellent spirits during our initial leg of the flight. My immediate thought was *Dear Lord, these troops seem so young!* I was also somewhat concerned because I had no idea what a "firebase" was all about. It sounded like this one was in the middle of the jungle, fairly near the demilitarized zone, or DMZ. I couldn't think of anything good that it might have going for it. It sounded uncomfortable at best.

The top speed on the helicopters was 135 miles per hour, and they had an operating ceiling of up to 19,000 feet. We had to refuel once at an air base near An Khe, where two more helicopters filled with supplies and troops joined us. The Hueys were refueled again at a brief stop at the air base at Da Nang. The helicopter engines were so loud that one could really talk or hear anything only while we were taking on supplies or fuel. Conklin and I had lots of questions, but because of the noise from the helicopter engine, we just sat strapped to our seats and left most of our questions unanswered. I couldn't even imagine what sort of dental facilities they might have at this firebase.

Chapter 8

FIREBASE 14, NOVEMBER 1969

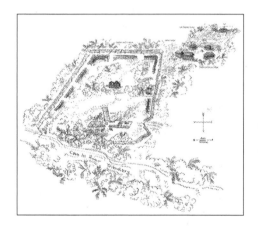

As we approached the firebase, the sun was just emerging from the mist. The landscape looked peaceful, beautiful, and emerald-green. The countryside was shimmering, almost glowing, in the early morning light. The landing zone at Firebase 14 wasn't much more than a field with tall elephant grass that had been flattened into approximately a two-hundred-meter circle. Our arrival must have awakened some of the locals. We began receiving some light, intermittent small-arms fire.

The waist gunner on the left side, a marine corporal, turned toward us and yelled, "There is a persistent rumor that any Vietcong who shoots down a US helicopter will receive an immediate battlefield promotion.

71

What we really have to be careful of is the 57mm antiaircraft fire. Although we know where most of those guns are located in this area, the NVA love to move them around to surprise us." That didn't seem terribly reassuring!

We shortly came under additional small-arms and machine-gun fire as we approached the landing zone. It sure felt like some of the local VC or NVA were trying for a promotion. Were they hiding in the ten-foot-tall elephant grass? The vegetation was so thick that they could be firing from almost anywhere.

None of us, including the new corpsmen, had any idea how loud a nearby large-caliber machine gun could be. I watched their bodies jerk and shake with the staccato firing. In addition, mounted on each side of the aircraft were two very loud 134mm Gatling guns, or mini-guns. The waist gunners were about three meters away from our seats on the helicopter. Jeez! My whole body shook with the noise. Conklin looked absolutely terrified. The standard-issue earplugs were of little value.

Whether any of the enemy combatants were hit was unknown, but the firing mowed down several small trees and a lot of tall elephant grass. Almost immediately, all of the small-arms fire abated. Our ears were ringing so much that there was no hearing anything for at least the foreseeable future. At this point my terror quotient was through the roof. The noise must have suppressed the need to move my bowels; my prayer was that the dampness on my legs was from perspiration. Perhaps we had all pissed our pants.

Reality Sets In

A marine patrol from the firebase appeared. They fanned out in a circle with their backs to the Hueys, which were landing two at a time. They fired into the bush and immediately finished clearing the landing zone, making it "safe" from the VC. Then the patrol came toward us, shouting directions we couldn't possibly hear, and started unloading the aircraft; we had no idea what they were saying. We were filled with anxiety, and it was nearly impossible to understand anything that was being shouted at us.

The marines wanted those helicopters unloaded quickly. There was a limited amount of space in the landing zone, and the VC were gone, but for how long? The sign language from the marine patrol got us moving.

They were herding us uphill toward the firebase—it felt a little like sheep being led to the slaughter.

The overpowering stench of smoke from the exploded rounds and the dampness from the lush green jungle made breathing difficult. I was so frightened that I was gulping for air; my breathing was labored and difficult. Outwardly, I hoped I appeared calm but excited. The ringing in my ears was mind-numbing.

Vietnamese village

We had to hike about two kilometers up a gentle rise to Firebase 14, where the rest of the marines and South Vietnamese soldiers were camped. The small village we passed on the way to the firebase seemed almost idyllic: small thatched dwellings around a central communal area. The villagers must have been farmers; we could see small plots of vegetables around the village. There were even plots of flowering bushes that gave off a nutty, peppery fragrance of cumin.

It did seem a little strange that the village looked deserted. There were no Vietnamese anywhere to be found. Perhaps the villagers thought that living so close to a marine outpost was dangerous. The thatched huts were a foot or two off the ground, probably to avoid dampness or wild animals.

The firebase encampment was another kilometer uphill, near a clearing about 150 meters from and approximately 30 meters above a bend in a small river.

Conk wheezed, "Jeez, Doc, I'm in pretty good shape, but climbing uphill in the jungle isn't what I signed up for. I hope that abandoned village we just passed wasn't the hot spot for nightlife in this godforsaken jungle!"

"Don't let it bother you, Conk. I'm sure there is some sort of nightlife or other excitement out here at the firebase."

There was a sense of peaceful confusion in the air. It was blissfully quiet, but it felt like chaos was lurking right around the corner. The lingering smell of cordite mixed with the fragrance of the lush vegetation. I couldn't see any permanent or even semipermanent structures. It looked like a firebase in the making and probably encompassed less than five hundred acres. The command center consisted of two large tents joined by a canvas tarp, positioned on a raised plywood platform with sandbags piled waist-high around its perimeter. Everything looked rather transient.

The marine captain who met us, Captain Darcy, certainly seemed glad to have some additional firepower and medical coverage. Solidly built with dark greenish eyes, Captain Darcy couldn't have been older than thirty, but his face was already a symphony of frown lines, and his short military haircut had that salt-and-pepper look around the temples. Although he seemed to have a kindly demeanor, his face was stamped with arrogance. It occurred to me that he had probably been through a lot of unnecessary bullshit to get to be second-in-command (when the major was absent) of this little hellhole.

He yelled, "Lieutenant, it is a pleasure to meet you and to have some additional medical personnel here at the firebase to help patch up my marines."

Shouting over the din, he said, "Please call me Jack."

Apologizing for the rustic condition of the encampment, he said, "This place may not look exactly like the Ritz, but it is all we have at the moment. We are trying to strengthen this firebase and ready it for our big guns. A 105mm howitzer is scheduled to arrive in the next two weeks if we can secure our perimeter."

The captain was the acting executive officer because the official XO was back and forth between the firebase and marine headquarters, meeting frequently with the CO of the division. The captain mentioned, "The executive officer's duties keep him at division headquarters almost continuously."

A little "girlfriend" light went off in the back of my mind when Captain Darcy mentioned the XO's back-and-forth trips to headquarters all the time. Now my suspicious inner self was competing with my terrorized inner self. I had to admit that the few Vietnamese young women I had come in contact with while at the hospital were very pretty. It was hard for me to determine whether they looked exotic compared with the round-eyed women from the States or were just outright gorgeous!

Captain Darcy continued to talk about the upcoming arrival of the howitzer. I kept my mouth shut. At that moment I couldn't tell the difference between a howitzer and any other type of large gun.

"The 105s can throw a thirty-pound shell approximately seven miles with excellent accuracy," Captain Darcy remarked. He also apologized for the VC welcoming party that had greeted us. "We know Charlie is nearby; we just can't seem to get them to show themselves. They melt into the jungle and disappear as soon as we start to outnumber them.

"Please remove your covers and officer ranks and get some jungle fatigues as soon as possible. We follow strict military protocol, but wearing an officer's uniform or insignia is just outright dangerous out here. Everything outside the firebase perimeter belongs to the VC."

He continued, "These dinks are dangerous. You do not want to venture outside the perimeter or, unfortunately, put your trust in any of the Vietnamese working inside the base. Even the children can be dangerous. Two weeks ago, we found a young Vietnamese boy with an American grenade strapped to his side under his shirt. He was trying to get close to the command center to do some damage. One of our Vietnamese scouts challenged, disarmed, and held him in the stockade for a week before releasing him. So please be careful!"

He mentioned that one of the upcoming projects was to clear a landing zone within the firebase. "There are just too many VC out near that landing zone on the other side of the village!"

My first thought was that I should break out the supplies and see who needed medical attention. It seemed to be a good idea to stay wherever the hell we were for as short a period of time as humanly possible. Some of the marines who had come with us immediately secured and helped strengthen the perimeter's fire zone; others were helping to load the most seriously wounded marines aboard the helicopters for the return flight to the base hospital at Da Nang. Conklin commented, "Jeez, Doc, this little corner of hell seems a long way from the *Kitty Hawk*!"

As we talked about getting the next possible ride back to Da Nang, Conklin asked, "How long do you figure we need to stay here?"

"Lord knows," I quietly whispered. "Our orders are quite open-ended. Let's see what needs to be done."

The gear we unloaded included two heavy rolls of concertina razor wire. Some of the marines were uncoiling and adding this wire along the perimeter. The morale and discipline at the firebase seemed excellent. However, every sentence the marines uttered seemed to include the word "fuck" as an adjective, adverb, noun, or verb, sometimes all in the same sentence! What was most interesting was that their language really didn't seem all that offensive at the time. I wasn't about to be critical of anyone living in these conditions.

Everyone else seemed busy making coffee and breakfast. Landing under fire had been so scary and nerve-racking that eating was the last item on my to-do list. But one of the medical docs (Gus something) encouraged us all to eat. "Hey, Doc, you never know when we might get another chance to wolf down some food." That wasn't terribly encouraging! I had gotten use to a three meal per day routine out on the ship. Gus was a chief medical corpsman, or senior squid in marine slang. "We don't do any major surgery out here," he said. "It is all patch-up and keep-'em-alive treatment until they can get medevacked back to the base hospital at Da Nang."

He could see from my insignia that I was a dentist. "Don't worry, Doc. We have absolutely no dental facilities, and our medical facility is pretty rudimentary."

Later it would become very clear that he possessed a tremendous range of medical knowledge; he was very talented. Gus was one of the few corpsmen who were truly older than the rest of us: he must have been in his midthirties and displayed some slight balding around a receding hairline. His "uniform" consisted of slightly soiled scrubs, but he still somehow looked very military, even with the sweat dripping off his forehead.

"Gus, how long have you been out here in the bush?"

"This is my second tour. The marines are my life, and I love the children in Vietnam!"

Meeting everyone in the medical trenches was an eye-opening experience. It seemed like there was an inordinate number of physicians at this firebase. We shortly learned that all the "doctors" at this firebase were medical corpsmen. If we weren't at war with the communist Vietcong and the North Vietnamese, we probably could have accomplished a lot of positive healing and other good things out there in the bush.

Conk remarked, "We should probably get the hell out of the country now and come back whenever this rotten, godforsaken conflict is over—or in twenty years, whichever comes first!"

"Conk, it might be good to keep your comments to yourself. No telling what the brass thinks about what we are doing out here."

The only pleasant surprise that greeted us was that all of the other corpsmen and medical personnel were very welcoming and grateful to have us there at the new firebase in the making. Although probably all of the corpsmen had much more practical field medical experience than I did, for some reason they seemed to like the idea of having an actual dental clinician in the bush with them. I didn't bring up the fact that I'd been out of dental school a total of six months. In addition, I really had no idea what I was supposed to do out here in the jungle. There was no identifiable dental equipment of any kind. All the medical instruments were sterilized in boiling water or used new right from the packaging. There were plenty of fears bottled up inside me. Later, on reflection, I found it strange that getting injured just wasn't one of them.

I thought about the chief's remarks about how he loved the marines and the children of Vietnam. Gus was one dedicated corpsman; he had dedicated his life to saving his marine patients and the children in South Vietnam. His attitude made our current situation a little more palatable. He was a true leader without bravado or a self-serving attitude. He inspired us all. At one time he mentioned that some of the children treated at the base were probably from north of the seventeenth parallel. We certainly had no idea whether they were North or South Vietnamese children.

The hospital area was a series of sandbagged trenches. Much of the complex was covered with tarps and ponchos because it seemed to almost always be raining or misting in this area of the country. The trenches were surprisingly neat and orderly. Gus had the entire complex designed to take care of the most badly wounded first. The waiting area was outside a sandbagged entrance and consisted of a selection of logs and rocks for seating.

Immediately inside the "hospital" entrance was a large triage area where the most seriously wounded were placed on plywood tables for treatment. The wounded who did not require immediate treatment were attended to in another trench branching out from the operating-room trench. All the supplies were located in "sterile" pouches in crates lining the trenches. The roof was quite rudimentary. The tarps and ponchos were designed to keep all the rain out and the light in. Occasionally some of the medical procedures had to be accomplished at night, and any visible light leaks could attract sniper fire.

Since my duty there would hopefully be for a very short duration, it was probably best not to complain or comment on the conditions. JB was sure we would be leaving in a day or two. His medical nursing skills would come in handy up here—wherever the hell we were. The ten cases of beer were stored in one of the medical trenches and were to be distributed on a limited basis around "cocktail hour."

It was disorienting and terrifying to have landed in an active "hot" landing zone, with the noise and confusion of the loud but brief firefight. The medical personnel who had come with us also had no idea where we were. We knew that we had to be pretty far north, perhaps near the seventeenth parallel or the demilitarized zone (DMZ). It was actually on the chilly side here at night. We all looked pretty shaken and definitely could have used a change of underwear.

*****

One of the corpsmen had been in action to help relieve a small Special Forces outpost near Laos and Cambodia that past July. Ben Het was approximately ten kilometers inside Vietnam from the Cambodian border. Since it was in the ARVN (Army of South Vietnam) operating area, the defenders of the outpost were relying on the ARVN troops to relieve them while they were under the siege of guns and rockets from the NVA. Once the ammo dump was blown up by a North Vietnamese rocket, US marines flew in for relief to save the base. Since that incident, it had been pretty clear to the brass that it wasn't always wise to rely on the ARVN during emergencies.

*****

After my first bite of packaged breakfast rations—it looked, but certainly didn't taste, like a health food bar—we heard what sounded like a car door slamming in the distance.

"That's an odd sound," Conk remarked.

Suddenly, everyone around me was shouting about "tubing" and looking for a rock to climb under while yelling, "Incoming!" Gus tackled me and pushed me into the mud.

The first mortar shell exploded in the river. The abrupt explosion confirmed my worst thoughts and scared the crap out of me as well as Conklin, JB, and the other corpsmen from the helicopter that had just arrived. After several more rounds that seemed to close in on us, the marines started to return some fire.

What was a little disconcerting was that the mortar rounds and small-arms fire seemed to be coming from the quaint little Vietnamese village we had passed on the way into the firebase, less than two kilometers away. Another perplexing realization was that everyone who was part of the medical group seemed to take the incoming mortar rounds as almost routine!

Then one of the radio operators took a sniper round in the heart, right through his radio. "Captain, watch out!" yelled his corporal. The radio telephone operators were some of the most important men in the platoon. They stayed close to the lieutenants or captains and served as their direct contact with the battalion when out on patrol. When the dead radio operator was brought into medical, I was sure I was going to be sick to my stomach. He was covered with blood.

A good-looking nineteen-year-old, he'd had his whole life ahead of him—and it had been snuffed out in an instant. What particularly bothered me was that he looked so young to be out here in the jungle in the first place.

The marine captain who had been standing next to his now dead and blood-soaked radio operator yelled, "That's it, guys! Give 'em the Willie Peter." This was a phrase beyond my immediate understanding, but my confusion was about to be cleared up.

The first round of W-P, or white phosphorous, landed in the center of the adjacent small village. It burst into several fragments—not unlike a Fourth of July fireworks burst, except that everything one of those fragments touched immediately burst into flames. The small group of thatched dwellings immediately turned into a boiling inferno.

"Jeez," I said to Conklin, "we're supposed to be here to help these folks, not burn down their homes!"

The mortars and firing stopped immediately. One of the marines explained that the village must have been taken over by the Vietcong. "The gooks probably have that village and are using it as a protective firing point," he said. It was later discovered that the Vietcong had built a labyrinth of tunnels connecting the village's structures and were directing fire on our base camp from several locations inside the village. This was certainly a dedicated, well-armed, and confident group of enemy soldiers.

As we started crawling out from under any protective coverings we had been lucky enough to find, the marine fire teams immediately organized themselves into rifle squads to search whatever was left of the village. A boot marine from one of the newly arrived squads had a shrapnel neck wound. He had been down by the river when the first mortar shell had arrived. He as well as the dead radio operator were attended to in the medical area.

The deceased radio operator was placed in a special body bag with some paperwork and readied for the next medevac helicopter.

I asked one of the corpsmen, "How many of these body bags do you have here at the camp?"

"Probably not enough, Doc," he replied, unnerving me.

The neck wound on the boot marine didn't look too serious, but it might have nicked the spinal cord. He screamed, "Hey, Doc, my legs ain't working right—hope it didn't affect my dick!"

I just shook my head. We administered seventy-five milligrams of Demerol, bandaged his neck, and marked him priority for medevac. Moments such as this made you really wonder what these marines considered most important in their lives!

One of the marines, led by a 2nd Lieutenant from the battalion, headed out to the village in an armored cavalry assault vehicle (ACAV) with a large-caliber machine gun mounted on top. This firebase had two of these vehicles courtesy of the US Army. The weapon looked very lethal. As he approached the still smoldering village, the lieutenant noticed movement out of the corner of his eye. "Corporal, what's that movement at two o'clock?"

"Watch it! Look out!" *Bang!* The corporal's warning came too late.

A Vietcong had come out of a hidden tunnel about two hundred meters away with what looked like a pipe up to his shoulder. The rocket-propelled grenade hit the antenna of the tracked vehicle and sprayed shrapnel down into the truck, injuring the lieutenant and two of the marines.

The lieutenant manning the machine gun, Ted Norris from Methuen, Massachusetts, swung the gun around, firing the entire time while bleeding profusely from his left arm. "You son of a bitch! Eat this, you little gook bastard!" One can only guess what happens to a person hit by several rounds of .50-caliber machine-gun fire. That stuff could tear a car in half. Ted exclaimed later that "the VC's body just flew apart. His head went airborne and spewed blood all over the trench."

On the way back to medical, Lieutenant Ted picked up a little five- or six-year-old Vietnamese boy who seemed terrified; he was probably from the village we had just burned to the ground.

The corpsman helped sew Ted's arm back together. Demerol dulled his pain, but he was going to be sore. It would have been wonderful to view a radiograph of the arm, in case there was a piece of shrapnel that we accidently could have missed. In addition, it looked like the lieutenant might lose at least part of his left foot. He would definitely lose his left small toe—it was gone along with part of his boot.

"Bandage it tight, guys; the ACAV troops need me to check for damage." These guys were extremely loyal to their men.

"Sir, you have an injury that will require hospitalization," Gus noted with some authority.

"No, thanks, Chief. Sew up my damn foot, will ya!" the lieutenant shot back. "You guys are apt to need me a little more before this fun party is over!"

Gus intoned that as long as the soldier wasn't a risk to himself or the squad, we couldn't make him leave for a real hospital. "Let's clean up his foot, cover him with antibiotics, and get him some larger boots to accommodate the bandage," yelled Gus before turning back to the lieutenant. "Sir, if you stick around here, we will have to change the bandage daily. In addition, there is a very good chance of an infection."

The lieutenant still refused to be medevacked.

Although we cheered the lieutenant's marksmanship, that was only the beginning of our problems. A heavy mist had crept over the valley, and low clouds gave only an occasional glimpse of the sun. The weather seemed to exacerbate the depression that was settling over the firebase.

The little Vietnamese boy, whom we called Joey, had watched the lieutenant's treatment with fascination. He was destined to be a firebase symbol for all the children in Vietnam. He was actually almost ten years old. One of the South Vietnamese soldiers spoke with him and relayed that the boy had lost his dad when the VC had come through on a recruitment drive; his mom had died of "sicknesses." The North Vietnamese had a rather effective recruitment policy: you could either join them and fight for liberation or get shot. Either way, it wasn't a wonderful set of choices.

There was one concept that was difficult to understand. As all of us eventually got to know most of the Vietnamese from the little village that we had burned to the ground, it was always a mystery to me how folks who were so desperately poor could be even somewhat happy. These poor Vietnamese folks, basically dressed in rags, were genuinely happy.

Sometimes the old women would sit in quiet groups talking with each other, and the men would sit smoking a pipe or American cigarettes and seem to be at peace with themselves and their surroundings; even with the chaos going on around them, perhaps they knew something the rest of us would never comprehend. Otherwise, how could these Vietnamese villagers, with virtually nothing in the world in the way of possessions, living in a war-torn country, possibly be even slightly happy?

*****

Most of our medical personnel were busy dressing wounds and dispensing morphine syrettes to marines who were in pretty rough shape. Three of the enlisted men from the tracked vehicle had substantial head injuries. A four-inch piece of jagged shrapnel protruded from the head of one of the marines, through his helmet. There's no telling what would have happened to him if he hadn't had his helmet in place. His helmet was unrecognizable.

Although we were reluctant to remove it, we eased the metal fragment out as we removed his helmet, flushed the wound with IV solution, shaved a patch of his scalp, placed eight sutures, bandaged his head up tightly, and administered antibiotic therapy. We didn't use any lidocaine while suturing him up. Oddly enough, the patient did not complain of any substantial pain and actually wanted to get back to his men on the vehicle. We loaded him up with antibiotics and anti-inflammatory pain meds and told him to take it easy for a couple of days.

Neither the lieutenant nor the enlisted marine with the head injury would consider being medevacked. Gus warned the marine, "Son, if you get any severe headaches or localized pain, let us know right away." Fortunately, the shrapnel had not penetrated the marine's meninges, or brain covering. Mostly, we worried about a secondary infection. The sutures needed to be cleaned daily; otherwise, they would make wonderful wicks for bacteria. The patient was told to check with medical every day for the next week.

Any scratch or open wound in this climate was an immediate breeding ground for all sorts of bacteria. The result was the very rapid spread of jungle rot, gangrene, and worse. All the corpsmen and JB were extra careful and did their best to maintain a clean environment for wound care. Our goal was to get every seriously wounded patient to a primary-care medical facility as soon as possible and without infection.

A daily dose of dapsone seemed to help the jungle rot. This compound (diaminodiphenyl sulfone) was also effective for the treatment of leprosy, which was not unheard of in this area. The once-a-week dose of chloroquine, derived from quinolone, kept the malaria in check but did nothing to limit the swarms of mosquitoes.

One of the "docs" was nowhere to be found while the rest of us were trying to patch up injured personnel. Later we discovered that Lieutenant JB was in the village with a squad of marines, looking for burned corpses or survivors. Fortunately, they couldn't find any corpses.

The medical area at this firebase was very rudimentary. Some of the trenches had sandbags around the openings. Most of the trenches had plywood or cardboard-box flooring. Because of the constant moisture, the cardboard in the trenches lasted only a day or two before it needed to be changed. The plywood also started to deteriorate almost immediately.

Most of the injured marines were on air mattresses. All the medical supplies were in crates that lined the walls of the trenches.

The operating-room table was a raised three-quarter-inch piece of plywood nailed and screwed to a couple of sawhorses. When I asked why the operating table was on a slight incline, the nearest corpsman replied in a concerned voice, "Doc, that just keeps the blood and the fluids used to clean the wounds from collecting on the table." I really didn't need to hear that right now. Canvas tents covered most of the medical area; some trenches had mosquito netting to keep out the smaller critters.

"Don't worry, Doc," commented one of the corpsmen. "We use a clean poncho for every grunt needing surgery. Anyone freaking lucky enough that they can't return to duty gets a medevac bird with a one-way ticket back to the world."

Everything seemed to be somewhat under control until the radio operator informed us that a spotter plane had reported a large group of North Vietnamese "regulars," battalion-strength, twenty-five to thirty klicks (kilometers) northeast of us, heading in our direction. *Oh, happy day*, I thought. *That's all we effin' need!*

The spotter plane pilot exclaimed, "The whole jungle seems to be a shit-storm of movement in your direction." The VC were so well camouflaged that from the air the entire battalion at first looked like a moving green carpet of jungle!

After burning down the adjacent small Vietnamese village, we discovered that it held a large underground cache of North Vietnamese arms, literature, food, and medical supplies. Perhaps this battalion-size group of VC was looking to supplement its own provisions. In retrospect, this wasn't the safest area for the marines to set up a firebase. Hindsight would tell us that there was no safe area in the entire country for these firebases. If you were not inside the perimeter of a firebase, then it was definitely not safe. At night, anyone outside the firebase perimeter was considered the enemy and extremely dangerous. During the day the marines continued to clear the brush and jungle fifty or more meters from the wire in order to have a cleared "kill zone" in case of attack.

The strategic idea for the series of firebases was to have interlocking fields of howitzer fire to interdict the VC and the NVA from flowing supplies and men freely into South Vietnam. The idea might have looked good on paper, but the NVA and the Vietcong were just not going along with the program. They seemed able to find a safer route down the back of the mountains in Laos and Cambodia directly into the southern part of South Vietnam. They had a virtual highway that could handle trucks, tanks, and other military vehicles. The Americans called it the Ho Chi Minh Trail.

The tunnels under the village weren't large enough for a good-size dog to enter, but some very brave men went into them headfirst with .45-caliber pistols and flashlights. These "tunnel rats" would slither through the tunnels and capture or destroy whatever the Vietcong had sequestered away. Often they encountered traps that wounded them, or they were forced to engage in hand-to-hand combat with a determined enemy. A common VC trick was to tie a poisonous snake from the root of a tree just inside the tunnel entrance. The snake could be pretty mad by the time a tunnel rat came along.

*****

One of our patients, José, was an official tunnel rat. He was only about five feet two, with a slight build, but he was absolutely fearless. He was Mexican American and claimed, "Those little cong are 'fraid of me!" He emphasized, "I don't dare fire the gun down there—too 'fraid to bring down the tunnel." Nothing ever seemed to bother him in the tunnels, but he had some concern about the limited air for breathing. He added, "I safe in the tunnels. I can only run into one cong at a time!" José didn't seem even slightly claustrophobic. "Those tunnels berry small; gunfire maybe bring more cong."

Many times he would have to twist his shoulders sideways in order to get through narrow openings. Our Vietnamese ranger scouts and ARVN regulars would never enter the tunnels, although they didn't mind going anywhere else in the jungle. They claimed there were too many snakes and rats in the tunnels. José had only once encountered NVA regulars in a tunnel system. "The little gook shits run like hell when they see me and my forty-five."

José had probably been in the bush too long; he was suffering from ringworm, crotch and jungle rot, and leech and various other insect bites,

85

in addition to a seven-inch gash in his right shoulder from an accidental injury in a tunnel that he claimed was from a "sharp rock." However, after his injury was treated and sutured up, he was anxious to get back to rat duty. After we sewed up his shoulder, we dosed him with antibiotics and dusted the rest of his body with insecticide powder. Like most of the other marines I encountered at the firebase, José was quite friendly and had a positive attitude about life in the service. He was very likable. One had to admire the guy, but was he brave and fearless or just crazy?

*****

In Cu Chi, approximately sixty kilometers from Saigon, the Vietcong had developed an extensive and elaborate tunnel system that totaled over 120 miles in length. Begun during the French war and expanded during the American war, these tunnels were used for protection from aerial attacks, for housing troops, and for transporting supplies. There was a complete hospital system in the tunnels, with operating rooms and beds for the wounded VC and NVA troops. After an attack, the VC would simply vanish into its tunnel system. It was particularly exasperating for the US Twenty-Fifth Infantry Division that called this area home. At the end of the war, it was discovered that over 43,000 North Vietnamese and Vietcong had died defending this Cu Chi tunnel system. Now it seems that the whole system is part of an elaborate tourist attraction. Some of the tunnels have even been enlarged for Western visitors.

*****

Up until 1968, our mission in Vietnam under General Westmoreland was to "search and destroy" the enemy. This philosophy relied on body count to keep track of our success. After the Tet Offensive in 1968, it became very evident that the North Vietnamese were going to pay any price to throw the United States out of their country and implement a communist regime.

Throughout the years that America and other countries were involved in the war in Vietnam, there was a lack of political and military leadership clearly defining our role and objectives. The North Vietnamese had no such problems: the North Vietnamese servicemen, politicians, and citizens had one common objective—the reunification of their country.

After a change-of-command ceremony, General Abrams, the new American general and leader in charge of the land war, instituted—at politicians' request—the political policy and theory of "Vietnamization" in 1969. This policy was to gradually turn defense of the country (South Vietnam—below the seventeenth parallel and demilitarized zone) over to the South Vietnamese Army.

General Abrams was a very different general with a very different mission. General Westmoreland was tall and good-looking and rarely drank alcohol. General Abrams was a short, tough ex–tank commander who believed in careful planning with violent execution. His instructions were to turn the war over to the South Vietnamese as quickly as possible. President Johnson was not about to authorize a continual escalation of troop strength in the summer of 1968. General Abrams's chief responsibility was to prepare our military for a negotiated settlement and the removal and withdrawal of American forces as soon as a negotiated peace could be obtained.

*****

It was getting late on our third day at the firebase, the sun was low on the horizon, and fog was developing in the valley below us along the river. This day had brought plenty of action for our medical group. Most of our patients were reasonably comfortable, although some needed more morphine while they waited for the medevac helicopter.

Only one patient, Sully, looked like he might not make it. "Doc, am I going to die?" he asked.

"Someday, Sully, but hopefully not today!" Conk replied. "You have a traumatic head injury, and we would rather remove the hunk of steel bullet under more ideal clinical conditions. In a hospital setting we could lessen the chances of infection or uncontrolled intracranial bleeding."

Sully asked, "Could you and the Doc come with me and remove the fragment for me at the hospital?"

Conk replied, "Trust me, Sully—you don't want me or the dentist doing any intracranial surgery for you!" Sully's condition would be best treated at the Ninety-Fifth Evacuation Hospital in Da Nang. For head wounds, this was the nearest facility.

It was time to pack up, call in the choppers, and head for the barn. One of the squids announced it was cocktail time and handed me a cold beer. It was a pleasure getting to know the new corpsmen. "Thanks, Doc," I said. "How do you keep it cold?"

"Well," he answered, "if we can't get ice, we keep it surrounded with cold packs or keep it cool in the river."

As a dentist, I would have been much more comfortable treating patients in an air-conditioned office overlooking the sea somewhere, with quiet oldies playing on the radio. It was not my preference to be in some godforsaken jungle, sweating profusely and fighting off bugs and leeches of all sorts while trying to comfort injured men much braver than I. I had to admit, however, that these marines were starting to grow on me, and the cold beer was delicious. I promised myself at that time that if at all possible, I would eventually practice with the ocean at my window, oldies on the radio, and a staff as knowledgeable and kind as these corpsmen.

I later learned that at this point in the Vietnam Conflict there were almost seventy thousand marines stationed in the war zone. It was a shame a few more couldn't be spared for this operation at Firebase 14.

The corpsman who offered me a beer, Carlos, was from the Philippines, and he seemed to enjoy the hot damp climate. He was from a mountainous area called Baguio in northern Luzon. "Our temperature there is usually in the eighties year-round." He had been attached to this marine battalion as a corpsman for almost five years and said it was his lifelong ambition to work with the US marines.

A shower and a change of clothes would certainly help. Tropical climates can be wonderful, but this was ridiculous. We were constantly wet from the fog, drizzle, downpours, or sweat. If we weren't wet, we were hot and wanted to be wet. Worse, this was only my first week in the bush; some of these marines had been out here for several weeks or months! The patients and the mission, especially the Vietnamese children, made conditions somewhat more tolerable.

Chapter 9

The Magnet Arrives

For the moment everything seemed quiet and peaceful in the jungle compound that made up Firebase 14. It seemed hard to believe there could be North Vietnamese regular army troops or Viet Cong anywhere nearby. There were strange bird and cricket-like sounds, but everyone seemed pretty relaxed.

That's when the first howitzer shell hit our area. It didn't make a sound, or at least we couldn't hear anything at the moment it was fired. As it passed right overhead, it sounded like a lightning-fast freight train. It exploded about fifteen hundred meters on the other side of the river. We had no idea what it was; we knew only that it wasn't anything good. The marine officers were having a hastily called conference in the CO's bunker when the second shell arrived. It landed about five hundred meters up and in the river. It occurred to me that we might want to vacate this particular area as fast as humanly possible. Two freight trains screaming overhead were plenty for me.

The officer in charge, the executive officer, was pretty calm, although he seemed to be chatting excitedly on the radio. That's when two more howitzer shells screamed overhead. The noise was deafening. Everyone could feel the heat from that salvo. The shells landed approximately one thousand meters into the jungle on the other side of the river: much too close for comfort. The concussion blew several marines near the river off their feet.

If abject fear hadn't gripped any of us yet, it certainly had me by the throat now. The blood was pounding through my body; this was building to be a real throbber of a headache. As I crouched down behind some sandbags in medical, nausea masked the violent headache that was starting to radiate down my back. Had any of us known where to run, we would have gone anywhere to escape that infernal thunder.

*****

A few minutes went by. It was almost dusk when in the distance there was a rumbling noise that none of could decipher. None of us had the slightest idea what was happening. It was like a distant thunderstorm on a hot, sultry summer's day. Sometimes a summer storm will clear the air and lower the humidity. This rumble of thunder didn't lower the humidity, but it did stop the freight trains that were dropping too close to our position. Less than a minute later an A7-E Corsair streaked over our position with a little wabble salute from the wings. "The Magnet" had arrived.

"Conk," I asked, "could that plane be from our ship?"

"Quite possible." The markings looked like VA-192. The pilot who buzzed us could well have been Daniel or another pilot from the *Kitty Hawk*.

Most impressive were the professionalism of the air wing squadron from the ship and the calm attitude of the young marines being shelled; they just seemed to disappear into the ground. It was also comforting to know that we had such immediate and accurate air support from the ships out on Yankee Station.

At the time, most of the marines were not even twenty-five: their average age was around eighteen or nineteen years old. Most were right out of high school. Their display of expertise, decision making, and calm demeanor under the most trying, terrifying circumstances was impressive. God got us through the mortar and howitzer barrage, and He gave us the peace of mind that helped us to concentrate on our patients care..

"Chief, it would be really helpful if the sweat would stop dripping off my face," I said. It was hard to determine whether the sweat was because of the heat and humidity, was an extreme nervous reaction, or both.

"You'll get used to it, Doc; we just try not to drip into any open wounds."

My uniform was as wet as if it had been dunked in the river. One of the corpsmen had lent me scrubs and odd parts of uniforms, reminding me again not to display any officer insignia of any kind—"they make excellent targets for gook snipers," he reiterated. In addition, the corpsman told me, "Unless you can get dry skivvies, the constant dampness can lead to jungle rot, so it is best to go without."

Marvelous, I thought.

We spent that night camped in the medical area of the firebase above the river. The corpsman who had given me the uniform parts and scrubs, Jon, showed me a "luxury" accommodation. No more than a narrow space adjoining the medical trenches, it contained an air mattress over some cut-up cardboard boxes with a poncho over the top of the trench.

The cardboard flooring was very temporary; in a day or two it would be so soggy that it would be unusable. Since medical was a bit of a priority, we could usually get some plywood for flooring from the cut-up ammo crates.

One of the corpsmen told me, "Doc, the Officers' Club should be open in a few weeks, where you'll be able to get a nice cold beer on tap, unless of course the fuckin' gooks overrun us before it's built." I appreciated his attempt at humor, but at that point all of us were too tired to care about anything but sleep.

That evening's "dinner" consisted of another C-rat with some canned peaches and more somewhat-chilled beer. Conklin asked, "Does anyone have any fishing gear? That might spark a positive change in diet around here." Most of the marines looked hungry all the time – probably because they were staping teenagers with excellent appetites and a need for food with a high calorie count. Good nutrition didn't seem to be a major concern of anyone at this firebase-in-the-making marine outpost. Most of the corpsmen and patients did seem to think that the canned peaches were a special delight. I finished all of mine, including the very sugary syrup. The date on the can was 1956. Fresh vegetables might have been available in the ground of the tiny village we had torched, but that area was turning out to be a dangerous place to visit.

*****

The nights brought a special set of problems. The moonlight that filtered through the cloud cover, fog, drizzle, and jungle canopy was not nearly enough to read by; we couldn't see much of anything. Any visible light source in the firebase itself, even a cigarette, invited enemy interest or sniper fire.

There was no additional shelling on this night after the A-7 passed by, so it was a pretty quiet night; sentries and patrols were out in the bush somewhere. But the night sounds were somewhat disquieting. There was a cacophony of insect and animal noises that were impossible to identify. In addition to the snoring of patients and fellow trench dwellers, there was the occasional growl of something larger. My guess was that it was not beyond the realm of possibility that tigers could add to our troubles in this godforsaken jungle. The growling reminded me of Chuck's story at the Officers' Club after the attempted assault in Po City. It briefly occurred to me, before drifting off to sleep, that I might have nightmares about tigers. Surprisingly, sleep came quickly, on this night. The next thing I knew, the early dawn light was filtering through the jungle canopy.

I was slowly learning that it didn't pay to overthink things or even speculate out loud, but one couldn't help but wonder where that battalion of North Vietnamese regulars was headed. It seemed to confirm our fears that they quite possibly were going to try to collect the arms and munitions under the small village nearby. None of us felt too comfortable with that kind of threat out somewhere lurking, planning and waiting in the jungle.

*****

At 0500 hours, when it was just barely light, one of the patrols came back into the firebase. All the marines looked dead-tired. They had a couple days' growth of beard, and they smelled like overripe garbage. They had dark circles under their eyes, and their uniforms were torn so badly that they looked more like rags than uniforms. All of them had scratch marks all over their exposed skin. They considered the firebase a refuge compared to the hell of uncertainty while patrolling the surrounding valley.

Their mental condition directly after one of their patrols into the bush was completely different from their mental state before the patrol. The constant state of alert while out on patrol and the constant fear of booby traps, snipers, and wild animals really got to some of the men.

No one liked going out of the firebase on patrol. Some of the men covered their fear better than others, but all of the men were relieved when they did not have any encounters with the constant dangers in the bush.

The squad leader, Lieutenant Aiello, was from a small town in central Florida near Ocala called Reddick. He looked like one tough marine. His curly dark hair was cut short in military fashion. Even though his uniform was shredded and he sported a three-day growth of beard, his appearance did nothing to detract from his military bearing and leadership.

The lieutenant brought in one boot-enlisted marine covered in leeches from the waist down. "Doc," the young marine said, "the little fuckers must have gotten on me in the river we crossed about ten klicks east o' here." The leeches lived in the damp jungle foliage and would frequently drop on the men as they went through the bush.

We powdered him up with some sort of pesticide and liquid "bug juice," and most of the leeches came off. He picked off the rest. Some of them were engorged with his own blood. "Hey, guys, watch 'em pop when I step on 'em with my wet boots!" said the boot marine. *Splat!*

Before leaving to report to the CO, Lieutenant Aiello mentioned, "There is some evidence of gomers near the river, but the little fucks were too smart to show themselves."

Gus said it was probably not a bad thing that they hadn't gotten into a firefight. "The little bastards only show themselves when they know they outnumber us." His respect for the VC and the NVA was obvious. They were very experienced and determined fighters.

*****

At daybreak two helicopters showed up to collect our wounded. Gus yelled, "Hey, Doc, the last medevac brought in a reporter from *Newsweek*. He wants to interview you!"

"Jeez, Chief, I've been here less than a week. He should talk with the CO."

"The CO doesn't do interviews with newspeople, and neither do any of the other officers; they all say they're too busy. Please humor this guy before anyone gets hurt. The news reporters have no idea how long you've been here."

The reporter was shown into the medical area by one of the corpsmen. "Doc, this is Mr. Michael Jacobs, a journalist from *Newsweek* magazine."

"Thanks for seeing me, Doc."

I quickly warned him, "You realize, Jacobs, that this is a firebase in development and our perimeter isn't exactly secure."

"Doc, don't worry about me. I've been all over the country. Can we get a picture of the medical area?"

"Absolutely not!" I replied emphatically. "We've been here less than two weeks, so our medical area is very rudimentary. You are not to photograph anything that might give aid or comfort to our enemy?"

Jacobs gave me a blank look.

"For your own safety you will be on the next Huey out of here. Do not take any photographs of our wounded personnel. In addition, I recommend you take photographs of the landscape only. Do not take pictures of or get near the perimeter; it is very unsafe. According to the XO, any jungle outside the perimeter belongs to the VC, and they are very active in the sniper department."

"Hey, Doc, like I said, don't worry about me; I'm no stranger to being out in the bush. I've photographed plenty of combat situations over the past six months—without even a scratch or close brush in a firefight. None of these Vietnamese Charlies bother me."

"Look, Mr. Jacobs, your enthusiasm is appreciated. However, you underestimate these gook enemy combatants at your peril. If you want to write a positive story or human interest story," I continued, "please talk to our chief medical corpsman, Gus. He has been out here as long as anyone and really appreciates what we are trying to do for the people of South Vietnam."

Finally, I reminded him, "While you are at this firebase, you are under the CO's command and responsibility. You will not write or photograph anything that reflects poorly on this firebase, its command structure, or the US military. And you *will* be on the next available flight out of here!"

As I walked away from him, it occurred to me this would be an ideal time for me to start back to the *Kitty Hawk* and enjoy a hot shower. Of course, with over five thousand men on the ship and the need to conserve desalinated fresh water, a navy shower consisted of annoying starts and stops. Even so, right now any kind of a shower would be pure luxury.

But the marine battalion commanding officer, Lieutenant Colonel Avery, had other ideas for us. The CO was a no-nonsense marine. He stood six-two without an ounce of discernible flab. Lots of worry lines flowed out from around his eyes and mouth, and his short hair was flecked with gray. I guessed he was in his mid- to late thirties. He was quite good-looking with terrific jaw structure. He probably would have looked great on a yacht.

Although the CO's leadership skills would have served him well anywhere in corporate America, it was hard to characterize his voice as commanding because there was always a touch of caring to it. He was never brusque or short with his men. He seemed to actually listen to his men when they had suggestions. This was his second tour in 'Nam. He was also concerned about the location of that North Vietnamese battalion. The aircraft from ships on Yankee Station had silenced the enemy's big guns, but what else did they have in store for us?

I kept all this in mind when he approached me and said, "Lieutenant, I would like you to remain at the firebase and help tend to the wounded. Your skills are very much appreciated here at the firebase."

My first thought was that the corpsmen probably had as much or more medical experience in the bush than I would ever have. My quick reply had more to do with admiration for him, the patients, and the dedicated men in the medical department than any altruistic desire to provide aid. "Yes, sir, I am happy to help any way I can." I hoped he couldn't tell my dominant thought, though, which was that *this whole idea of a firebase in this particular area could turn into a real clusterfuck.*

After washing in the shallow part of the river, most of us ate a little breakfast out of packages. Today was Friday. It was difficult to remember what was on the *Hawk's* menu: would it be bacon and eggs over light or sausages and pancakes? Jacobs was just coming back over to the medical area. Getting rid of this turkey might not be easy. I could suggest he go out to the *Hawk* and interview the air boss or down to the hospital at Tan Son Nhut and interview some of the doctors. But I just couldn't in all fairness do that. This news reporter would be an intrusion on other officers' busy time. But I certainly thought about it.

I realized that news reporters had a specific and important job to do in getting news about this war to the American people. It was just painful to me at the time to have Jacobs taking up the time of these marines who were doing everything possible to aid and defend the local population while staying alive and healthy in the meantime.

Unwelcomed Guests

The initial hint of enemy activity came from one of our Vietnamese rangers (the marines called them Kit Carson scouts). The radio message was short and to the point: "Elements of the NVA battalion crossing the river approximately fifteen klicks east of our position, possibly in order to outflank our firebase."

In addition, aircraft had scattered an array of very sensitive noise and motion detectors between us and the NVA battalion that had been spotted heading toward the firebase. These detectors utilized small radio transmitters to send data to intelligence monitors, who would attempt to guess at enemy strength and direction of movement based on whatever signals they received. The only problem was that the sophistication and effectiveness of the devices were never foolproof. Their use never seemed to relay any real useful information.

Our first problem was that we didn't know the strength of the opposition. What seemed to be even more of a concern to the CO, however, was that the enemy knew a lot about our strength. The CO knew that the NVA battalion leader would not even consider getting this close to our outpost unless they outnumbered us at least six to one. The CO also suspected that the enemy was very aware that this base still lacked howitzer firepower.

*****

A battalion can have anywhere from four hundred to twelve hundred men. The marine battalion at this firebase had approximately 380 men left, plus the two squads of marines that had come with us from the air bases at Tan Son Nhut and Da Nang. We were spread over perhaps three or four hundred, or at the most five hundred acres of real estate. Although we had razor or concertina wire, listening devices, claymore antipersonnel mines, and some trip flares all along much of the perimeter, the frustration in our commanding officer's face was evident. His puny reinforcements didn't give him a lot to work with. Without a howitzer this was turning into a real head-scratcher.

The nice part of having a 105mm howitzer in the camp would have been that the gun could be lowered, in case of a human wave attack by the enemy. It could be loaded with antipersonnel "beehive" canisters. These projectiles held over 8,000 fléchette darts that would spread out after the canister exited the barrel of the howitzer and act like shotgun pellets to mow down charging enemy combatants.

*****

Right after the radio report, José the tunnel rat came back with confirmation of a large amount of firearms, munitions, and medical supplies in the tunnels under the small village we had burned down. Our collective thought was *Jeez, now we are really in the soup!*

In an additional complication, one of the marines out on sentry duty in the bush brought in what were probably the remaining residents of the village that had been torched. There were approximately twenty-one people. All of them were women, children, or older folks. We saw a lot of them at our makeshift hospital; most of them were in pretty rough shape, with burns, leeches, and other pustulating wounds.

One of the female Vietnamese kids had an infected, abscessed permanent maxillary molar tooth. There were no thirty-gauge needles around, so we infused the area around the abscessed tooth with lidocaine using a twenty-five-gauge needle and removed the tooth. I used a thin tissue retractor and a marine Ka-Bar knife as an elevator.

Her mom had looked justifiably terrified as we sterilized the knife with an open flame from a lighter and then wiped it down with alcohol, so we had to get her out of the medical area. She was upsetting her daughter too much with her screaming. I hid the "surgical" instruments behind the little girl so that she wouldn't get even more frightened. She looked quite small and pitiful lying on our plywood operating table. My heart went out to her. However, she seemed comfortable while I was elevating and removing the tooth. Perhaps she was just too frightened to move. Mom and daughter seemed to relax after the extraction; the abscess had immediately drained. Her family thought it was a miracle: it was a first for me!

The villagers brought to the firebase claimed that the North Vietnamese had taken all the young men and would kill them if they didn't agree to "fight for liberation." This did prove to be an effective recruiting tactic.

*****

Across the river from the battalion, there was open jungle and tall grass for several miles. In the background were some low hills and mountains. The mountains must have been at least ten or fifteen miles away. Gus told me these mountains were part of the Annamite Range. It seemed so peaceful there. The weather had cleared slightly. Except for the drenching humidity, it looked like it was going to be a pretty good day; we must have been between downpours. From May through October, this area of the country could see some horrible monsoon storms. Although it was November, the air was stagnant and still and just as muggy as usual.

One of the Vietnamese rangers explained to the villagers about their homes. Some of the marines were going to try to rebuild them or give the villagers some tents for shelter at a new location. Captain Darcy thought the safest location for these refugees was probably within the perimeter of the firebase. A quiet section near medical was set aside for their tents.

The jungle area along the river was usually alive with the sounds of birds and all sorts of other wildlife. In many respects, the rural areas of Vietnam epitomized what many of us hoped would be the outcome of this conflict: a calm, orderly transition to self-government and political freedom for all of the population. On this particular morning, there seemed to be a quiet disconnect along this stretch of the river near the firebase: a period of calm, but no bird or other jungle noises. The hush was somewhat disconcerting.

Even the river seemed to slow down. Normally a meandering lazy flow, it almost seemed to stop. There was little movement anywhere. The peace and quiet signaled concern for the chief. "Something doesn't seem quite right, Doc. Keep an eye out for snipers or any sort of unusual activity."

"Chief, you're making me nervous. It isn't as if we don't have enough to think about here."

The CO had patrols and scouts out in several directions, but now he was fully aware of why the NVA wanted our position. To us in the medical area, the response seemed obvious: rig the tunnels with explosives and let's Dixie. Our CO, however, had a better idea. He conferred with the officers in the battalion, and the consensus was to lure the NVA into a trap near the village. Although that might work, we didn't have to like the idea of being part of the bait.

The entire battalion was busy constructing additional makeshift fortifications with logs, sandbags, ponchos, and brush over some dug-in trenches. These "hooches" would be their homes and sleeping accommodations until a more permanent base could be constructed. Most of the men were digging holes or filling sandbags. It was a little troubling that one of the corporals digging a foxhole next to his hooch had the bottom of the foxhole collapse into what appeared to be part of the VC's tunnel system.

The CO told José to investigate the hole as soon as possible. No one liked the thought of having enemy tunnels within the camp perimeter.

*****

In the medical area, we used air mattresses for the patients. On board the *Kitty Hawk* and at the base hospital, there were clean sheets and comfortable beds for injured sailors and marines. None of us would ever make fun of shipboard life again. Conklin mentioned that almost everyone on the ship complained about the monotony of institutional food, the 24-7 duty and working conditions, the navy showers, the constant drilling at general quarters, and the strict shipboard regime. We even complained about the movies being old and that we had steak only once each week! All of us at the firebase would have instantly traded our sleeping accommodations and C-rats for the monotony of shipboard life. Conklin said he had "never realized how delicious the food was on the ship and enlisted clubs."

It was a pleasure to reminisce about the ability to easily sterilize instruments and the ready access to radiographs and a wide variety of medications. Some sailors on our ship referred to the *Kitty Hawk* as the "shitty kitty," and no one ever spoke very positively about the base hospital at Tan Son Nhut until they found themselves out at Firebase 14. While I sat in the makeshift hospital with these thoughts going through my head, it looked like lights were twinkling in the distant Truong Son Mountains that cut across the country.

Within two or three seconds, the entire jungle and tall grass several hundred meters across the river erupted in a sea of flames. Most of us either were blown off our feet by the shock wave or dove for cover. The twinkling lights must have been large-caliber muzzle flashes from unfriendly fire coming from the distant mountains. The shells landed a lot closer than any of us cared to think about. We could feel the heat and shock wave from the explosions. Trees on both sides of the river were mowed down or stripped of their foliage. Some of our men near the river were injured by the torrent of shrapnel from the shells and splinters from the flying foliage. The marine brass was on the radio immediately.

*****

The chances of getting out of this crazy dung hole in one piece seemed to be getting more remote by the minute. The injured were packed into our makeshift hospital. The corpsmen were busy administering pain medication, starting IV lines, digging out shrapnel, and stitching patients back together. Some of the men had broken bones and were pretty badly injured. An immediate "dust-off" medevac was called into headquarters. Even with their injuries, many of these men wanted to get back to their squads for support and action.

It was too bad the dental techs from the ship weren't there with the docs to help out. One in particular, Gary T., who was from somewhere in Montana, always seemed able to anticipate every need whenever there was an emergency. Gary T. was very intelligent, could improvise, and was always thinking ahead.

At least we would have no trouble convincing the journalist from *Newsweek* to get on the next bird out of the firebase. He almost seemed anxious to leave!

About fifteen minutes later, our marine scouts reported enemy activity on our side of the river. They were taking small-arms fire from about twelve kilometers up the river to the east. *Crap! This is all we need*, I thought. Suddenly, the entire river exploded less than one kilometer to our east. We didn't notice the twinkling lights in the mountains, but then all the troops seemed pretty busy.

*****

Everything seemed to be happening at once. It was difficult to concentrate on our patients. Conk remarked that his gloves had to be changed—they were soaked with blood. The entire river seemed to erupt in a huge rush of water, rocks, shrapnel, and logs. Even though our base was quite a way up from the river, the patients were getting soaked with water, sweat, and debris. *Surely, things can't possibly get any worse than this*, I thought. It was amazing how fast things could go downhill.

The first distant roll of what sounded like thunder came before we saw the jets streaking toward the mountains. Then a loud whooshing sound was heard up the river and to the west. It sounded almost like someone had opened a giant can of soda and resembled the rumble of a sustained explosion. We saw a vapor trail of what looked like a flying telephone pole against the horizon. That couldn't be good. Was that a surface-to-air missile going after our aircraft?

"Hey, Chief, what the hell was that?"

"Doc, I hate to tell you, but that is a SAM!"

"How the hell is that even a possibility, Chief?"

The North Vietnamese must have had a surface-to-air missile battery within a few kilometers of our firebase. Was it a mobile site? Why hadn't the Vietnamese ranger scouts found this site? In the next instant, the whole side of the distant mountain seemed to catch fire. It looked as if the NVA had purposely made a target in the mountains in order to lure our fighter-bombers out into the open. The little bastards! It was time for payback.

Chapter 10

SURFACE-TO-AIR MISSILE SITE, NOVEMBER 1970

Our CO, Lieutenant Colonel Avery, was on this new intelligence like a cat on a frightened mouse. He asked one of the recently arrived squad leaders to investigate and, if possible, eliminate the threat of the nearby SAM site. The lieutenant squad leader requisitioned two rocket-propelled grenade launchers (RPGs) and a 60mm mortar team.

Colonel Avery also sent a message to the fleet admiral and to the "Wild Weasel" combat command in Thailand, notifying them of the threat of a possible nearby SAM site. The Wild Weasels were a group of air force pilots and electronic warfare officers (EWOs) who formed an anti-SAM fighter group to counter the threat of the Soviet surface-to-air missiles.

These brave air force officers would fly behind enemy lines in North Vietnam in order to evaluate the SAM radar location and kill the missile site before the site could launch a missile and kill them. The motto on their arm patch included the initials "ygbsm" ("you gotta be shitting me"). These were the first words of EWO Jack Donovan when he learned of the Weasels' mission: "fly behind enemy lines in the backseat of a crazy fighter pilot who thought he was invincible and try to raise the SAM radar in order to destroy the SAM site before the enemy could launch a missile at you that flew at three times the speed of sound."

The twelve-man investigatory squad requested by Lieutenant Colonel Avery was organizing near our makeshift hospital when the squad leader, Lieutenant Jack Monari, decided it would be a good idea to have a corpsman or a doc with them in case there was any sort of medical emergency. The lieutenant had impressive leadership skills and talked with a bit of a southern accent, which gave the impression that he might be from farm country somewhere in Alabama. His speech was deliberate and clear, even if a little difficult to understand.

The only emotion any of us felt at the time was anger that this hidden SAM site was trying to kill our pilots. Some of those pilots could also be shipmates from the *Hawk* out in the Tonkin Gulf. Anger wasn't a beneficial emotion right then, but it was very evident that none of us were happy about a hidden SAM site anywhere near us.

Maybe it didn't look too busy in medical at the time because the squad sergeant asked, "Hey, Doc, can you and a corpsman come along?" It sounded not like an order but more like a hopeful request; sergeants didn't give orders to navy lieutenants. But my agreement was immediate.

"Sarge, let's make this SAM site history! If you think I would be an asset, I'd be happy to help." Emotions were running pretty high. It wasn't that anyone was anxious to go out beyond the confines of the base, but I guess the thought at the time was that the missile site was just too close for comfort.

After a quick course in firearms management, the sergeant handed me a .45-caliber handgun and an extra clip of ammunition. He admonished, "Don't let the gooks get close enough to have to use this, and keep the safety on!"

As I loaded some bandages and pain meds into a backpack, I wondered which after-dinner movie they were going to be showing tonight in the wardroom on the *Hawk*. "Hey, Sarge, about this time of evening, our wardroom in officer country on the *Hawk* turns into an air-conditioned movie theater with comfortable seating for everyone. It doesn't look like there is much chance of that happening out here in the bush."

"No, I don't think so, sir." There was something very likable about this seemingly grizzled old sergeant who was actually in his late twenties. He was probably my age!

Monson, one of the other docs from medical, was asked by the chief to join us. No one ever seemed to enjoy working with Monson. His attitude seemed a little severe out here in the bush. He was, for sure, concentrating on staying alive, but he had a subtle way of putting down anyone of lesser rank or rate; his rating was that of a first class petty officer. Although he was competent, he had a habit of talking down to other sailors or marines, especially those who were our patients and under our care. If he had pulled crap like that at the dental clinic on the ship, our chief would have corrected that attitude problem in a New York minute.

Perhaps the laws of civility were relaxed or overlooked when everyone was under the constant danger of enemy fire. The instinct of self-preservation is understandable, but should people whose existence is threatened just disregard all rules of polite and moral behavior?

In Germany after World War I, inflation and hyperinflation turned even some law-abiding citizens into the criminal element.[*] Normal citizens under the duress of wartime activity were known to exhibit deviant and uncivilized behavior toward their family, friends, and neighbors. Was it possible that conditions here in the jungle were causing Monson to denigrate his fellow marines?

The patrol took off so fast that there was no time to think about what a crazy idea this whole patrol was or its possible consequences. We were heading west along the riverbank with two South Vietnamese scouts leading the way. The mosquitoes and flies were so thick that you could inhale them if you weren't careful. Many of the troops had scarves made from T-shirts over their mouths so that they could breathe without swallowing the proliferation of bugs.

Our main goal was to prevent a second launch of another SAM. Monari decided we would follow the river for a few kilometers. It was the most exposed route, but at least we could make good time. He warned us, "Stay in ankle-deep water so the gooks won't spot our footprints."

*****

Our clothing and feet were continuously wet, or at least damp and spongy from the constant high humidity, mist, and intermittent rain. Walking in the water was a reminder to check the troops for trench foot after this fun trip in the river. Continuously wet feet could lead to a malady known as immersion foot disorder, which in turn could lead to gangrene and amputation.

---

[*] A. Fergusson, *When Money Dies*: W. Kimber & Co., London, 1975, 237.

Occasionally, if a man was desperate enough to get out of the bush, he would incite this condition by not changing his footwear or socks for weeks on end. But most of the marines at Firebase 14 seemed to have a positive attitude about their circumstances. Even though everyone, except perhaps some of the lifers, wanted to get back to American women and the world they knew. Since I was a little older (mid 20's) these men seemed very young. Most were really a collection of older teenagers who seemed quite dedicated to doing their job. It made me proud to be associated with them.

No one really liked being out in the bush, and everyone complained about something: the food, the supplies, the weather, the enemy, the lack of reliable mail, the lack of women, or their superiors. Mostly, the complaint was no women. When possible, the admin officer would rotate the troops to one of the more major cities in Vietnam for a little R&R. Unfortunately, most of the troops would come back with some version of drippy dick disease. However, getting laid with some hot whores and a few cold beers seemed to go a long way toward curing a lot of difficult problems for the troops in the bush.

*****

Our patrol consisted of fourteen men. The stealth and speed with which these marines moved was astonishing. As the next-to-last one from the back, I heard almost no sound except some faint splashing noises as we quickly walked along the river near the right bank. The issued handgun made a slight swishing sound in its holster against my pants as we all hurried to keep up. It was still daylight, so we could see where we were going, but twilight was coming on quickly. We had gone about twelve to fifteen kilometers up the river when our squad leader signaled us to halt and get down. Then we heard it.

There were people speaking in low voices somewhere off to our right. It sounded like barely audible murmuring. They were so quiet that it wasn't clear what language they were speaking, but it sounded like Russian. Although my experience with the language in the Russian Club at Reading Memorial High School had been minimal and I was nowhere near fluent, some of the words were recognizable to me.

I crept up to the squad leader and whispered my thoughts in his ear. He didn't seem at all pleased. "The little fuckers have Russian advisors!" he whispered.

If we were near the SAM site, we certainly couldn't see it. Our squad leader sent one of our Vietnamese scouts into the jungle, away from the river, to investigate. The rest of us hid in the jungle brush adjacent to the river. After our brisk and nimble progress down the river, we were all a little tired, dirty, and wet.

This small scout was incredible. You couldn't hear or see him as he went through the jungle. He must have spent most of the trip on his stomach. He returned after forty minutes or so with his uniform, face, and hands caked with mud and green jungle slime. He confirmed our worst fears: there was a SAM site about four to five hundred meters into the jungle. It was in a concave depression in front of a rocky ridge. The scout relayed that there were seven men near the missile area. He said that the site was virtually impossible to see and that he never would have found it if it weren't for the sound of their voices. Their voices carried because of the rocky ridge behind the site. He was virtually on top of it before he realized that it was a missile site. The Fan Song radar screen was camouflaged on the back with vegetation to make it look like trees and vines.

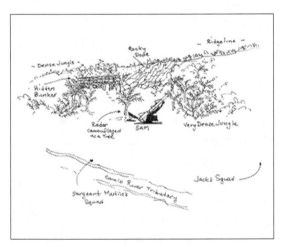

Surface-to-Air Missile Site Area

Although at the time we couldn't see any overt aircraft activity, there were some distant, faint, silvery vapor trails catching the last glint of sunlight. All looked quiet in the sky until we heard a low but very audible hum from the direction of the SAM site. What were these little creeps up to? Were they getting ready to test the system or launch another missile? But at what?

I thought of home. Both of my parents were relatively sane people and lived in an old family farm home above the road to the high school in the quiet, picturesque country town of Sudbury, Massachusetts. What the heck were we doing in this hellhole, eating mosquitoes and breakfast nut-bar C-rats next to this rock-strewn river in the fetid jungle?

*****

Our squad leader was in conference with a Sergeant Mestilo. He was the Top Sarg at the firebase; everyone respected him. The sergeant must have had Native American blood in him. When he moved through the jungle, he was almost invisible and perfectly silent. His corporal said, "Mestilo definitely has his shit together." Although not very tall, perhaps five feet six or so, he was very powerfully built and probably a lifer. Scars on his face and arms indicated he'd had some experience with a blade. His face was a symphony of pathology. Between the broken nose, penetrating dark eyes, and interlacing scars, it was hard not to stare. Even with all his surprising facial features, he wasn't particularly ugly, just unusual-looking.

Mestilo's camouflaged uniform was bleached out to an almost monochromatic pale-brown color. His men respected and trusted his leadership skills. He consistently made sound decisions, and his first thought was always the protection and safety of his men. He probably could have done well in a leadership position in almost any large company in America. He told us he had grown up in the Texas Panhandle near Amarillo in a small town called Masterson, but he had never really known his parents; they had both died when he was young. His relatives, including aunts, uncles, and cousins, had brought him up, and they all worked on the same farm, helping with the crops and cattle.

The conference between Lieutenant Monari and Sergeant Mestilo ended with the sergeant declaring, "Let's rid this valley of one friggin' SAM site as soon as possible." The idea of eliminating the missile site was admirable, but the how-to was a little confusing. The lieutenant almost immediately had a plan.

Lieutenant Monari was always thinking about two pages ahead of everyone else. If those writing his fitness reports had any brains, he would always be up for early promotion. He was the sort of officer any organization would be proud and eager to employ. In the private sector of American business, he would be looked at as presidential material.

His most impressive quality was his absolute calm. It was as if he were mapping out the solution to a math problem while lecturing to a class in a university. How did these marines stay so collected under what had to be extreme pressure? His calmness under pressure seemed typical of the marine officers and enlisted men I had encountered in Vietnam. This calmness and leadership under pressure gave the rest of us a good dose of much-needed confidence.

The lieutenant advised us, "We are going to split into two groups." He would lead one patrol with one of the Vietnamese scouts, and the other scout would go with the sergeant. His primary concern was stealth and missile site defenses. "Our goal is to leave the SAM site inoperable."

The lieutenant continued, "My group is going to try to get up behind the gook bastards. If we get in trouble, there will be two clicks on the radio. If that happens, Sergeant, you attack the site—don't wait for us. Otherwise, we'll take the first shot." Lieutenant Monari, five marines, a scout, and the corpsman Monson backtracked about one klick east in the river and then slipped into the jungle.

It was starting to get foggy and dark; visibility was getting somewhat difficult. It was an overcast, wretched, dismal evening. Perhaps the rain would hold off until this scary mission was over. The rest of us went with the Vietnamese scout and the sergeant. The plan was to backtrack to the scout's last site visit and wait until the lieutenant's group could get above or on the far side of the site to launch the attack. Each group took a rocket-propelled grenade launcher with three RPGs. We left the heavier 60mm mortar equipment and the three-pound shells covered with vegetation near the river, in case we needed to retrieve them for a defensive position.

Jack Monari was to fire the first RPG round into the site before we were to attack. Since our distance to the site was shorter, we were to fall back after the attack and wait across the river for covering fire in case

Monari's patrol was followed. It all sounded quite logical. Logic, however, has a way of going south just when you don't want it to. All of us were wet and grimy by this time, but we knew that the SAM site could not be left to bring down our aircraft. The tension kept the adrenaline flowing; I was on the edge of crawling out of my skin in abject panic. The thought that a higher power was looking out for us kept me sane. *Dear Jesus*, I prayed, *please protect us!*

The Vietnamese scout traveled the four hundred or so meters stealthily. After the first fifty or sixty meters, we were on our hands and knees. After another hundred meters or so, we were flat on our stomachs. It was as if we were becoming part of the jungle floor. The troops carrying the RPG launcher were struggling somewhat; that sucker was a little awkward when you had to crawl through the jungle with it.

We moved extremely cautiously. It was hard to see: the undergrowth in the jungle was a wall of damp leaves, brush, vines, fungi, and small trees, and there was continuous sweat dripping into our eyes. We could hear and feel the crawly insects as we inched our way through the damp, soggy jungle.

The loudest sound I heard was my own terrified breathing. Feeling completely inept and out of my element, I found it difficult to control frequent, frantic gulps for air. We had blackened our faces, which were now covered with splotches of mud and green vegetation stains. The sweat drenched us so much that most of the black face covering was running off us in rivulets. After about thirty minutes of inching along, the scout held up one finger, signaling us to wait. He whispered, "We' here."

Low voices and the hum of equipment were audible, but we still couldn't see too much. But no one questioned Mestilo; he seemed to have a handle on what was going on. We all wondered how the NVA and the VC had gotten these missiles, the launcher, and all this assorted radar equipment down into such a remote spot in the jungle. There were no roads. Most of the equipment had to have been carried in by handcarts, water buffalo, or elephants. We had to be fairly close to the seventeenth parallel and North Vietnam. This was an ingenious enemy that at the very least deserved our respect.

A deep humming sound began to emanate from the radar site. Suddenly, it turned into a claxon warning, interrupted by distant sounds of droning aircraft. The claxon tone wasn't particularly loud, but something was definitely about to happen. I heard movement and activity slightly to our right, some seventy meters away.

Suddenly, we spotted a streak of fire coming directly into the missile site from a small rise about one kilometer away. Monari's first RPG shot exploded against the rock ridge about thirty meters behind the site. Then all hell broke loose.

Just to the left of the SAM site was a well-camouflaged bunker that our scout hadn't spotted. This hidden structure must have been housing at least twenty North Vietnamese troops. The NVA poured out of the bunker like ants to an overturned picnic basket. The gomers made a beeline directly for the source of the incoming fire. They had a mortar team lobbing shells in Monari's direction within a minute. In addition, they had some sort of heavy field gun that started firing toward Monari's position. Another RPG round missed the missile site but exploded just behind the hidden bunker.

From our position and angle, our patrol couldn't get a clear shot through the jungle, but at least we now realized the site's exact location. The launcher had raised a missile on its platform and looked about ready to go.

"Holy shit, Doc, look at the size of that missile!" whispered the sergeant. It was huge. A strange, low growling noise was coming from the vicinity of the missile.

"Hey, Sarge," I whispered, "what the hell is that sound?"

"Crap, Doc, you got me by the short hairs. I don't have a friggin' clue!"

We didn't realize it at the time, but the low growling noise was the rocket engine on the missile. The next sound we heard was the very loud explosive whoosh of the launch. The missile practically exploded off the launcher track. It was out of sight in an instant.

These missile operators were, if nothing else, fast and efficient. They had another missile on the launcher within two minutes. That's when Sergeant Mestilo whispered, "I've had about a fuckin' 'nough of this crap."

He took the two-man RPG team to a less sheltered area where they had a clear line of fire about ninety meters from the SAM site. Stealth wasn't so critical now because the NVA seemed focused on the other RPG team. The RPGs had an effective range of two hundred to five hundred meters, and their maximum range would not be more than approximately nine hundred meters. The rocket itself usually had to travel at least thirty meters in order to arm itself. *Please, God, let them be accurate*, I thought.

Mestilo's first grenade rocket missed the launcher by at least three or four meters. The RPG rocket launch was much louder than expected, but we were enmeshed into the jungle floor and inconspicuous and at least fifty to sixty meters away from the RPG launching tube. The second RPG caught the missile launch mechanism itself about halfway up the rail. Initially, it looked like the grenade rocket hadn't done too much damage, but in an instant the entire rail and launching pad was engulfed in flames.

It wasn't clear whether it was the SAM rocket fuel exploding or the payload or both. In a moment the entire site was in flames. The results were spectacular! We flattened ourselves into the slime to avoid the blowback and the intense heat. The fireworks probably alerted every North Vietnamese and Vietcong for miles around.

The sergeant must have been thinking the same thing because he said, "Okay, guys, let's get the fuck outta here!" Our scout led us back through the jungle to the river, and our patrol was not particularly stealthy on our way back. The SAM missile crew had too many other problems at the moment to worry about us.

*****

Meanwhile, the lieutenant's patrol was really catching heavy fire. "Heads down, ladies. Charlie wants to fight back," yelled Lieutenant Monari. The mortar rounds were exploding above them in the thick jungle canopy. The loud chatter of AK-47 rounds strafed across their position; the firepower peeled the bark right off some of the trees and flattened small vines or brush more than waist-high. "The fucking gooks must have had a patrol out here," yelled Monari over the din.

The incoming mortar rounds actually saved them since they were all eating dirt within a second or two of the first explosion from our patrol's RPGs. The mortar shells were going off in the jungle canopy above them, and some of the shrapnel rained down harmlessly around them. Although Monari's squad couldn't see the missile site, they could feel the heat and shock of the explosion and knew Sergeant Mestilo had been successful and the site had been destroyed.

The SAM site exploded in flames. "Mission accomplished, ladies; let's bingo toward the river," yelled the lieutenant.

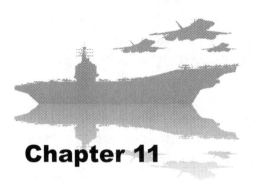

Chapter 11

THE LONG WAY BACK

"Lieutenant, the gooks are all around us!" shouted Corporal Herbert, the youngest marine in the patrol.

Monari shouted, "Keep a low profile, men, and hug the mud! We need to keep moving toward the river. Fernandez, you take point, and we will slither south until we hit the river. Absolute silence, and keep your safeties off with fingers over the trigger guards."

Everyone felt comfortable with Fernandez at point. He was bright and quick-thinking and had excellent bush instincts; he weighed decisions carefully. Not only was he likable and in possession of a terrific sense of humor, but the men trusted him with their lives. Point position required lightning-fast reflexes and was never enviable. The point man needed nerves of steel and a steady hand over the trigger. He had to be constantly on alert for booby traps, mines, and any evidence of enemy activity.

Halfway to the river, Fernandez saw a fresh footprint and heard some rustling in the bush. He let go with his M-16 on full automatic. A moan from the jungle indicated a possible hit.

"What the fuck are you doing?" cried Monari.

"Gooks up ahead, sir," snorted Fernandez. He didn't have time to bring his rifle up again before a gomer came crashing through the bush. The VC put one bullet into Fernandez's back before Monson, who was second in the patrol line about ten meters back, put two M-16 rounds into the gomer's face. Monson's credibility had just jumped in the minds of his fellow marines.

"Keep moving, you pukes," Monari admonished in a low voice. "Leave the launcher. Just keep crawling south."

Monson helped Fernandez with a pressure bandage and a morphine syrette. AK-47 rounds kept snapping overhead, but the patrol made steady progress. As they approached the river, Hutchinson took a round to the shoulder. Monson grabbed him by the flak jacket and pulled him into a small clearing. He applied a pressure bandage and gave him a syrette of morphine. Since Fernandez was clearly in pain and having trouble crawling, Monson gave him another morphine syrette. The morphine seemed to put a smile, or at least a more relaxed look, back on Fernandez's face, and he resumed crawling toward the river.

"Carmody," the lieutenant ordered, "head out to the river and signal the other patrol; they should be across by now. Keep your fucking head down. We'll wait for your confirming signal, two clicks on the radio; we need absolute silence."

It wasn't hard to stay quieter than the explosions and the commotion from the SAM site. Another marine caught a round just above the knee— even while crawling on all fours. That took Monson's last morphine syrette.

*****

Our patrol with the sergeant had gone east along the river for about two hundred meters and then waded across at a shallow spot at a bend in the river. We all hid up in the jungle with the mortar launcher team. There were seven mortar shells, an RPG launcher with one grenade rocket left, five M-16s, and an assortment of small arms. I felt ridiculous carrying a .45-caliber pistol and seriously hoped it would never have to be used. Our clothes smelled like sewage and were caked with mud. Our movement was somewhat constricted by our wet, sticky clothing, but we were too frazzled and tired to notice or care about anything except getting back to the firebase.

In civilian life, some of my family members had a license to carry a firearm; however, these licenses were for duck hunting with a twelve-gauge shotgun or target practicing with a .22-caliber pistol at the Cape Ann

Sportsman Club's indoor range in Gloucester, Massachusetts. It hadn't occurred to me until that moment that I might actually have to shoot someone. As we were climbing into the jungle on the far side of the river, a secondary explosion from the SAM site told us another SAM missile must have cooked off.

*****

We sent a radio signal to Lieutenant Monari in order to let him know we were in position, but we didn't get a confirming signal on our radio. He and his team had their hands full, but the lack of acknowledgment was of some concern to Sergeant Mestilo.

Mestilo hissed, "The little fuckers have 'em in a shit sandwich. Jeez, I wish I had gone with 'em."

As this mission wore on, our respect for the sergeant increased greatly. He had been a marine for about eight years and was one tough character with a minimum of BS. His best attribute, even though he was undoubtedly a lifer, was that his first concern was not the enemy body count, but returning his men home in one piece. He never spoke down to his men, yet he was firm and definitive about his orders. You got the idea that you never wanted to cross him. The sergeant had us spread out along the riverbank about ten meters apart.

The mortar team went looking for a suitable position to set up their weapon: they needed a clear area without any jungle canopy blocking their shots. The rest of the patrol was hoping that the mortar team would get a good distance away; all we needed was something else to draw enemy interest.

We could hear lots of small-arms fire, AK-47s, and M-16s from east of us up the river, indicating a probable firefight between Monari's RPG team and the folks who had streamed out of the hidden bunker. What we did not realize at the time was the professionalism of the enemy troops in the bunker. They were crack NVA support troops for the Russian missile site and had roving patrols in the area. It was one of these patrols that had Monari's support team in its crosshairs.

The next visible sign of Monari's patrol was an orange streak blurred by the low fog and jungle foliage about two hundred meters to our left and about half a klick into the jungle. It sounded like a larger-caliber shell or RPG round; the glow of the round striking something was followed by heavy machine-gun and automatic-weapons fire. It looked like Lieutenant Monari had stirred up a bit of a hornet's nest! The lieutenant knew how to handle himself in a firefight, but we weren't sure whether he knew the numbers he was up against.

In a few minutes, one of the men in Monari's patrol popped out to the edge of the jungle about 150 meters to our left, on the opposite bank of the river. He signaled with an infrared light, and our sergeant flashed back with a confirming signal. The marine on the far side of the river immediately ducked back into the undergrowth.

Our sergeant got on the radio to the battalion commander to alert him of our situation. We were told to evacuate the area immediately after the patrols had linked up and get back to the base camp ASAP. The battalion CO mentioned extraction, friendly aircraft cover, and fire-suppression activity. The CO did not want our patrols to be in the way of any friendly fire directed at the enemy.

Our sergeant now heard from Monari's patrol; they were making their way through the jungle toward our position and were being pursued by an enemy force of unknown strength. We were informed to lay down a mortar barrage about one hundred meters into the jungle in a direct line in back of their exit point out onto the river, indicated by the infrared signal.

Two or three minutes later, the patrol came out of the undergrowth about 125 meters west of us on the other side of the river. Our sergeant was watching intently with a monocular night scope. After flashing their infrared signal, they moved as quickly as possible, but it looked like they had taken a few casualties. Two men were being carried on the backs of other marines, and one marine was walking with a splinted and bandaged leg. They quickly disappeared to the east of us down the river. Everything was quite visible in the night scope. Then our luck took a better turn.

*****

The first thing we heard were several muffled poping sounds from somewhere in back of us in the jungle. Our mortar team had put down a pattern of shells in the area Monari had requested. Although it was impossible to tell whether these mortar shells had landed as planned, or whether they were effective, there was one secondary explosion. The VC were probably protected by the heavy jungle canopy. We were busy covering the other patrol's exit from the jungle and their retreat down the river toward our firebase site to the east. We would follow shortly behind them if nothing else came out of the jungle. It was at least twelve to fifteen kilometers back to our firebase camp. Then we saw movement through the fog; the enemy was outlined against the river.

It looked like twenty to thirty NVA troops streaming out of the jungle and onto the far riverbank. There was barely enough light to see their movement against the river. On the sergeant's command, our mortar team immediately fired the last four shells. One landed and exploded in the river, but the rest seemed close enough to scatter the troops. As the NVA was melting into the jungle, our RPG team let loose with our last rocket in their direction. It was hard to determine whether this rocket was successful; it seemed to explode in the jungle along the river. We were pretty busy assessing the other squad's condition. The sergeant was on the radio to the base CO, who again requested our immediate evacuation; suppressive air support had been ordered.

We hoped we hadn't stirred up additional enemy activity. Our immediate priority was to link up with the other squad and return safely to the firebase. We all wondered if we should be concerned that the air strike pilots might not know our exact coordinates. But it was too late for second-guessing.

When the mortar team joined us, we all needed to hustle in order to catch up with Monari's patrol. At that moment the first aircraft came in low and straight, screaming down the river. It was so dark we couldn't tell what squadron it was from or even the type of aircraft. There was no spotter plane or other warning of friendly aircraft activity. That plane came straight down the river, roaring like an angry lion, in complete darkness without releasing any cluster bombs or mini-gun fire.

The five-hundred-pound canisters of bomblets or cluster bombs were called Rockeyes. They were particularly lethal against personnel or trucks. When dropped or deployed, over two hundred bomblets would spread out and pretty much devastate anything in a three-hundred-foot-long by two-hundred-foot-wide area. One bomblet could disable a tank. We knew we didn't want to be anywhere near that scenario. At least now we knew we had some backup.

The lieutenant had to be at least two or three kilometers up the river in front of us. We stepped lively down our side of the river for about 100 meters. We wanted to avoid a friendly-fire incident from the incoming aircraft. We hadn't realized at the time that the pilot could visualize the river and objects on the landscape in his radar thanks to a heat-sensitive black box on the aircraft. This particular piece of equipment was able to give the pilot a real-time read of the terrain and information about exactly what he was visualizing, even in total darkness and inclement weather.

The immediacy of the air support indicated that the aircraft had to have already been in the area in order to support our patrol. Daniel informed us later that there were often air patrols around twenty-five thousand feet that were always ready for immediate deployment to support the firebases and troops in the bush. Those brave pilots were a constant reminder that someone was always looking out for us.

*****

Sergeant Mestilo informed us, "Get undercover men. If nothin' else comes out of the jungle, we will follow the first patrol; otherwise, we will provide protective cover fire for them." Part of the twenty-third psalm came to mind: "Even though we walk through the valley of the shadow of death, we will not fear evil, for you are with us; your weapons comfort us." This patrol didn't have too much firepower left; it was comforting not to have to use it.

*****

"Damn," breathed Mestilo. "There are three gomers creeping along the opposite riverbank heading east." The night scope had just proved its value; the problem was that there was only one night scope. The enemy was moving low and fast in pursuit of Monari's patrol.

Mestilo immediately whispered a plan. "All right, marines. Dig in and find some protective covering. Although there are only three gomers visible, there could well be more in the immediate area. They could cross the river and get behind us or outflank us. When they are directly opposite us, follow my fire into the riverbank. The little pissers are walking in the water. Wait for my command and then empty your weapons along the opposite bank. Reload and quietly head east along the river; cross at the bend where it's shallow."

This was a turning point for me. I was not looking forward to shooting another human being. The thought of someone shooting back at us was turning my legs rubbery. This definitely had not been part of the job description. These feelings were embarrassing because the young marines in our patrol seemed to harbor none of these hesitations.

On Mestilo's command, all the weapons were unloaded; even my .45 was emptied. The M-16s mostly fired on automatic.

"The way we were spread out made us look like a much larger force," commented the sergeant. The total skirmish took less than thirty seconds. There was no return fire. The sergeant watched the VC retreat into the jungle, and our patrol carefully picked its way east along the riverbank.

The Charlies weren't able to return fire, and no more came out of the bush. Still, we just knew there were more out there somewhere. Perhaps the low-flying aircraft had spooked them back into the jungle. It wasn't clear whether the pilot was from the *Hawk*, but a silent prayer of thanks was sent for all the men out on Yankee Station.

*****

As we entered our base camp, directly after Monari's patrol, everyone in the makeshift medical area was busy looking after the wounded. The sergeant requested a replacement patrol to ensure the Cong wouldn't come storming into the firebase behind us. That replacement patrol left immediately to strengthen our perimeter and set up a couple of LPs, or listening posts.

The LPs were approximately one hundred to two hundred meters outside of our perimeter. These two-man listening posts were designed to give the perimeter troops time to adjust and arm the claymore mines and make sure they were ready for a possible attempted breach of the perimeter.

The men in the LPs were to stay hidden and not reveal their presence to the enemy. An LP was a nerve-racking and extremely dangerous place to stay, especially at night.

The nights were so dark that you literally could not see anything outside of your area of touch. Sometimes you could hear or even smell the gomers crawling near the LP, but you could almost never see them. If the men in the LP heard close-in enemy sounds, they would toss a grenade in that direction. Firing the M-16 would give away the position of the LP and mean certain death. The early-warning LPs were not at all popular duty.

*****

Mestilo asked me, "Doc, would you mind going with me to the CO's bunker for the debriefing?" It wasn't clear if he was nervous about stirring up the NVA or proud about disrupting and destroying the SAM site and needed confirmation.

"Sure, let's bring the CO up-to-date, Sergeant."

Lieutenant Colonel Avery's so-called bunker included two tents hooked together with ponchos. The sandbags on the tents' perimeter were to help stop small-arms fire and shrapnel. The bags reached about waist-high. The plywood floor was a definite luxury. The command post certainly wasn't elaborate, but it served its purpose. Like everything else at the firebase, it looked very temporary. The more information gleaned at the debriefing, the more everyone's concern deepened for this entire firebase and its mission.

Although surprised, the CO didn't seemed shocked at the proximity of the SAM site. "How did those little bastards get so close undetected?"

"Sir," I said, "they probably were exceedingly stealthy in order to avoid an air strike. We must be quite close to the DMZ."

The sergeant added, "No need of an air strike now, sir."

It almost seemed that the lieutenant colonel felt as if his options were being limited. His immediate goal was to strengthen and fortify this firebase into a vital link in a chain of command centers that would protect the people of South Vietnam from an invading enemy. No matter how hard he tried, the CO could not ensure success of the operation at this firebase. All of us worried that any minor victories and magnificent opportunities could at any moment unexpectedly turn into unmitigated catastrophe.

Lieutenant Colonel Avery seemed to be handling an immense amount of adversity under pressure in a difficult-to-win situation. It was clear that he was on his way to full colonel after his stint in the bush as commanding officer of the battalion. His plight was similar to that of the British in our own Revolutionary War. The enemy in Vietnam did not want to confront anyone in a firefight unless they had overwhelming odds. In addition, the VC knew what they were fighting for—a reunification of their country. Most Americans knew we were fighting a political war, designed by politicians. Our circumstances in this "politician's war" made the loss of our most valuable personnel even more frustrating and sad.

*****

There were marines and service personnel from various races and ethnic groups at the firebase. The CO's views on racial problems within the firebase were rather unique and straightforward: "we have no racial problems now, and we will not have any—*ever.*" He warned that if you had racial prejudices or any other prejudices, they were to be ironed out while you were on patrol away from Firebase 14.

This was a pretty interesting way of solving the problem. Anyone who has ever been out on a patrol in the bush knows that everyone is dependent on each other. There is no room for petty bickering or cronyism. Your life literally depends on the grunt in front of you and the grunt behind you. Skin color or ethnicity does not enter into the equation. The CO was crystal clear with all his direct orders.

*****

Early the next morning, two squads of marines took off into the jungle, looking for NVA or VC to the west of our position in the direction of the SAM site. My fervent hope was that they would find nothing and come back to report no activity.

The marines venturing into the bush were confronted by myriad dangers with every step. They probably most feared the ambush. The VC were masters at silently waiting for our troops to enter into a killing field of fire; they would then attack from more than one direction with automatic weapons, usually AK-47s. In addition, there were booby traps, land mines, and snipers to worry about.

One of the VC's favorite booby traps was a marine helmet with a grenade attached inside. The pin would be strung to a nearby root covered by the helmet. Once the helmet was kicked or picked up, the grenade pin would be jerked out, exploding the helmet and killing or maiming anyone within twenty feet.

The punji traps were especially terrifying. Sharpened bamboo stakes tipped with poison, usually human excrement, were placed in large holes covered with brush. Often the lighter Vietnamese villagers could traverse a trap without falling into it; the larger American soldiers, however, would fall down into it. There were thousands of these traps all over Vietnam. Schoolchildren were often recruited to sharpen the bamboo into spikes.

One of the new men from the battalion, Private Winterspoon, had fallen into a punji trap the day before I arrived. Although his wounds were cleaned and he initially survived, even the intravenous antibiotics that were dripped into his veins couldn't stay ahead of his infection. He was medevacked back to Hawaii almost immediately but died of massive infection shortly afterward. The excrement-tipped punji stakes had plunged the infected material deep into his flesh. It was a horrible way to die.

*****

After digesting the after-action report on the SAM site to the west of the firebase, the brass had concern about the number of North Vietnamese troops from the missile base who might be heading in our direction.

The acting XO, Captain Darcy, explained the importance of channeling the NVA from our west into a narrow one- or two-kilometer area in a natural valley that snaked its way along the river through the jungle. His game plan was to hit the peaks on both sides of the valley with air strikes and drive the enemy toward the thickly dense jungle valley floor. He then planned to call in an air strike with napalm on the narrow remaining corridor. Two squads were planned to move out in a pincer movement toward the river.

As Gus outlined this plan to me, I thought, *There must be a death wish for all the vegetation within reach.* This operation sounded scary and harebrained.

*****

By noon, the first report from the northernmost squad came into headquarters. The patrol had found evidence of enemy troops in the valley. There were footprints along the river and areas of flattened elephant grass. Listening devices in the area also confirmed the presence of human activity, but the patrol hadn't spotted any troops.

These marines were tough and jungle-savvy; they didn't miss much. A spotter plane also indicated some evidence of enemy activity, including flattened elephant grass and an area of a possible recent cooking fire, but again, the NVA seemed to have melted into the jungle. Our CO knew that if you didn't spot the enemy, that didn't necessarily mean they weren't there. In medical, the fact that no VC or NVA could be located was indeed a blessing.

The medical area had been so busy that some of the docs' sleep was fitful and disturbed by horrible nightmares resulting from the plethora of traumatic injuries suffered by the young marines. Many of the men working in the medical area at Firebase 14 reported frequent sleep difficulty. Some said that they were afraid to fall asleep at the end of the day. Exhaustion would cause them to collapse on an air mattress at odd hours of the day and night. Watching the death and dismemberment of our most precious resources had a lasting and chilling effect on all of us treating them. It is no surprise that sleep was difficult and that nightmares often woke us. If we hadn't been so busy in medical, we probably would have been even more depressed and suicidal.

The enemy activity at this firebase was almost as bad as at Peleliu or Okinawa during World War II and just as terrifying. A marine survivor from Okinawa once tried to explain to me the combat situation there: "Son, you know how you can be startled in the night by a sudden noise or movement that causes you to jump? Well, it was like that for seventeen straight days and nights on Okinawa!"

*****

The second squad was operating in the area near the destroyed SAM site, fifteen kilometers west, but on the other side of the river. One of the men on the patrol spotted a lone enemy soldier high in the crotch of a tree, partially concealed by vines and vegetation. The marine waited until they were out of range and then whispered to his sergeant, "Hey, Sarge, check out that tree we just went under, about ten meters up where it branches out."

The squad leader immediately formed a defensive perimeter, but it was too late. The enemy attacked from two directions. The marines didn't realize it at the time, but they had wandered into the middle of a heavy concentration of professional NVA troops intent on surprising and overrunning our firebase. This attack could have been disastrous for what was left of our battalion.

As JB later told me, "Our defenses on the river side of the encampment were really exposed. There were no trip wires or razor wire or claymore mines on the river side of the battalion encampment. Although the base was elevated, it was an open field of fire. If this patrol of NVA and VC had coordinated their attack with the others who eventually attacked our northern perimeter (which evidently had been their intent), they could have easily overrun the firebase."

The NVA opened up with a burst of automatic weapons. The marines immediately hit the deck, but two of them were cut down in the first volley. After regrouping, the sergeant called in for medical evacuation and reinforcements. He knew that he had to get his squad to safety before they were overpowered.

The patrol leader, Sergeant Cassidy, was as tough as they come. An African American from Nevada, he stood around five feet eight and weighed about 190 pounds, much of it solid muscle. He was completely devoted to his men—as they were to him. He knew it wouldn't take long for the enemy to assess their vulnerability and cut them to pieces.

The first squad was several kilometers away on the other side of the river. They would be unable to add any firepower. Also, the second squad had no way of knowing the size of the NVA force that had them trapped.

Within minutes, it was evident from the heavy AK-47 fire that they would be overrun if they didn't get out of the area quickly. Two of the men were badly injured, one with a sucking chest wound and the other with a nasty gunshot wound to the right shoulder. The river was three or four hundred meters to their right.

The sergeant ordered his men to detonate two smoke canisters and use the cover to retreat to the river. The sergeant's second command went out over the radio: "Air strike on the smoke area south of the river. ASAP." Now they had to hustle to get out of the way of an air strike that could commence anytime within the next thirty minutes.

As they carefully wormed their way to the river, the enemy was all around them. One of the injured marines, Private Kastinopolous, moaned to Cassidy, "You should leave me, Sarge. I ain't gonna make it."

"You'll make it," growled Cassidy, "or we will all die trying to haul your sad ass to safety!"

Although slowed by their injured, they carefully shot their way to the bank of the river. Without Sergeant Cassidy's careful and professional guidance, they probably never would have made it. "Hey, Zeek, you and Nigro defend this spot for about five minutes and then follow us back through the jungle to the river. Try to keep them off your backs until we can clean 'em out with an air strike."

The sergeant had the two corporals hang back and fire their M-16s on full automatic so that the enemy would have difficulty assessing the number of men retreating. All remaining grenades were tossed into the jungle to further confuse the enemy. The explosions helped to camouflage their retreat. Because of the dense jungle canopy, the mortar was useless. Although two more marines were hit, they finally made it to the river and crossed at the shallow bend just as the first aircraft came screaming in low over the valley.

If the pilot dropped any bombs, damage seemed limited. The aircraft was soon long gone, and only a faint roar of the afterburner was heard as the plane climbed into the distance.

The next second, the entire jungle across the river seemed to ignite in flames. The napalm had a distinct petroleum odor. The patrol heard several secondary explosions, indicating that the enemy had moved in some munitions for larger-caliber weapons. Even though the trees, vines, and brush were almost always soaked with dampness, the napalm seemed to immediately consume the vegetation.

Sergeant Cassidy's squad never knew where the aircraft had come from. It went by so quickly and low that the marines caught just a fleeting glance at it. Although they couldn't tell at first whether any ordnance had been dropped, the plane's low angle had fully unleashed and spread the napalm's destructive power. The five-second-delayed fuse also ensured a wider distribution of the explosive jellied gasoline. Those brave pilots were fantastic! The hornet's nest the second squad had stumbled into was no longer returning fire.

When the sergeant's squad returned from their mission, we all had our hands full patching them up. Another medevac unit was called in to get the four new patients to Da Nang as quickly as possible. One marine corporal was suffering from multiple splinter wounds from an AK-47 close-in round that had hit a nearby tree. One large splinter fragment had lodged in his neck and was dangerously close to his carotid artery. JB bandaged the splinter right into his neck wound and administered antibiotic therapy and pain medication. "Son, surgical removal will be much safer in a regular hospital in case your artery needs repair."

*****

The first squad returned with relatively minor injuries that included insect bites, leeches, and a sprained ankle. Although they had detected the presence of the NVA, they could not find any enemy combatants. One marine was suffering from a high fever and hallucinations. Another had suffered a gunshot wound to the leg, but the sergeant thought it might have been self-inflicted since no enemy snipers were found. If a man stayed out in the bush too long, anything was possible. Self-inflicted gunshot wounds frequently sent the patient to the rear or a safer area. If it was serious enough, the wound could lead to a one-way ticket back to the world.

Gus also thought the soldier's wound looked suspicious, so he asked, "Corporal, how long you been out here humping around in the jungle, having all this fun?" Even though he was in obvious pain, we held off administering any morphine.

"Doc," he whimpered, "this is my seventh month of duty in the bush with only one three-day R&R."

His state of mind seemed even more fragile than his leg injury. After a short conference with Gus, it was decided to give him medication, dress his wound, and tag him for evacuation. We didn't want any of the other men in his patrol to follow his example, but we also didn't want him hurting or shooting anyone else. These types of judgment calls were very tricky; it was a blessing to have someone as experienced as Gus to help weed out these difficult psychological cases. Both squad leaders and their sergeants were called in for immediate debriefing.

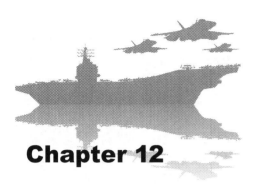

Chapter 12

TOO CLOSE FOR COMFORT

Although the battalion CO was pleased that the SAM site had been destroyed, it was painfully clear that the NVA had successfully moved into this area of operation and had us trapped in a position that was very difficult to defend.

The brass thought of Firebase 14 as a potential command and control center for this entire northern area of South Vietnam (Quang Tri Province). They were attempting to expand the firebase to include the 105mm howitzer. Although this big gun could fire a thirty-plus-pound projectile and offer protection for the firebase for almost ten kilometers in any direction, the facts were that one, we had no howitzer or shells, and two, the NVA and Vietcong were now much closer than ten kilometers in probably every direction. The CO knew there was a pretty good chance we could be overrun by a determined enemy.

Although the 105 howitzer would have been very handy, the overall plan of the allies was to gain arterial support over the central and northern portion of Vietnam through interlocking firebases and outposts to interdict and defend from an invasion of the army of North Vietnam. This was a fine theory, except the NVA didn't seem to want to buy into the program. It was pretty well known that they were hustling most of their supplies and reinforcements down through Laos and Cambodia along the Ho Chi Minh Trail, directly into the southern part of South Vietnam.

There was at least a battalion of angry and well-motivated enemy forces approximately ten to fifteen kilometers to our east and an unknown number of enemy combatants from the SAM site to our west. Unconfirmed reports from listening devices (LDs), long-range reconnaissance patrols (LRRPs) and Vietnamese scouts estimated that there could be a full regiment of North Vietnamese Army hidden in our area along this quiet tributary of the Cam Lo River.

Although we were dead-tired, our biggest concern wasn't going to be lack of sleep. We were outnumbered at least six to one. The battalion CO, however, was very positive; he kept mentioning that the brass at headquarters had some very smart people involved with this operation. *My question was, were they related to the same geniuses that had gotten us into this debacle of a war in the first place?*

*****

Our dreams of glory in Vietnam were sinking faster than a large animal in soft quicksand. Nothing seemed to be going as predicted. The frustration of the senior officers in charge of this firebase and throughout Vietnam was evident. They probably felt some of the same chagrin that many Japanese admirals felt after the Battle of Midway in June 1942. After losing four of their top-line aircraft carriers, the elite brass of the Japanese imperial navy came to realize that their offensive in the Pacific had turned around and had become defensive in order to protect the home islands.

In Vietnam the offensive position of aggressive body counting and bringing the battle to the enemy was gradually turning defensive, with a focus on not losing any more of these valuable marine, army, air force, and other naval and service personnel—in addition to curbing the hundreds of thousands of civilian casualties. There was a hidden suspicion in the US military and among many of the US politicians that the Army of South Vietnam was not as dedicated and as interested in defending its country as it should be.

*****

As dawn approached, the enemy was probing our outer perimeter about twelve klicks to the east. There was no evidence of large-caliber weapons, just patrol activity and probing by the Vietcong or elements of the NVA. We could hear some of the distant small arms firing, and our radio operator from a spotter plane alerted us to some closer-in enemy activity to our north. In addition to spotter aircraft and the LDs, one of the LRRPs (long-range reconnaissance patrols) had alerted our CO of movement of the NVA battalion in the northeast sector toward our position. As 1969 came to a close, there were still over 54,000 marines in Vietnam. A few more of these seasoned marines would have been comforting at this firebase.

The LRRPs acted very independently of our firebase marines. They darkened their faces with green and brown camouflage paint and slithered through the jungle. They had very little contact with our CO unless something critical was happening, and they purposely avoided engaging the enemy unless they were inadvertently discovered. On one occasion, an entire company of NVA decided to camp almost on top of one of the LRRPs. The soldiers in the LRRP turned off their radio and stayed silent for ten hours until the NVA moved on.

*****

The chief petty officer in medical was helping stabilize a patient for the next medevac helicopter when our 81s let loose. Located in a clearing near the burned-out village, these three heavy mortars were still within the base perimeter. They made a distinctive hollow, loud *thunk* when fired, but they couldn't take the place of air cover.

"Jeez, Doc," yelled Gus, "these little fuckers are going to get us in a shit squeeze play if they get any closer."

This was probably a stupid question, but I asked anyway. "Chief, what's the range of those mortars?"

"I hate to tell ya, Doc, but they only go out about two or three kilometers, maybe up to four and a half, depending on the arc. They do have a pretty decent kill radius, around twenty to forty-five meters. Each round weighs fifteen pounds, so it can get through the jungle canopy growth pretty well. Doc, don't worry about the mortars; just pray for some air support."

None of us wanted a repeat of the battle up northwest at the much larger base at Khe Sanh. It had begun at the end of January 1968 and lasted seventy-seven days. We lost almost five hundred brave US marines and ARVN rangers in that battle. Over ten thousand North Vietnamese were killed or wounded. After the siege, the base was abandoned. Later it looked as if the attack at Khe Sanh had been planned as a diversionary effort for the coming Tet Offensive.

Perhaps the NVA had planned another Dien Bien Phu, a decisive and historic battle waged in the spring of 1954. General Giap of the Viet Minh forces overran the French outpost in western Vietnam, which led to the French expulsion from Indochina. We hoped the enemy didn't realize that our position at Firebase 14 was as just as tenuous.

*****

As the sun crept over the jungle canopy and turned the Cam Lo River pink, we could distinctly hear small-arms fire that couldn't have been more than a few kilometers away. Although it was only 0700 hours in the morning, our CO was in a high-level meeting with some of the other officers in his bunker. By 0730 hours, the entire firebase knew what was in store for us.

We were told that at exactly 0930 hours, a flight of B-52s from Guam would do everything in their power to disrupt the battalion, or perhaps full regiment, of the NVA that was moving toward our position. All our outlying defenses and patrols, including the LRRPs, were to disengage immediately and return back to within the main perimeter of the firebase. The wounded from Monari's patrol were in serious need of medevacking if they were going to make it home alive.

Small-arms fire and machine-gun rounds were beginning to penetrate the firebase. Two marine squads were defending the northern perimeter; two .50-calibers on the half-track assault vehicles were returning enemy fire to the east. A couple more ACAVs would have come in pretty handy right about now. In the distance, I heard a distinct hollow *thunk*.

Chief Petty Officer Gus yelled, "Doc, d'ya hear that sound? That's our sixties returning some closer-in fire. Those suckers only have a range of around two thousand meters! Now we have to be careful!"

There was a distinct urine smell from inside the main medical trench. Some of the docs or patients must have pissed their pants. Most of us in the medical trenches knew we had at least two hundred marines out on the perimeter defending us. All of us knew that probably wasn't enough firepower to deter a carefully planned and coordinated attack. We also knew that the average age for these marine defenders was probably under twenty years old.

A few of the claymore mines were being detonated on the northern perimeter, indicating that some of the enemy troops were quite close to breaching our northern defenses. The seven hundred small steel balls in the mines should slow down any gomers who ventured too close to the perimeter wire, but it was well known within the firebase that we had only a limited number of these weapons.

Some of the marines were being carried to our hospital area with significant wounds. One marine came into medical hopping, dragging what was left of his right leg. Shrapnel had torn much of the muscle off the leg, and he was bleeding profusely. After we tightly bandaged his leg and administered morphine, he wanted to get back to his squad! We had to order him to stay in medical with his head down. As he hesitated in a crouch, we tried to convince him to stay put by telling him, "We may need your firepower and help if the gomers get too close."

He shot back, "Doc, if they're that close, we're all screwed."

The chief looked at me and just shrugged his shoulders. We all knew this wasn't going to be pretty. It was too late for second-guessing. Most of us in medical realized the brass didn't have a clue about what to do in this exceedingly dangerous predicament.

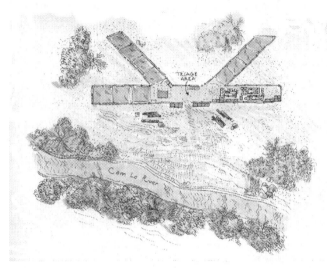

Medical area (not to scale) above the Cam Lo tributary

The chances of our being overrun by the NVA and Vietcong were increasing by the minute. All of us were trying not to think of that scenario. We could hear incoming mortar rounds advancing from the east, getting closer to our position. According to Gus, everyone was too busy to be terrified. Scared shitless was more like it.

Suddenly, there was a tremendous explosion, and we all hit the deck. After lying terrified in the bottom of the trench for a few moments, one of the docs looked out and discovered that the top half of the closest ACAV was just gone. A mortar shell or an RPG round had instantly taken it out along with its .50-caliber gun. That vehicle was only a couple hundred meters from our position! All that was left of the ACAV was a smoking hulk.

"What the hell happened to the guys on the ACAV?" I asked Gus. "Where are they? There was a whole crew on that vehicle!"

"They bought it, Doc. Let's just save whoever we can. They never knew what hit 'em."

One of the marines who had been near the ACAV came staggering into medical. He was completely deaf, and most of his clothing had been shredded or torn off by the explosion. Although he had multiple flesh wounds, none of them seemed life-threatening.

I yelled at him to lie down on the makeshift operating room table so we could clean him up, but he just kept screaming. The corpsman grabbed him, and I administered 100mg of Demerol in his backside, but he kept whimpering about his mates on the ACAV.

I pointed to the table, and he grudgingly climbed onto it. "Doc," I shouted to the corpsman, "let's wash him down with Betadine, bandage him up, and hope he doesn't go into shock on us."

*****

Saving whomever we could consisted of trying to stop the flow of blood, making sure everyone was still breathing, and administering morphine and Demerol in order to keep down the screaming. With too much pain medication, a patient could die from respiratory arrest—he could just stop breathing. But with too little, the patient's pain would cause the release of endogenous epinephrine from the adrenals, causing hypertension and heart failure.

What a mess. Between the mud, bloody gloves, bandages, and heavy smoke and fog, it was surprising we could breathe or function at all. The worst of it was the continuous earsplitting crashing of mortars and RPG rounds. *Zoom! Bang! Boom!*

The mortar rounds were landing closer now; some were landing within the firebase and too close to our makeshift hospital. If there was any lull in the explosions or automatic weapons firing, the sound of the mortar tubes would get through to our ears. "Tubing!" someone would shout. The machine-gun and automatic-weapons fire was all too close.

One of the wounded marines shouted, "Hear that, you guys? That's some AK-47 rounds coming our way."

You never forget that sound, especially if the round is heading in your direction; it has a distinct clacking noise. The louder cracks were probably from a recoilless rifle. These rifles seemed to be in good supply for the NVA. They were a form of lightweight artillery that allowed some of the gasses from the projectile to escape out the back end of the firing tube. They could be very effective against lightweight armored vehicles.

The AK-47 is a Russian .30-caliber in a gas-operated magazine for semiautomatic or full automatic firing. The weapon was developed by a

Russian named Kalashnikov in 1947. These guns are accurate and deadly bastards, especially at close range. They don't weigh too much at under ten pounds, with a range of four hundred meters. The Cong seemed to have an unending supply, along with plenty of Russian and Chinese RPGs.

One of the injured kept yelling about his mother and wanting to go home. "Hey," shouted Gus, "for Chrissake, will somebody give that jarhead more morphine to get him to shut the fuck up? We got enough trouble here without the screaming!"

The cacophony of explosions, enemy whistles, automatic weapons fire, and the cries of the wounded was deafening and threatening to drown out our sanity.

All of us were trying to stay low in the medical trench to avoid any stray shrapnel or bullets. It also seemed a little quieter while we stayed low. Some of the close-in explosions were knocking down the medical supplies that Gus had so neatly arranged on shelves lining the trench.

One of the wounded marines kept replacing the packages of bandages and medicine that kept tumbling out of the shelves on top of him. "Jeez," he exclaimed, "can't these idiots let up for a few minutes! I don't want to be buried in bandages!"

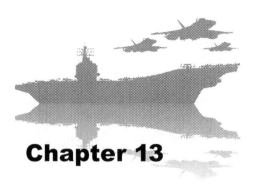

Chapter 13

Overrun—December 1969

Conklin kept yelling, "Jeez, Doc, keep your friggin' head down. Nobody needs to be a hero today. Let's concentrate on staying in one piece and patching up our wounded brothers."

My shoulders were sore. It felt like my back, legs, and shoulders were turning to mush. It was as if the stress of a great weight was pressing down on me. It was easier to crawl around on all fours than to crouch all the time. It was strange, but crawling around in the mud just didn't seem too bothersome or even unnatural at the time.

Gus yelled, "Let's get an inventory of all our weapons; it looks like we may need 'em!" The chief medical corpsman quickly located two M-16s with partially loaded clips that had come in with some of the wounded marines.

Embarrassingly, by the time the chief got to me, he had to reload my .45. Hopefully, he thought it was just ignorance and not that my hands were shaking too much to load the clip. It was interesting: my hands never seemed to shake while treating patients.

*****

We had two major concerns in our medical trenches. Of course, we worried that the VC could overrun the firebase before the air strike from the B-52s showed up at 0930. It was only around 0730. But of more immediate concern was that we could run out of trench room for our patients. The trenches were wide enough so that two stretcher bearers could pass each other, but we had only about forty-five meters of trench space for patients. It was perilous and extremely hazardous for patients to be outside the trenches because of all the incoming fire and mortar shrapnel.

Roots of nearby trees were serving as hooks for some of the IV solutions. Our on-deck waiting area was a series of logs and rocks outside the trenches. Some of the less seriously wounded marines were lying there behind some of those logs that were normally used for seating in the waiting room area. The violent and abrupt noise from the close-in explosions was making it difficult to think. The term "hellacious" kept pounding through my head.

In later years, when I discussed the situation with colleagues, they were unable to describe their feelings at the time of the attack. One person said,

The closest I could come was to compare the attack to what happens to someone in a dark room who is startled by a sudden loud noise or flash of light. The event causes you to jump, and your blood pressure spikes. But you immediately identify the noise or event and calm down. During the attack at Firebase 14, there was no opportunity to calm down. My stomach was churning the way it did after eating undercooked Tijuana tamales. I had an immediate and constant feeling I was about to vomit or mess my pants; the startling effect kept me looking for a place to puke.

Once we had treated the most seriously wounded, I flopped down on a piece of soggy cardboard to rest my sore knees and shoulders. Gus came over with a canteen of bug juice that tasted a little like warm, sour lemonade. My throat was still constricted and chalky-feeling. The drink was delicious.

Joining me on the soggy cardboard, Gus asked, "Doc, do you think any of those incoming rounds are coming from inside the firebase?" He was screaming in my ear, but it was still hard to hear him. Incoming rounds and shrapnel from RPGs peppered the trees and logs near the entrance of the hospital. The larger explosions caused the trees to sway and the ground to shake.

I retorted, "How the hell can anyone tell where all this crap is coming from?"

His response was unnerving. "Doc, the only way we could receive so much small-arms fire is if the gomers are within the perimeter. I just treated several men who had been stationed on our northern border who'd been shot in the back."

It took me a moment to let that sink in. Fire had to be coming from behind our lines! Rather than sit there and think about it, I got up in a crouch and got back to work. Gus joined me. Our next patient was Jefferson, the operator of a .60-caliber machine gun. He had received a fleshy shot in the ass by someone hiding just behind a tree, only forty meters behind him! It was the only structure of any sort where someone could be hidden. Fortunately, the round just caused a furrowed opening across his right buttock.

"My loader went to investigate, but there was no one there. They're like freaking ghosts!" exclaimed Jefferson. "We see the underbrush move, but they never show themselves."

After patching up Corporal Jefferson's flesh wound, Gus administered some antibiotic and pain medication and asked him if he would show him where he had been shot.

"I guess you're not talking about seeing my ass again, are you?"

"No, Sergeant, take me to the area you were defending."

"Sure, Doc. I ain't feeling too much pain at the moment."

Gus grabbed one of the M-16s, and I watched them snake their way up a slight rise in the jungle to an area so covered in low vines and thick vegetation that I lost sight of them and went back to work on another hurting marine. It was almost an hour before Gus returned to tell me what had happened.

*****

Apparently, the smoke and early morning mist had been so heavy that it was difficult to see where they were headed. Staying low to avoid incoming rounds and shrapnel, Jefferson yelled back to Gus, "Doc, our position was up about fifty meters in front of that large dead tree stump right ahead."

Gus raised his weapon, and Jefferson exclaimed, "Doc, what the hell are you doing? We have marines on that perimeter!"

Gus replied, "We are just going to put a few well-aimed rounds into that dead tree—just to make sure it's really dead! And then we'll put a few into that big log next to it to make sure that's dead too!"

After a short burst of fire, he went over and pushed on the stump of the dead tree. It toppled over, exposing a tunnel entrance partially covered by brush.

"Jefferson, get me a frag." Gus tossed the grenade into the tunnel, and he and Jefferson hit the dirt behind the adjacent hollow log. After the muffled explosion, the chief noticed blood oozing out of the log he'd shot up. "Jefferson, tell your loader we just killed one of his ghosts."

Gus's next trick was to get Jefferson safely back into the medical trench before the morphine wore off.

*****

Gus placed the M-16 in the corner and sent a slightly wounded marine to get a message to the CO about the tunnel. Meanwhile, it was difficult to keep Jefferson still. "If you want to help with the wounded men, Jefferson, fine, but ask Monson to locate José. We need a tunnel rat in that tunnel immediately."

Monson found José on the eastern perimeter, in the area of the remaining ACAV unit. When the two returned to medical, Jefferson advised José of the situation. A reply from the CO had arrived in the meantime and was definitive: investigate and eliminate any tunnels within the perimeter of our firebase.

"Hey," yelled José, "I need a .45 for tunnel work. I no go into tunnel without gun."

I said, "Here, take mine." He grabbed the firearm, checked the clip and chamber to make sure that it was fully loaded, borrowed a flashlight from medical, and ran uphill to the tunnel entrance with Gus in a low crouch.

After leading José to the tunnel, Gus returned to medical. "He is one brave tunnel rat, Doc; we just need him back in one piece. That tunnel was still smoking when José took a deep breath and disappeared into the gloom."

Lieutenant Monari, after being briefed on the discovery of the tunnel, stationed Corporal Mastronami next to the entrance in case more gomers came out of it, or in case there were any VC within the firebase who might be looking for an escape route. The lieutenant had no idea whether the tunnel system extended to other areas within the perimeter or whether it went directly outside the camp, but it was imperative to find out soon.

Monari went to confer with the commanding officer. Since Colonel Avery's tent had been completely shredded by incoming fire and shrapnel, they crouched behind what was left of the sandbag wall that surrounded the command area. It looked like both were conferring with the radio operator.

Gus returned to medical after meeting with the brass at what the command center with some sobering news. "It looks like the NVA may breach our northern perimeter, and there is no telling how many VC may be in or under the firebase!" He said that Avery kept yelling into the radio, "Broken Arrow, Broken Arrow, Broken Arrow—Firebase 14!"

At first I wasn't sure what Gus was talking about. "Gus, what the hell are you saying?"

Gus explained, "That's code for the shit has hit the fan! That code means we're being overrun. This is only the second time during this war that the 'broken arrow' code has been used. The first time was in 1965 when Lieutenant Colonel Hal Moore was surrounded by NVA regulars and the Vietcong while leading men through the La Drang Valley."

We gathered some weapons together and hunkered down in the mud in the bottom of the trench. Even our remaining injured patients looked concerned as the noise level ratcheted up. Gus yelled that he wasn't ready to give up, but "If we have to go, Doc, we're in good company with these injured marines," he said.

Within six or seven minutes we heard the high-pitched scream of a jet engine over the din of the firefight on our northern periphery. Sounding out of place, it came right at us and was over us and gone in a second. We had no clue at the time where it had come from but later learned it was part of a squadron from out on Yankee Station. It included Daniel in his A7-E Corsair II from VA-192 and his wingman. They let loose a couple of five-hundred-pound Rockeyes to disperse the NVA from our northern perimeter. A second later a whole section of the jungle to our north exploded with hundreds of bomblets from the Rockeyes.

Although grateful, we were too busy to look up or even think about anything but keeping our patients and ourselves alive. The close-in fire made us think that there was just no place to hide. Even the trenches in the medical area were vulnerable to incoming mortar rounds.

Daniel told me later that he'd had to get permission to break away from his original assignment: interrupting the North Vietnamese who were bringing Russian and Chinese weapons and supplies down the Ho Chi Minh Trail into South Vietnam. When he heard the radio chatter about the predicament and 'Broken Arrow,' his CO, Commander Parker, said, "Go out and see what can be done to give those marines a hand out near Firebase 14."

The next sound I heard after the Rockeyes was the close-in droning of an enormous aircraft that turned out to be music to our ears. It was an AC-47 gunship, a slower prop plane that had been converted from a C-47 transport plane. It carried three General Electric mini-guns that could fire four to six thousand rounds per minute of 7.62mm shells. It circled our northern perimeter slowly, banked, and turned to train the firepower on the enemy below.

"Chief, what the hell is that?" JB yelled. It looked like a tongue of flame had cleansed the jungle about two to three hundred meters northwest of the camp.

The chief shouted over the roar of the mini-guns, "That, Doc, is Puff the Magic Dragon, call name 'Spooky.' It should at least slow down anyone wanting to overrun us. A ten-second burst from those motherfuckers will blanket every foot of an area the size of a football field."

*****

After a brief lull in the incoming fire, we heard the unforgettable flutter of medevac helicopters. This time they brought along two friends: AH-1 cobra helicopter gunships. These choppers carried twin M-60 7.62mm machine guns and two M-134 Gatling guns that could fire up to four thousand rounds per minute. In addition, they also carried twin pods of seven XM-158 air-to-ground rockets. Their timing couldn't have been worse.

The firebase had a predicament. The NVA had the marine battalion in a box, and they knew it. One of the cobra helicopters started smoking. It must have taken direct fire from somewhere just north of the small Vietnamese village we had torched with the white phosphorous rounds. The chopper was going down fast—too fast. It exploded on impact. Surely no one could survived that explosion.

Amazingly, though, twenty minutes later, Monson dragged one of the pilots into our medical area with severe second-degree burns and a broken leg. He'd actually jumped clear at the last minute. Monson had found him on fire at the edge of the landing zone. His flight suit must have had some sort of flame retardant; the corpsman had been able to extinguish the flames on the burning airman by removing his own shirt and then rolling the pilot in the wet jungle growth.

It was a miracle he survived. There was no such luck for the second pilot or anyone else aboard. This guy deserved a medal, or at least some beach time at Cam Ran Bay. Once he was stabilized, he would be on his way to the hospital ship, one of the hospitals at Tan Son Nhut, or the 510th Evacuation Hospital near Da Nang. After that he would be sent to Japan or the continental United States for lengthy rehabilitation—assuming, of course, the firebase was not overrun by the VC. After we injected him with one hundred milligrams of Demerol, he became quite chatty. He yelled over the din that he was from a small town in Maine, near Skowhegan, and he really wanted to see it again.

Gus said encouragingly, "We'll medevac you out with the second bird as soon as the landing zone is clear."

JB went over to him, laid a hand on his shoulder, and said, "I'm from New Hampshire, and I love Maine. I have friends in Kennebunk and Damariscotta."

"We're just a little north of there in Newcastle, on the great Salt Bay. Ever hear of Harrington Corner?"

Monson piped up from the marine he was helping. "I got an air force buddy who was stationed up near Dover-Foxcroft."

JB added, "Jeez, I haven't heard a Maine accent in quite a while. It reminds me of home and honest people!"

I finished coating the pilot's burns with bacitracin and ointment and watched as JB slowly and carefully splinted his broken leg. Fractures were problematic since there was no x-ray equipment yet at the firebase. It was always a relief not to see any complex fractures visibly poking through the skin.

JB told him, "You might be able to get your rehab at the Chelsea Naval Hospital near Boston. That way your friends and relatives can drive down to visit."

That seemed to make the pilot happy, or perhaps it was just the absence of pain from the narcotic medication.

His smile vanished when JB warned, "But captain, it's a lot easier gettin' into this firebase than it is gettin' out!"

*****

Outside our medical trenches, we were taking fire from every direction. The ground appeared to bubble occasionally. Only later did we discover that this was from direct fire and ricochets. The VC were getting much too close.

It began to rain again. It wasn't a driving rain but a continuous body-soaking rain that chilled us to the bone. Even though I was sweating profusely from fear and abject terror, I felt cold. Our clothing always seemed wet, grimy, and torn. Still, our scrubs looked absolutely pristine compared to the uniforms of some of these brave marines.

When the marines returned from patrols in the bush, their uniforms were always filthy and stank of dried blood from the leeches, pus from sores, sweat, and jungle rot. If a man stayed out in the bush too long, his clothing would rip, fray, and actually disintegrate on his body. If a marine's boots or clothing got too foul, any infections or immersion foot disorder could eventually kill him.

*****

Between the weather and incoming fire, the base was turning into a muddy shambles.

Two of our corpsmen carried in another wounded marine. It looked like something had scraped his face. Most of his left ear was missing. In addition, his left leg was bleeding through his shredded pants in several places. He was clutching what looked like a single-barrel sawed-off shotgun.

Seeing it, Gus exclaimed, "Hey, they could use this little puppy on the perimeter." He reached to grab the gun, but the wounded marine didn't want to let go.

"Hey, Doc, don't take my weapon!"

"Easy, marine," said Gus. "Let's get you patched up first. JB, this marine could use some pain meds."

"What the hell is that, Gus?" I asked. "Is that a rocket grenade launcher?"

Through the din he yelled, "That, sir, is what we call 'the Persuader.' It's an M-79 grenade launcher—although with this crap flying all around us, it can also be used to fire shotgun-like pellets or darts."

Another marine was trying to crawl into medical. Corpsman Monson went out and dragged him into our trench. It looked like part of his face had been blown away, and he couldn't stand up. We put him on the operating table and washed off his face with IV fluid. His legs looked like they had been caught in barbed wire. There were multiple cuts and possible shrapnel wounds. The corpsman cut off his pants and cleaned and bandaged his legs; his privates seemed okay. Gus and I examined his facial wounds.

"Corpsman," I said a little louder than I had to, "he has lost part of his nose and most of the flesh off the right side of the mandible. We will clamp off the facial artery and hope the external carotid hasn't been nicked. Let's get a compression bandage on him A-SAP."

Surprisingly, the marine was quiet and didn't complain of any pain. We had to be careful he didn't go into shock. At least he didn't ask or complain about the condition of his privates!

*****

Many of us had heard stories about a famous battle in the A Shau Valley in the northern part of South Vietnam. The entrance to the valley was close to Laos, and the NVA could easily resupply their soldiers by going down the back of the Laotian mountains and into South Vietnam. The hill that the VC and NVA were using as a staging point for resupply to

South Vietnam was on a small plateau. The battle for "Hamburger Hill" occurred in May 1969 and was very costly: fifty-six American and South Vietnamese soldiers were killed.

They called it Hamburger Hill because of the illusionist similarity to a meat grinder: it ground up human flesh. It was some politician's assessment of that victory that left a bad taste in everyone's mouth. A Massachusetts senator, the illustrious Edward M. (Ted) Kennedy, claimed that the position so many of our fellow patriotic American warriors fought for was of "no strategic value, and the assault was senseless and irresponsible." Although his assessment of the battle may have been correct, the area certainly had strategic value to the NVA. Kennedy's diatribe didn't help the morale of the troops who were stationed in that valley.

It would be another few months before this famous senator would cause the drowning death of Mary Jo Kopechne in an automobile accident off the Dike Bridge on Chappaquiddick Island, Martha's Vineyard, Massachusetts. The accident, on July 18, 1969, at 11:15 p.m., cost the senator from Massachusetts his presidential ambitions. The media seemed to gloss over the fact that Kennedy, although married, was drunk and partying with an unmarried schoolteacher. The fact that he didn't report the "accident" until the next morning was unforgivable: it certainly cost Mary Jo her life.

*****

The second cobra helicopter had circled the downed chopper with its mini-guns, mowing down anything that moved in the bush. After the landing zone was cleared, the second medevac helicopter landed. The corpsmen got the most seriously injured—including the pilot from the cobra that had gone down earlier—from our facility to the evacuation helicopter. We were all hoping the cobra pilot from Maine would make it home to Harrington Corner.

More intense mortar and small-arms fire began coming in from the northern sector of the firebase. The battalion CO came over to our position and asked if there was any way we could evacuate the rest of the wounded. Doc Gus looked around and said, "To where, sir?"

It was a good question. It was getting close to 0800 hours, about an hour and a half from the B-52 drop. The firebase could be overrun before the B-52s could give us enough time to discourage a very aggressive enemy.

The CO wearily responded, "The nearest hospital ship." It sounded like a question. At the moment, he knew we all were just trying to keep our heads down and crouch behind some shelter. It was getting difficult to move within the firebase. It was almost as if the muck was trying to suck your soul into the ground.

Sergeants Mestilo and Cassidy came toward us in a running crouch. Under the circumstances, they both seemed pretty calm. Sergeant Mestilo shouted, "Keep your heads down. The VC are within the firebase perimeter, so pick your targets carefully. We can't afford to lose any more of our men."

It was chilling to remember that the VC wouldn't have attacked us unless they significantly outnumbered us. It felt like the entire NVA battalion had decided to make our area their home.

In retrospect, the high brass had made a miscalculation. They had assumed the NVA would not target our base because we were small and inconsequential; we didn't even have a howitzer. It hadn't occurred to any of us that what they really wanted was directly under the burned-out village right next to our firebase. In addition, the North Vietnamese were fighting a war of reunification for their country. The number of their losses was really of no consequence to them.

*****

The NVA attacked the Khe Sanh base located in Quang Tri Province on January 21, 1968. The North Vietnamese Army sent three divisions (approximately twenty thousand men) against a single marine regiment of approximately five thousand men. The NVA lost between ten and fifteen thousand men. The entire siege lasted seventy-seven days, until July 1968. The marine casualties included almost five hundred men killed in action.

Early that morning of January 21, 1968, the NVA had made sure all hell would break loose at the Khe Sanh base. The North Vietnamese fired hundreds of 82mm mortars, artillery shells, and 122mm rockets into the base. The firepower was immense. It set off the ammunition dump and fuel storage areas. The attack destroyed the mess hall and damaged several helicopters and trucks.

The US Air Force flew B-52s against the NVA in an attempt to hold the base. The B-52s, also known as BUFFs (Big Ugly Fat Fuckers), could carry 108 five-hundred-pound bombs or a mixture of 500-pounders and 750-pounders. One of the captured NVA prisoners told of how one B-52 Arc Light strike had killed 75 percent of his entire regiment. The use of the B-52s and their ability to drop their bombs within one thousand meters of the perimeter was probably the deciding factor in the marines holding the base.

*****

The reason the North Vietnamese Army was so intent on resupplying itself in a hurry was that they knew that approximately 2,200 marines were making a sweep across the northern part of South Vietnam near the seventeenth parallel. We didn't know this at the time, but Operation Dewey Canyon would be the last major marine offensive of the war. It would take place between January and March 1969. It was probably this force that drove this North Vietnamese battalion to seek food and weapons for resupply even though these supplies were adjacent to our firebase.

Although Operation Dewey Canyon would be a tactical success, with 130 marines killed in action compared to 1,617 of the NVA, the army of North Vietnam would continue to move south.

*****

Our perimeter on the north side of the firebase was taking heavy small-arms fire, and Sergeant Mestilo thought that the NVA could breach the razor wire at almost any time. Two more claymores had been tripped, and several of the marine defenders had been injured by small-arms fire in that sector. An additional platoon from the eastern sector of the firebase was redeployed on the northern perimeter to reinforce the marines left in that section.

The sergeant and Lieutenant Monari were trying to bring more claymores and heavy machine guns to the north side of the base, but unfortunately, much of the extra firepower was needed elsewhere. In addition, the base was running low on claymores and .50-caliber ammunition. These were items that were just not easy to come by out in the bush.

The claymore mines would fire almost seven hundred steel balls waist-high and were very lethal up to about fifty meters. The balls were propelled by electronically detonated C-4 explosive. The purpose of the mine was to rip the spine out of the enemy's back with maximum efficiency—unless, of course, the enemy was too close; then it would just take off a person's legs. The large print on one side of the mine stated "This Side Toward Enemy" in bold letters. The steel balls would explode in a fan-shaped pattern for maximum effectiveness over a wide area.

Suddenly, we heard the first of several explosions on the northern perimeter. The NVA was in the habit of breaching razor wire defenses with Bangalore torpedoes. These explosive devices consisted of a series of thin two-and-one-eighth-inch steel tubes, each five feet in length, that could be snapped together to form a long extended tube of explosives. These torpedo devices were ideal for clearing a three- to ten-meter breach in razor- or barbed-wire defenses.

Some marines were hastily establishing a secondary perimeter, one that was 150 meters inside the northern perimeter wire and would isolate the last sighted tunnel. Other marines were planting a new set of trip flares, razor wire, and whatever claymores were left.

Gus growled, "Where the fuck is José?"

The lieutenant was not going to abandon the outer northern perimeter until our tunnel rat came back from exploring the tunnel under the dead tree stump that Gus had discovered. The machine gunners on the northern border of Firebase 14 were to be hurriedly brought into a smaller arc of the new defensive position in order to provide interlocking fields of fire. Several marines were building new bunkers out of logs and sandbags.

As we were trying to keep everyone comfortable, or at least breathing, in our makeshift hospital, a smiling José poked his head into our trench.

"Jeez, José, where've you been?" yelled Gus.

"You 'member village with tunnels underneath?" exclaimed José.

"Yeah, sure, what of it?" returned Gus.

"That's where I been," claimed José. "It take long time. I watch for snakes and keep good lookout for Cong. I get so tired, I look for way out of tunnel. I stuck my head out somewhere in jungle and see many Cong heading toward you guys."

Gus told him, "You have to report all this immediately to Lieutenant Colonel Avery at his command center."

José replied with a contorted face, "I'm a little scared to go to CO, Doctor Gus. Maybe you tell him."

"Jeez, José," Gus snapped. "I can't stop in the middle of clamping off this artery!"

"Gus, I'll take him up," I heard myself say. "C'mon, José, stay low while we visit what's left of the command center."

Gus yelled, "Remember, Doc, no heroics today. We need you here!"

*****

As we sprinted across the camp, I could see that most of the tents had been shredded or blown away. All that was left of the command center was a pile of shredded sandbags. We crouched down behind the sandbags, and José filled in the CO. Cupping his ears, the CO listened and digested this new intelligence report. It looked like he was trying to block out the cacophony of noise from outgoing and incoming fire as well as formulate a plan.

He asked, "José, could you lead a rifle team and a .60-caliber to that area again?"

"S-sure," stammered José. "But they got to be skinny like me. No use to send big ones into tunnels—they no fit."

"Lieutenant," the CO said, turning to Monari, "get together a fire team of skinny marines and let José take them up behind the enemy lines with the skinniest sergeant. Let's see what trouble they can visit on our Cong friends north of the firebase."

Monari got Mestilo and Jefferson together in sick bay for a conference. Although Jefferson was wounded, he volunteered to be a part of the squad, adding that his backside wound wasn't too sore and he was the right size to fit in the tunnels. He also knew how to handle the M-60. He immediately suggested three other slightly built African American marines to go with the "skinny squad."

The M-60 gun required at least a two-man team. The gun itself weighed almost nineteen pounds, but the several hundred rounds of munitions (.308-caliber) were also heavy, and the ammunition belts had to be carried in a tightly lidded steel container to avoid dirt and jungle vegetation from clogging the belt during firing. The machine gun came with a five-pound detachable tripod.

The gun itself could fire up to 550 rounds per minute, up to a distance of almost four thousand meters (approximately two and a half miles), but its most effective range was around a thousand meters or less. Its chief detraction was that under sustained firing, the barrel would seize due to heat. Although that problem could be remedied by quickly changing the barrel, there were no replacement barrels yet stocked at Firebase 14.

*****

Jefferson was from Fort Myers, Florida. He had grown up just off Anderson Avenue, which later became Dr. Martin Luther King Jr. Boulevard, in the northeast part of the city. He had always known he wanted to be a marine. His schoolmates and even his older brother had always teased him because of his slight build. He was constantly getting into fights with boys who were much bigger and stronger, but he never complained. Instead he was always plotting revenge for his tormentors.

Once he had put dog feces way up in the toe area of a tormentor classmate's sneakers during gym. Another time he had buried a brick in the bottom of his tormentor's school book-bag. His biggest coup had occurred when he found a group of his tormentors smoking in the boys' room in high school. He very quietly, minding his own business, entered one of the stalls and then lit and flushed a cherry bomb down the toilet. He then strolled out to the hall and informed one of the teachers that "some boys were doing something they weren't supposed to be doing in the boys' room."

Bang! The toilet blew off its seal, and water cascaded everywhere. All the smokers got into trouble, and Jefferson achieved monumental street cred with his tormentors for this little stunt.

*****

Although small in stature, Jefferson was big in the guts department. Monari said to him, "Jeffers, you don't have to go on this mission. You've already got your ticket back to the world."

"I know that," replied Jefferson, "but can you think of anyone better on the M-60?"

The lieutenant said sternly, "Look, you men pick your skinny squad, and just be careful. We cannot afford to lose you guys. And make sure you're underground at 0930 hours for the B-52 strike."

José and eleven other men, all weighed down with equipment and ammunition, slithered into the tunnel where the dead tree trunk had stood. Only one of the South Vietnamese scouts agreed to enter the tunnel, and Jefferson probably shamed him into going along. Gus had given Jefferson a couple of capsules of Fiorinal with codeine to take if—and only if—his wounded backside decided to kick up on him. Fortunately, his gunshot wound involved no vital organs and impacted only the fleshy part of the gluteus maximus muscle. The wound made it difficult for him to sit, but he wouldn't be doing much of that on this little caper.

*****

We watched the skinny squad follow José up toward the tunnel. The rest of us went back and hunkered down in medical. Although the noise from the intermittent firing and incoming rounds was disconcerting, nothing seemed to be coming toward our medical department at the moment. We were fortunate that the enemy hadn't found the range on their mortars.

Our small field hospital was on the back side of the base, closest to the river in a swale, or depression, that protected us from direct fire. However, any enemy firing from the valley across the river could have picked us off quite easily. We really needed the promised howitzer for better protection and to return enemy fire. Fortunately, much of that area had been cleared by howitzer shells from the NVA. This meant that we had a clear fire zone across the river from the medical compound and could see if there was Charlie movement in that area. For all of us in medical, it was a case of hunkering down and trying to make our patients comfortable.

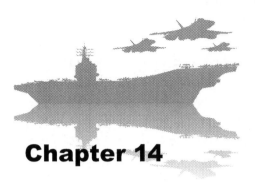

Chapter 14

BEHIND ENEMY LINES

The "skinny squad" had traveled for about forty minutes when José made a sharp right turn and headed up a slight incline toward daylight. One of the squad leaders, Sergeant Jennings, asked, "Hey, José, is this where you came out before?"

"Yeah, Sarge, but we have to be careful. Last time up, there were at least a couple a dozen gomers in the area."

José stuck his head through some brush and looked around. "Maybe Charlie has run away for now, but I no see no one."

The men carefully climbed out of the tunnel entrance and formed a defensive perimeter. Sergeant Jennings had Jefferson deploy the M-60 in the direction of the base camp in case the VC were located on the northern perimeter of the base over a kilometer away. Meanwhile everyone was in the process of finding and then digging a defensive position. Jennings sent two of the men slithering into the jungle about one hundred meters north and south to act as early-warning lookouts or listening posts. Both men were given the same password: Geronimo. If they detected any movement, they were to hustle back to the perimeter established near the tunnel entrance.

The jungle seemed strangely quiet except for the incessant firefight back at the base. The level of the fire seemed to be abating. By now it was 0915 hours. The smoke, low-hanging fog, and mist in the air lent a feeling of unease and tension to the skinny squad as it huddled around the M-60 that guarded the northern approach to the firebase.

This waiting really got to some of the men. No one knew what was out there in the jungle, and everyone eyed his watch, knowing what was about to break loose in fifteen short minutes. Jennings tried to relax his troops by chiding them. "Why can't you skinny bastards gain some weight? Y'all know you can eat all the C-rats you can get your hands on!"

Jennings was from the New Orleans area, across the river near Houma, Louisiana. His actual hometown was a little town called Bayou Cane. Whenever he talked about it, he would make some sort of redneck joke. He made the place sound like it was on the edge of nowhere. He was a little difficult to understand sometimes, and he would just say that was the Creole coming out of him. He did say that the people were genuine there and that he hoped to bring up his family there.

He was the "old man" in the squad, having just turned twenty-six that month. He was young to have made sergeant and was a dedicated marine. He thought about a career in the marines. Although he didn't consider himself a "lifer," he did enjoy the responsibility of leadership and was dedicated to the safety and survival of his men.

Moreover, his girlfriend Kendra was waiting for him back home. She was a committed Christian, and they had an understanding that they both felt was as strong as any vows they could make at the altar. Although dedicated to the mission, he wanted all his men to get home safely. He definitely wanted to see his girl and family again. He planned his life around Kendra.

*****

Suddenly, someone screamed "Geronimo!" from the listening post closest to Firebase 14. A few seconds later, Jamison came crashing out of the jungle and made the hundred-yard dash into the makeshift perimeter; he made a flying leap and dove over Jefferson's M-60 position.

Jamison was extremely agile. He had held the record for stolen bases while at Methuen High School in northern Massachusetts. He really wasn't too wild about being a marine, but his uncle had gone up through the naval ranks and made admiral. The motto that had gotten him through boot camp was "If Uncle Sal can do it, I can do it."

"They're right behind me!" he breathlessly shrieked.

"Keep it in your sneaker," yelled Jennings. "We've got you covered. How many gomers would you estimate coming our way?"

"How the fuck do I know! I didn't stick around to count noses." Jamison was always a little dramatic, but it did look like there was some enemy activity coming from the base camp area. Enemy whistles and distant shouted orders could be heard.

Jennings looked over at some men clustered near the M-60 machine gun. He signaled to the two carrying RPGs and to one with an M-79 grenade launcher, aka the Persuader, which was loaded with fléchette rounds.

"Spread out a bit," warned Jennings, "at least five meters between shooters. And be careful with the Persuader. Those arrow rounds tend to spread out after being fired."

Fléchettes were small, arrowlike projectiles that covered a wide thirty- to forty-degree arc and were ideal for jungle or close-quarters engagement. These darts were nasty little critters. One of them could shred an entire arm. Sergeant Jennings and his band of skinny marines had no idea that the NVA was well aware of an impending B-52 strike coming their way.

The next movement they noticed came from the area where Jamison had charged out of the jungle. The underbrush swayed with activity. It was obvious that a large group of something was coming their way. The marines could hear shouts and whistles of communication. Even though it was undoubtedly enemy activity, they were hidden by the tangle of vines and thick jungle growth.

It was at this point that Jefferson's backside pain decided to kick into high gear. "Jeez, where are those pills the doc gave me? Man-oh-man, this is the last thing I need right now. Fuck, it even hurts to squat." He fished the pills out of his flapped camouflaged pocket and downed them both with a swig from his canteen. It was then he remembered that he was supposed to take just one every four hours for pain. Talk about maximum stress—his head felt like it was about to explode!

The marines were locked and cocked. Most fingered their weapons and flicked off the safe mode.

Less than a minute later, a fully charged platoon of approximately thirty-five Charlies came directly at Jefferson's position without the slightest idea that there was a dedicated marine reception waiting for them a hundred meters across a jungle clearing. Abject shock registered on their faces as Jefferson's M-60, RPGs, and withering M-16 fire greeted them at a range of less than eighty meters.

The sergeant had some concern that the RPGs might not arm themselves since they usually needed at least thirty meters of flight in order to arm the fuse. Some of the rocket-propelled grenades exploded in the trees and vines behind the charging VC. The M-79 Persuader boomed again and again. Some of the NVA escaped back into the jungle, and two made it within ten meters of the marines' makeshift perimeter before being cut down by flying-arrow fléchettes.

The barrel of Jefferson's M-60 was glowing red when it seized up and stopped firing. "Jeez!" he yelled. "I knew this could happen!" It had just never occurred to him that it might happen when he needed the weapon most. He had gotten carried away with trying to put down the enemy force and save the base and hadn't been paying attention to how many rounds per minute went through the gun barrel.

"Hey, Jamison," yelled Jennings, "where in hell did you find all these little fuckers?"

"Don't ask me," Jamison retorted. "They came streaming out of the jungle from hidden positions near what's left of the abandoned village and firebase!"

Two elements helped Jefferson's skinny squad defeat the larger NVA force: preparedness and surprise. This platoon of NVA regulars was caught completely off-guard. Most of them never even raised their weapons to defend themselves. What was most remarkable was that these were not battle-hardened "lifer" marines, but young men just barely out of high school. It was possible a few were high school or college dropouts.

Sergeant Jennings yelled, "Look, Jeffers, you're due a bronze star for this effort if I have anything to say about it!" The entire area was covered in a mixture of low mist, smoke, and bloody enemy bodies.

After the brief firefight, Jennings, Jefferson, and their squad hurriedly searched the enemy bodies for any useful information. This platoon was part of the NVA battalion that had been planning to, or perhaps already had, overrun the firebase. One of the enemy soldiers was alive and had gone down with a flesh wound to his leg.

When questioned by the Vietnamese scout, the enemy soldier revealed that the platoon was hustling to get underground before the "bombs fell from the sky."

Sergeant Jennings was perplexed that they knew about the supposedly secret B-52 strike. He yelled to Jefferson, "Make sure the CO hears about how these bastards knew almost to the minute the time and location of the drop."

The distant rumble of thunder presaged an ill omen for those above ground. The skinny squad hurriedly edged into the tunnel system, bringing their NVA prisoner with them. It was unusual to take prisoners in the bush. They frequently caused trouble and often had explosives strapped to their bodies. But this prisoner was frisked and was truthful, so his wound was bandaged, and the skinny squad took him into the tunnel system and back to the firebase.

*****

The medical section was receiving a steady stream of wounded. Doc Gus thought we might have to start stacking the less seriously wounded soldiers on air mattress in one of the trenches. We needed three things to happen immediately: reinforcement of our perimeter, especially the northern border; evacuation of our most seriously wounded; and additional air support to check the large number of VC and NVA who were starting to breach our outer perimeter wire.

We had no idea at the time that Sergeant Jennings and Corporal Jefferson had successfully reduced the enemy force on the northern perimeter. Without the interdiction of the skinny squad, our northern perimeter would have been breached within an hour of the B-52 strike.

All of us were concerned about the issue of equipment and instructions that would help get us through the B-52 air drop. In medical we had a limited number of surgical masks and earplugs. Gus told those who did not receive these supplies to make earplugs out of cotton or the small rags used to clean the rifles and to make mouth coverings out of T-shirts or rags.

We could hear claymore mines detonating closer to the eastern edge of our perimeter. These mines were very effective for close combat operations. Hearing the claymores go off meant the enemy was close to, or in the process of, breaching the outer razor wire.

It was difficult to get around even within the firebase because of the chance of being hit by incoming fire. It was no longer the occasional stray round that went whistling through the trees, but a sustained cacophony of ungodly noise. All of us were concerned that the enemy would soon use heavy mortars in order to reach deep into the elevated position of the firebase.

Suddenly, approximately eight minutes before the scheduled B-52 drop, incoming fire completely ceased. The quiet was almost overwhelming. Within the firebase we knew of no apparent reason for the VC to break off contact. There were no bird or animal sounds, just the sucking sounds of men trying to walk through the mud, avoiding the myriad of puddles from the incessant rain.

The CO informed us that during the strike, we were to leave our mouths open, remove eyeglasses, and lie facedown in a bunker or protected position. In addition to the earplugs, we were instructed to place our hands over our ears. Someone also suggested it would be helpful to scream during the ordnance drop. Jeez!

In medical, we were thankful that the most severely injured had been medevacked out. Our spaces were in total disarray, and we were getting low on IV fluids. The trenches were spongy-wet and smelled of jungle rot and death.

JB later remarked about that December day, "When I think back on that day in the early winter of 1969, it is surprising that conditions weren't even more terrifying. Perhaps we were just too busy getting our brave wounded marines comfortable in the makeshift hospital; none of us knew what to expect. The incoming fire had been alarming in the extreme; the sudden cessation of incoming fire around 0920 hours was even more perplexing. Even today, when I remember the problems we had at Firebase 14, it causes nausea, sweating, and fear."

*****

The B-52 Stratofortresses were originally designed as long-range nuclear deterrence aircraft. The B-52F version was modified in 1964 for aerial bombardment use in Vietnam. This aircraft carried twenty-four 750-pound bombs in external bomb racks in addition to the twenty-five bombs loaded in its internal bomb bay.

These huge aircraft were first used in Vietnam on June 18, 1965, in Operation Arc Light. The mission targeted the northwest area near Saigon, which was thought to have been a haven for the Vietcong, and was originally designed to reduce the threat to the capital city from the North Vietnamese and Vietcong guerrillas. They were thought to be preparing for an offensive operation in an area known as the Iron Triangle. The first mission was accomplished with the use of thirty large eight-engine aircraft. These B-52 aircraft dropped over a million pounds of high explosives on that June day in 1965, but the results were only mixed. Although some Vietcong supplies were destroyed, only two guerrilla bodies were ever found.

Unfortunately, during the mission two planes collided while refueling and crashed into the South China Sea. Only two of the twelve crewmen from both planes were rescued. The total mission cost: twenty million dollars! The real cost, however, was much more: ten invaluable, priceless US Air Force personnel lost.

Chapter 15

THE B-52 DROP

At approximately 0930 hours, distant explosions started rumbling in our direction. The thundering got so close that most of our equipment and personnel on the deck were bouncing around like beach balls. Even our remaining ACAV overturned. Several of our men were now bleeding from head injuries received during the close-in explosions or from hitting their heads on logs on the roof of their bunkers. All of us were lying down, hugging our knees or blocking our ears. Without earplugs or rags blocking our ears, the explosions would have been deafening. One of our patients started bleeding from his ears.

Terrific flashes of light, almost like lightning slapping the earth, were immediately followed by thunderous explosions that sent logs, rocks, and parts of trees flying through the camp. Most of us were tossed around like rag dolls. The furies of hell had been unleashed.

The earth seemed to have been torn apart. All the poncho coverings in medical were ripped away. It seemed for a few moments that the 500- and 750-pound bombs were coming right through our camp, even though the closest detonation was probably several hundred meters from the camp perimeter. Our ears were ringing, and our eyes were watering. Even with our eyes shut tightly, the lightning flashes of the explosions were painful. We were clutching our throats as the blasts seemed to suck the air out of our lungs.

Each blast and shock wave hit us like an invisible linebacker kicking our backs and flinging dirt and debris down into our clothing. Finally, the earth stopped shaking, and all was quiet except for the moaning of the injured and the constant ringing in our ears.

No one would ever want to experience anything like that B-52 strike. We never heard or saw the bombers. How in the world did they ever get those bombs to hit so close to our firebase without hitting us? Even though the lightning and explosions seemed to be right on top of us, in reality the closest explosion from a bomb was probably not as close as we thought. Most were at least one thousand meters from our perimeter. But the smoke, smell, sound, and terrific flashes of light that seemed on top of us made the B-52 drop terrifying.

Almost immediately, patrols were up and out. The VC seemed to have melted into—or were blasted out of—the jungle, although our patrols later found a few mangled body parts. An eerie, smoky fog and mist-shrouded quiet settled over the firebase as the marine patrols checked on what was left of the NVA.

Although our CO was concerned that the enemy might take advantage of the period directly following the B-52 raid and could be coming our way from the SAM site to our west, we were all thankful for the air force and their excellent targeting.

Still, the CO had good reason to be watchful for additional gomers.

*****

For the first hour after the bombardment, not only were many in our camp dazed and injured, but some had difficulty performing even basic tasks. Waves of nausea engulfed many of us in the medical area. Bile was being pumped into my stomach; vomiting threatened to overwhelm many of us.

It occurred to me that the bombardment must have wiped out or severely disrupted the entire NVA battalion. Only the good Lord would know how anyone subjected to that kind of vicious bombardment could survive.

One marine whose body was brought in had his head nearly severed from a piece of shrapnel. The sight was so grotesque that we placed him immediately in a body bag. No one needed to see that bloody mess. His body was marked for graves and registration. The war was over for this poor soul. I never did find out where he was from or anything about him. I was pretty sure that not even his parents would have recognized him.

Our medical team gathered everyone with overt signs of injury around the makeshift medical area. There were so many troops bleeding from the nose and ears that they had to sit on rocks and logs near the entrance. Some of the injured Vietnamese civilians began to show up. The most serious injuries got treated first. Many of the injured had received burns; most of the children were terrified and crying.

The intense small-arms fire from the northern perimeter had fully abated. Unfortunately, no one had any idea how many troops the enemy had stationed in the tunnels during the air strike. José and the rest of the skinny squad hadn't been seen or heard from since they slithered into the tree-covered tunnel.

*****

José tied a white T-shirt to the end of an M-16. Staying flat on his stomach against the tunnel wall, he poked out the flag before slithering out and showing his face. The white flag was a good idea. A marine corporal had his M-16 trained on the tunnel entrance by the dead tree trunk, to drop anything that moved. This area was now outside the closed-in perimeter, and the tunnel rat didn't want any friendly fire coming his way.

The members of the skinny squad were treated like returning heroes. Jennings and José reported to the CO at the command post. They related that they had taken only one prisoner out of the entire platoon, but some of the NVA might have escaped back into the jungle. The body count was twenty-one dead and one prisoner.

Back at sick bay, we patched up the NVA prisoner. He sat there trembling and silent, his hands secured with plastic ties behind his back. Immediately, the CO ordered a South Vietnamese soldier to begin his interrogation. What he most wanted to learn was how the enemy had known the exact time and location of the B-52 drop. With the prisoner destined for a POW camp near Saigon, this might be the CO's only opportunity to find out. Actually, we would all find out much later.

*****

160

One of the problems with the effectiveness of the air strikes was the early warning given to the NVA. The Russians had trawlers patrolling directly opposite the end of the runway of Anderson Air Force Base on Guam. These observers would radio Hanoi whenever B-52s lifted off. The North Vietnamese radar would pick up the bombers as they approached the coast. The radar plotters would give the NVA a pretty good idea of the general target location and the approximate time of the drop. The information was then relayed south to the NVA units operating in South Vietnam. This answered Sergeant Jennings's question of how the enemy had known in advance about the time and location of the bombing runs.

However, we were to find out much later that there might have been a more accurate—and sinister—reason for the North Vietnamese's pinpoint knowledge of our air force movements and plans.

In the fall of 1967, Chief Warrant Officer John Walker had decided to balance his checkbook and improve his cash flow by selling out US naval secrets to the Soviet Union. After being captured eighteen years later, he would spend the rest of his life in prison. During his time as a spy, he sold our adversaries key lists for some of this country's most sensitive cryptographic systems and data on the United States' newest secure telephone system.

During the Vietnam War, Walker served in the combat theater on the USS *Niagara Falls*, a combat stores ship. It is speculated that Walker, while serving aboard, could have compromised the navy's theater cipher settings. This information, filtered through Moscow's spy chief Boris Solomatin, easily could have helped the North Vietnamese in listening to our internal communications.

*****

The radio operator called in an additional helicopter to help evacuate the most seriously wounded and the three we had been unable to save. It was gut-wrenching and heartbreaking each and every time we lost a marine. Inevitably, their fellow soldiers would tell of their selfless heroism. What might have been the future for these courageous men?

All of us were dog-tired. The bloody gloves, soaking wet scrubs, and muddy footing were beyond depressing. It was hard to believe that the Lord could be anywhere near this jungle hellhole.

One of the survivors suffered from a chest wound, and two appeared to be in deep shock and couldn't hear anything. Several of the others were moaning from severe burns. Six of the men had been injured from flying debris from the impact made by our own B-52 strikes.

One patient in particular had me worried. He was bleeding from his left ear, and nothing we tried could stop it. He could have been suffering from a crushing injury of the auriculotemporal artery that is found in front of the ear canal. A hard enough backward blow to the left lower jaw could easily cause this arterial injury.

The patient told us he'd received a blow to his lower jaw during the bombardment and could not get his teeth to close together properly. He complained of extreme pain on clenching. Palpation of the mandible and condyle area seemed to indicate that he had suffered a fracture. What I wouldn't have given for any kind of portable x-ray machine.

As the sound of rescue choppers filled the air, the CO asked me, "Lieutenant, would you accompany this first group of wounded back to the hospital at Da Nang?"

My first thought was *Wow! We're headed back to clean sheets and sanity.* The next words out of my mouth changed my life forever. "Sir, is there any way that my corpsman could take these brave marines back? It might be more useful for me to remain here."

If I had a reason behind this crazy statement, it certainly wasn't bravado or a measured calculation of the risks. On reflection years later, my only conclusion was that perhaps we were all suffering from the shell shock of the close-in B-52 strike.

The CO's reply gave me something to ponder. "Lieutenant, okay, you stay here. The corpsman who came in with you will take the patients back to Da Nang. And thank you." He continued, "Our patrols have detected enemy activity approximately eight kilometers to our west. It might be part of the contingent of NVA that was guarding the SAM site." He then requested my presence at the 1300-hour briefing at his headquarters.

I spent the rest of that morning taking care of the less seriously wounded. In addition to their wounds, most of these men were suffering from insect bites, leeches, and jungle rot. The leeches were particularly insidious. They couldn't be easily detected. They would drop off the wet foliage and cling to exposed skin, and when they bit you, they released a type of local anesthetic. They were noticeable only when they were full of blood.

All our more serious cases, including three dead marines and our prisoner, had flown off on four medevac Hueys. The death of one of the wounded marines surprised us. His leg had been shattered by machine-gun fire and was a pulpy mess of tissue and bone below the knee. We had stopped the blood flow with tourniquets and blunted his pain with narcotics. While we were trying to resuscitate him from respiratory arrest, blood started oozing from his mouth. It wasn't until we turned him on his side that we noticed he had taken some small-arms fire to his back. Indeed, the wound looked minor, about the size of a pencil eraser, but it had probably torn up one of his lungs, making our treatment only marginally successful.

Gus and I looked at each other: had we killed him by giving him too much morphine? We knew his parents and loved ones wouldn't hear of his death for days. The official statement would probably read, "Corporal Willard died instantly from the result of enemy fire." At some point we all realized there were going to be many more victims of this war than just those who didn't come home from the jungle.

Gus, as senior medical corpsman, was essential in helping everyone make decisions when medical got busy and swamped with wounded soldiers. His home was in Irondequoit, near Rochester, New York. He had attended the Rochester Institute of Technology but had dropped out after some challenging math courses his first year. After joining the navy, he'd had no trouble with the ninety-six-day Hospital Corpsman "A" School. His first duty station had been at sea in the Mediterranean on a sub tender. He had then attended "C" School at Camp Pendleton in California to take an advanced training course on emergency medicine and wound trauma. His skills were critical and especially valuable at this firebase.

Gus had set up a system of air mattresses that led up to our plywood operating table. The closer a patient was placed to the table, the more serious his wounds and the more likely he would be to get immediate treatment. If someone looked in horrible shape and wasn't likely to make it, we would administer morphine and place him in an adjacent trench.

One patient, a second lieutenant, was shot up so badly that we decided he couldn't be medevacked with the recently injured and deceased. He had lost a foot and had taken several rounds to the chest and abdomen. He had been directing fire on the northern border of the firebase. Since we knew he wasn't going to make it, we applied a tourniquet to his lower leg, administered a high dose of morphine to keep him comfortable, and relegated him to the "death" trench.

About an hour later, we heard a raspy voice call out, "Hey, Doc, could I get a little water?"

Gus and I looked at each other in shock. Had we heard correctly? "Who the hell was that?" I shouted. There shouldn't have been anyone over there except the dead or near-dead lieutenant.

Gus said, "Let's take a look!" He went over to the death trench and looked down. "Doc, you gotta get over here!"

When I got there, I saw that the lieutenant's eyes were open and tracking us! We carefully lifted him up and carried him over to the empty operating table.

Gus looked at me, still flabbergasted, and said, "I guess we better give him some water. "Let's change his bandages and stabilize him with an IV."

We adjusted his tourniquet, dosed him with antibiotics and a bit more morphine, and tagged him for immediate evacuation. He was able to tell us that his hometown was near Boston in Haverhill, Massachusetts, so he was probably another patient who would eventually wind up at the Chelsea Naval Hospital. All our spirits were lifted that another marine hadn't died in this trench, and we hoped he would make it safely back to the continental United States, Okinawa, or Japan for recuperation. It looked like God had more plans for that marine!

*****

Our ears were still ringing from the B-52 strike. Many of the marines remaining at the base seemed to be getting back to important but routine tasks, such as clearing more and more jungle and brush away from the wire. This clearing or "killing zone" made it more difficult for the enemy to sneak in close at night for sniper fire. Since the firebase was on a gradual plateau, about twenty to twenty-five meters above the rest of the jungle, it was a little easier to defend.

The marines were also busy fortifying or rebuilding their hooches. A hooch was a marine's home until something more substantial could be constructed. It was essentially a foxhole with a poncho over it. Some were a little more "luxurious," with an adjacent trench for lying down. Most had an air mattress, making sleeping somewhat more comfortable.

Ideally, a tent would sit on a plywood platform. This raised-platform tent would help to keep out dampness, jungle rot, leaches, and all sorts of crawly creatures that were frequent inhabitants of dug-in hooches. However, there was a problem with this: raised tents made great targets for snipers, and our primary goal at this point was just to survive. We constantly worried about gomers sneaking through the perimeter or surprising us with another tunnel entrance.

If the marines were sleeping several to a tent, there was a good chance no one would hear a sapper sneaking into the firebase. In a small hooch, you could easily hear anything moving close to you. Several patrols were also out in the bush, looking for evidence of NVA activity. No one was suffering from boredom.

*****

Sergeant Mestilo was hastily directing the reconstruction of the CO's command center. The tents had been shredded, the sandbags had been torn apart, and large holes in the plywood floor needed repair. The wooden pallets used to transport mortar shells were used to reconstruct the flooring. New tarps replaced the tents, and more sandbags were piled waist-high, giving the command center a bunker-like appearance. It was quiet, and a smoky mist made it difficult to see.

Mestilo came up with a pretty good idea. "Hey, Corporal, have the men dig out and enlarge the inside shelter beneath the flooring. Put a solid, heavy wooden trap door over it, right in the platform floor, just in case things get too dicey around here again."

"Sure, Sarge. How deep?

"At least five feet, with room for three men," he answered quickly.

*****

The briefing from the brass turned out to be a very somber affair that put everyone on edge. The battalion's acting executive officer, Captain Darcy, sketched out on an easel map our general position and the position of reported NVA movements. It looked like an untenable situation. Much of the jungle across the river had been denuded by earlier howitzer and mortar activity. The nearby village had been leveled by the white phosphorous rounds, and the areas to our east and north had been pretty much decimated by the B-52 strike. But the area to our west still provided excellent cover for covert enemy activity. It was pretty evident to the brass that there could be an entire NVA regiment in the surrounding area. If their intent was to retrieve supplies from under the burned-out village, there wasn't a lot we could do about it.

*****

The final part of the XO's report hit me especially hard. It left me speechless and trembling. All four of our most recent medevac helicopters had come under enemy fire while near the coastal city of Hue. The aircraft with my corpsman and the four patients aboard had been hit with triple-A antiaircraft fire and was lost in the jungle. The other three aircraft made it safely to the air base.

The news was devastating to the entire medical team. Only the CO knew that it was supposed to have been me on that helicopter. Although I was already a believer at the time, this incident made me realize that perhaps someone upstairs was looking out for me.

At the end of the briefing, the XO gave us a pep talk about how important it was to be careful in the field and to look out for each other.

JB mumbled loud enough for me to hear, *"The best way to avoid danger in the jungle is to get the hell out of the jungle. Doesn't anyone else think this is insane? What we are supposed to be doing out here in the bush? Does anyone care?"*

Everyone's nerves were still a wreck from the morning's B-52 carpet bombing and close encounter with Charlie; it took me several hours to calm down and stop shaking. The shaking wasn't visible, but my insides were still on a roller coaster. If we were supposed to be on a search-and-destroy mission, it appeared that Charlie had the same goals.

That evening, Gus suggested I take the medevac flight out the next day with some of the other marine officers.

"What's up?" I remarked. "I'm not injured—yet."

"After a significant battle, many of the officers plan a little R&R at one of the local watering holes in Da Nang," replied the chief. "It is strictly off the record, Doc, and it might be a chance for your nerves to settle down. No one is ever charged for leave on these missions. Think of the trip as a necessary mental health break. You would be surprised how a little TLC from some understanding young women can go a long way in soothing your nerves."

My thought process went something like this: First, I thought there must be plenty of officers who deserved time on the beach a lot more than I did. Second, I thought it might be a nice break to get away for a couple of days. Third, I thought, *Frig it, I'm outta this hellhole at first light tomorrow morning.*

Chapter 16

R&R Vietnamese-Style

The trip the next morning into Da Nang was a quick, easy ride on one of the Medevac choppers—less than forty-five minutes. The weather was sunny, with calm wind and oppressive humidity. The helicopter was flying pretty low to avoid the chance of enemy fire, but there was a nice breeze washing through the aircraft that kept us comfortable.

There were five of us heading into town for a change of scenery. One of my fellow officers was someone I hadn't met yet; an older warrant officer, he might have been anywhere between thirty and forty, on loan from the navy. He introduced himself as George and said his specialty was marksmanship. He had a deeply lined face with short salt-and-pepper hair. He spoke in a very refined, quiet manner, almost like a college professor addressing a seminar class.

"Oh, you're a sniper?" I suggested.

"Well," he retorted, "we prefer to think of ourselves as neutralization personnel. If it weren't for this little junket, you'd probably never know I was at the firebase."

"Where are you normally stationed?" I asked.

The increased whine of the helicopter engine drowned out his reply, but he explained later that he typically was attached to an LRRP unit or would look for a very secure "hide" somewhere outside of the firebase with a high and long-range view of the terrain.

"I am a very patient man," he explained. "Sometimes I sit or lie down for several hours at a time without moving except to survey the landscape through very powerful binoculars. If I detect movement of any kind, I zoom in on it with my telescope mounted on my rifle."

"Isn't that pretty boring?" I suggested.

"Well, yes, it can be. You do have a lot of time to think; your own movements have to be very slow and deliberate because you never know who is watching you. Most of the time, what you think might be enemy movement is caused by the wind or an animal. But I used to hunt turkeys back in Arkansas, so I developed a pretty good sense of what was worth shooting and honed some pretty good marksmanship skills."

George was quiet and reserved. I liked him right away. And though we were certainly not going into the city to hang out at the library, he had a family at home and was not interested in getting drunk and laid.

At George's suggestion, we found a good restaurant and bar at the One Star Hotel. The name sounded a little shaky, probably because many Westerners consider a three-star hotel to be borderline. The hotel was very near the Han River and market and not too far from a fairly large church, St. Joseph's Cathedral. The hotel was old and dated but pure luxury compared to what we had been used to recently.

Our first order of business was a long hot shower. But the showers seemed to have been made for smaller people. I had difficulty getting my hair wet without bending or kneeling down.

George had been to Da Nang before and advised that there were certain areas to avoid, but he said, "Most of the area is a whole lot more secure than around the firebase."

We spent a delightful two days in Da Nang. The Vietnamese were friendly and went out of their way to make us feel welcomed. In the evenings we spent time at the lounge at the One Star Hotel and reminisced about home. Several of the young female bar girls were absolutely stunning, but you just never knew what you could catch from being with them.

The music from the piano was totally relaxing, and the beers were pretty cheap (draft beer went for twenty-five cents per glass). "Jeez, Doc, we could get absolutely wasted for a couple of dollars in a joint like this." After a few beers, George loosened up some and talked a bit about one of his missions.

*****

His LRRP group was shadowing a patrol of Vietcong soldiers who were in the process of setting up an ambush near a clearing north of Loc Ninh, near the Cambodian border. It was during the dry season, and the temperature was near 100 degrees in the daytime. "Even in the heat, the undergrowth was damp and smelled almost moldy," said George.

"My spotter and I slithered away from the LRRP patrol and hiked far around the area of the ambush. We set up on a ridge overlooking the valley and the probable ambush site. We were both covered with camouflage face paint and blended into the jungle fauna pretty well. An enemy soldier would have to be close enough to step on us in order to see us.

"We had a decent view of the area, so we covered ourselves with brush, leaves, and grass and waited to see what the Cong were up to. Our only movements were a slow sweep of the valley with the high-powered binoculars and an occasional sip of water while we baked in the heat.

"We were in radio contact with a patrol of the Fifth Cavalry Regiment, First Air Cavalry Division. They were about three kilometers from the ambush site. The problem was that my spotter and I couldn't detect any movement anywhere in the valley.

"We were baking in the sauna-like heat. Suddenly, my spotter noticed a flash of a reflection down in the valley. We both focused our attention on the vegetation in that area. Through my rifle scope I noticed some movement in and around the vegetation. It looked like there were two Cong setting up some sort of explosive devices along the trail.

"I messaged the American patrol to warn them about the Cong activity. The First Air Cavalry sergeant thought this might be an opportunity to trap the Vietcong at their own game. 'Sir,' he asked, 'is there any way you could keep them in their current position while we flank them to the west? Their natural tendency would be to head for the Cambodian border. It is less than ten clicks from their position. Perhaps we can surprise them.'

"'We'll try,' I whispered. 'Give me two clicks on the radio when you want me to try to pick them off.'

"About twenty minutes later, our radio hissed with two audible clicks. I slowly squeezed the trigger of my sniper rifle. My first round was on its way. A moment later, my target lurched back into the brush. That brought additional movement and activity in the area. I focused on the tallest enemy fighter visible through the jungle cover, hoping he might be the Cong leader. He went down with a halo of a fine spray of blood.

"I'm sure the Cong could hear the distant crack of the sniper rifle, but sounds get distorted over distances in the jungle. The two quick kills or serious injuries caused confusion and maybe even panic for the Cong. They started heading west.

"This is where my work got interesting. I had to balance reducing the enemy ranks with the knowledge that every shot could be giving away our position. My spotter and I could see movement heading west, but no discernable targets. About every two minutes, we would send a round toward the last movement on the trail, hoping the patrol would think the rounds were coming from behind them.

"Within minutes the Cong patrol was confronted by the patrol from the First Air Cavalry. Their sergeant had the Cong in a crossfire and eliminated the threat. Some of them might have slithered off into the jungle, but not many! It was a good day to be a sniper."

*****

The next morning we had no trouble getting a bird out to the firebase. Not a lot of folks were anxious to head out into the jungle unless they had orders. We had food, medical supplies, and ammunition on board, but no other replacements for all the injured who had been evacuated.

My stomach was still a little jittery from the attack the previous week, but we had no incoming fire all the way to the firebase. We landed just north of the burned-out village in the cleared area of buffalo grass. After we landed, George said good-bye and immediately disappeared. I guessed he was off to some LRRP unit or another assignment.

He never did talk much about what he did or where he operated. The only time he even mentioned his work was after those couple of beers at the One Star bar. Every other time I questioned him about his personal life, navy duty, or operating area, he would change the subject and talk about his hometown. He said he had grown up in a little town south of Little Rock, Arkansas, called Sheridan. He said he loved to hunt in the woods or out by some river. He mentioned that he was never really comfortable being inside and much preferred to stay out in the bush as much as possible.

*****

By now our battalion commanding officer fully realized that we were sitting on real estate the North Vietnamese wanted very badly. Not only were more arms and ammunition discovered beneath the village we had burned down with the phosphorous rounds, but José and our troops also located large quantities of rice, propaganda leaflets, and medical supplies in those tunnels. These valuable supplies were needed by the NVA and VC in order to, as their propaganda stated, press their "battle against the infidel American forces." Much of the translated propaganda got right to the point: "Kill American Soldiers."

The brass was coming around to the idea that our remote valley near the river just wasn't the smartest area to contest. It wasn't clear to the battalion CO whether Firebase 14 was essential for the initial mission of "search and destroy" or whether it was needed for the "Vietnamization" process endorsed by the new general and Washington politicians. It was beginning to look like this real estate would be tricky to hold for the long term.

It was December 1969, and the North Vietnamese leader, seventy-nine-year-old Ho Chi Minh, had died the previous fall. If possible, the North Vietnamese seemed more resolute and determined than ever to unite their country with the South.

The Vietnamization process seemed to be working out pretty well— for the North Vietnamese. It was well-known that the new American general in charge, General Abrams, was to turn the war over to the South Vietnamese soldiers as quickly as possible.

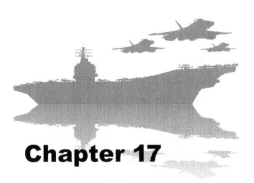

Chapter 17

POLITICS AND THE WAR EFFORT

In the 1968 presidential election, the Republicans nominated Richard Nixon, and the Democrats chose Hubert Humphrey, President Johnson's vice president. Both men had pledged to continue President Johnson's policies in Vietnam. Since both candidates were hawks on the war in Southeast Asia, the American public had little opportunity to have a clear voice in what was happening in Vietnam.

The only other voice on the war policy was that of a third-party candidate, Governor George Wallace of Alabama. His stated policy of "bombing North Vietnam back into the Stone Age" was hardly an alternative for those who wanted to end the conflict, which at that time was nearly half the population of the United States.

Perhaps the military brass in Vietnam was beginning to have second thoughts about the direction of the war. After all, in January 1968, North Vietnam had announced a seven-day ceasefire to celebrate Tet, the Vietnamese New Year. However, on January 31, the NVA launched a simultaneous attack on 126 South Vietnamese cities—every provincial capital of South Vietnam. This was soon known as the Tet Offensive.

Some of the fiercest fighting was in Hue, near the seventeenth parallel, the border of North Vietnam. It took US marines nearly a month to retake the city, at a tremendous cost in casualties. Over fifteen thousand Americans were killed in Vietnam in 1968. The Vietcong were able to penetrate even the American embassy in Saigon. The success of the Tet

Offensive surprised and sensitized the American public to the nature and direction of the war in Vietnam and caused a seismic negative shift in the popularity of the war for the American people.

By this time well over 50 percent of Americans felt that fighting a land war in Southeast Asia was a monumental mistake. Even many senior officers at the Pentagon felt that ensuring political freedom for the South Vietnamese people was not worth the losses of our precious military personnel. Added to this was the increasing dollar cost of replacing equipment and supplies.

The senior brass at the Pentagon were also questioning the South Vietnam political and military commitment to the overall war effort.

Our military losses and our strategy in the firebases in the northern part of South Vietnam were having minimal effect on North Vietnam's ability to increase the number of troops and supplies brought into the southern part of the country. The NVA sent most of its supplies at night down the mountainous roads and passes of the Ho Chi Minh Trail in Laos and Cambodia, directly into southern South Vietnam.

*****

The results of the 1968 election were quite close: Nixon won with 43.4 percent of the vote to Humphrey's 42.7 percent. Governor Wallace actually received 13.5 percent. With this narrow victory, President Nixon earned the right to dictate American policy regarding the war in Vietnam for the next four years. This political victory proved to be very expensive for America and for Mr. Nixon.

Unfortunately, the South Vietnamese Army had not made much progress with Nixon's Vietnamization policy, which was intended to enable the South Vietnamese to press on with the war while slowly reducing, unit by unit, the American presence in their country. President Nixon took much of his advice from his national security advisor, the brilliant Dr. Henry Kissinger of Harvard University.

Dr. Kissinger's policy was really a ploy he called "linkage." In other words, if the Russians and Chinese would stop supplying arms, equipment, and war materials to the North Vietnamese, then America would facilitate the flow of world oil and agricultural products, mainly wheat, to the

Russians and Chinese. These communist countries were North Vietnam's main suppliers of technology and war materials. They basically completely ignored the US national security advisor.

Regardless of the intended high-minded purpose, President Nixon was able to keep the war going for another four years. The long-term result was disastrous. The people of South Vietnam and America quickly lost trust in the Nixon administration, and our status as a strong, moral nation came under worldwide criticism. Our greatest loss was that of an irreplaceable treasure: the men and women of our armed services who were killed in accidents or by friendly or enemy fire.

In addition, the South Vietnamese *and* the North Vietnamese were losing thousands of soldiers, civilians, and children to this war. The eventual final body count would be much higher.

Although the ratio of combat deaths to injured was lower in Vietnam than in Korea or World War II, the statistics were still overwhelming: approximately 300,000 men and women, US citizens, were wounded, many of them crippled for life.

As of 1970, 46,000 American troops had been killed in action. What, if any, were the benefits to the American way of life? And what were the benefits to the people of South Vietnam? The total number of North and South Vietnamese lost, killed, maimed, or wounded during the war is so large it is difficult to calculate. The number could be in the millions.

Many Americans felt that President Nixon was continually trying to extricate our country from this war. However, our presence in the country only continued to prop up the South Vietnamese president, Nguyen Van Thieu. In June 1969, Nixon announced the first reduction of US troops from the war theater. Our total high number of troops serving in the Vietnam War zone came in that year: 541,500 in 1969.

Nixon claimed that by August 1, 1969, twenty-five thousand American troops would return home to the United States. This was the first sign of the reversal of President Johnson's war policy of continued escalation of the conflict. The fact that public opinion and demonstrations in America had forced Nixon's change in policy was not lost on the American public. Nixon's new approach of de-escalation was also used to cover up a much more sinister and disastrous policy.

The NVA had launched a general offensive campaign against the South Vietnamese Army and the American forces in February 1969. President Nixon had responded by secretly bombing the NVA supply lines in Laos and Cambodia. He kept his campaign of aerial interdiction from the American public and Congress. Of course, it wasn't a secret from the American pilots who were regularly told where and when to bomb, nor was it a secret from the Cambodians, Laotians, or NVA.

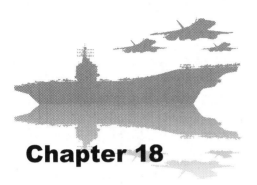

Chapter 18

RETURN TO "REALITY"

In late February 1970 the *Kitty Hawk* was due to rotate back to the shipyard in Bremerton, Washington, for a complete overhaul. Our ship had four propeller screws and eight steam boilers feeding four steam turbine engines developing 240,000 ship horse power. With the air wing on board, we had over five thousand men in a ship that was over one thousand feet long. The flight deck was approximately sixty feet above the ocean. The boilers provided steam for the catapults, heat, and hot water for the crew in addition to the power for the engines. The ship had been built in Camden, New Jersey. Construction began in December 1956, and the ship was launched in May 1960. It was retired to the Bremerton Naval Shipyard and decommissioned in 2009. In between it took a lot of abuse and wear. Minor repairs were accomplished right away, and complete overhauls, including all exterior and interior maintenance, were done approximately every five years. Complete cleanliness was required in all of the ship's spaces at all times.

My orders to return to the *Kitty Hawk* came while I was serving out at the firebase. JB had left Firebase 14 in late February and had come out to our ship for R&R in March. It wasn't unusual for those men serving in Vietnam to request leave on an air-craft carrier. He related in some detail his own temporary additional duty (TAD) orders and his activities while serving at the firebase after I had left. Although it was difficult for me to leave the remnants of the battalion, I have to admit it was a relief. It was especially difficult leaving Gus, JB, and the rest of the "docs."

I was able to take the next scheduled medevac flight out of Firebase 14. It took me back to the air base at Da Nang, where we were able to get a helicopter flight to Ton San Nhut. Right after leaving Firebase 14, we received some small-arms fire. Other than that, the flight from the firebase was uneventful.

The huge air base at Ton San Nhut had a different story. The base had sustained several rocket attacks. Firefights and probing fire at the perimeter of the base were becoming more frequent. As we made our approach to the helicopter pad, we could see muzzle flashes from the adjacent rice paddies.

Our helicopter received a strong jolt and careened sideways as we were descending to land. We must have been hit by some small-arms fire or a near miss from an RPG. The pilot shouted, "Strap in tight, ladies—this might be a hard landing!" The waist gunner kept looking for targets. With farmers out in the fields, it was difficult to pick out who was directing the fire or actually firing on the aircraft.

Bang! We landed so hard that I was surprised to see the aircraft was still intact. The pilot yelled, "Get away from the copter!" I grabbed my duffel and ran. There were holes in the fuselage, with fluids running out. The pilot had taken about ten running steps from the bird when—*whomp!*—it burst into flames: another success for Charlie. The concussion knocked us all flat, but only the pilot's clothing caught fire. He was burning alive. I ran over to him and shouted, "Lie still, Captain!" and put out the flames by smothering them with my duffel bag. Medical help arrived immediately and carted him off for treatment at the base hospital.

My subsequent COD flight to the *Kitty Hawk* was smooth as silk compared with the helicopter rides that had taken us from the ship to the hospital at Ton San Nhut and to the firebase four months earlier. Memories of the COD accident the previous fall had given me horrible nightmares.

The month after I returned to the ship, I was reunited with JB. That first evening in the wardroom, he told me about how a COD had brought him out to the *Kitty Hawk*. "It's difficult to describe the relief I feel," JB said. "Life on the *Kitty Hawk* in the middle of the Gulf of Tonkin, even during flight operations, is relaxing compared to being in a firebase in the middle of a jungle!"

Even though he was technically on leave, JB saw patients with us on the ship for a few days. He later joked, "The schedule in the dental and medical department was a surreal experience. The cacophonous sounds of flight operations, the roar and whine of jet aircraft, and the constant hum of the ships systems were a welcome relief from the shrieks, growls, and even deadly quiet of the jungle."

*****

Our typical day out in the Tonkin Gulf began with sick call at 0800. Anyone with a dental problem was allowed to come to the dental department and explain his problem to our first class petty officer. If the petty officer felt that there was a problem, the patient received an emergency sick-call visit with one of the four staff dentists assigned to the *Hawk*.

Since a great many of our sailors on the ship were between the ages of eighteen and twenty-five, a lot of them had troubles with their third molars, or wisdom teeth. None of the other dental officers wanted the difficult, tiresome task of removing impacted wisdom teeth, so that project was left for me, the youngest on the staff.

My time working and seeing patients with my then roommate, Dr. Jim A., was pretty good training for shipboard oral surgery. At least he had a bit more experience, which he shared with me on a few patients before letting me loose on the hundreds of sailors I eventually treated. No one in the dental department enjoyed or wanted to practice oral surgery, and all the officers were senior in rank, so I was "promoted" to the position of ship's oral surgeon.

After a few straight weeks of impacted wisdom tooth duty, few of the dental impactions were troublesome for me. The first hour of sick call was set aside for all the dental emergencies, after which patients were scheduled until late afternoon. JB thought the medical department was terrific duty. He flew back reluctantly to Tan Son Nhut to resume his duty at the hospital as our ship headed for the Philippines.

*****

We would see emergencies anytime, no matter the hour. While at sea, we worked seven days a week and all holidays. While in port, all of us took liberty except for the dentist on emergency duty. Our dental department CO often took on this responsibility. Although this was very gracious, in reality he wasn't interested in seeing a foreign port if he'd been there several times before.

The experiences at Firebase 14 were difficult to talk about with anyone on board except JB and the two marine captains. When we got together in the wardroom, we would talk for hours about the politics of the war and the strange futility of our being there. Both marine officers felt that the brass high command did not want to waste our precious resources on this conflict.

However, both marine captains also felt that there might be two positive outcomes from our involvement. First, a free and democratic South Vietnam would be a welcome ally for the United States in Southeast Asia. And second, our involvement had given our military an invaluable proving ground to test new weapons systems and electronics, such as listening devices and scent detectors. Their enthusiasm for the whole conflict was tempered by the losses of so many colleagues in our armed forces. There was nothing these marine officers detested more than losing a fellow marine.

*****

The only interruption to our routine aboard the *Hawk* was when a group of state and federal legislators came out to our ship on one of their "political fact-finding missions." One of the visitors was from Boston, Massashusetts congresswoman Louise Day Hicks. I had been aware of her when she was a councilwoman known for her radical antibusing stance in south Boston. None of us had any use for people breaking the rhythm of our day. It also bothered me to think about who was paying for this "fact-finding" trip to Southeast Asia. My thought at the time was that the taxpayers of Massachusetts and Boston could probably find and deserved better representation.

The CO of the dental clinic called us into his office to brief us on protocol. "Please, guys, look busy, but don't do anything too exotic while the dignitaries are going through the medical and dental spaces."

*****

When we returned to the continental United States and the Bremerton Naval Shipyard near Seattle, Washington, the ship's executive officer asked me to share a ski lodge with his family and the ship navigator's family at Crystal Mountain Ski Area. Alex and his wife Marcia and their two daughters were avid ski enthusiasts. Our ship's navigator, Commander C. E. M., and his family had already signed on to the idea. Being an ardent skier from New England, I thought it sounded like a fabulous opportunity.

It was an honor to be asked by these high-ranking, decorated naval officers to join their families for skiing. It was so radically different from being out on the ship or in the jungle that it didn't seem real. The skiing and the fellowship with the officer families from the ship were terrific, until the last run on May 2, 1970.

My last run was particularly exhilarating. It was a picturesque, sunny spring day. On a three-diamond run down a dangerous trail, I became airborne going over a mogul. When I dropped back down to earth, I landed on loose granular slush. My skis stopped on impact, but I kept going and fractured my left medial malleolus (ankle).

This resulted in a two-day stay at the local hospital. The medical staff repaired my ankle with two pins and a screw, and the pain was significant. However, that pain could not compare with how sick I felt upon hearing on May 4 that Ohio National Guard troops had opened fire on students demonstrating against the war at Kent State University.

Surely, there had to be a better way of dealing with student demonstrations. Although the National Guard troops were inexperienced and must have been in fear for their own safety, it was hard to justify their actions. To this day, the nausea I felt hearing about this tragedy while lying immobile in the hospital still comes back to haunt me.

*****

Living on the *Hawk* in dry dock while working at the base hospital in Bremerton wasn't too much fun in a cast, although the sailors who ran the huge aircraft elevators did help me avoid most of the ship's ladders. One day while I was working in the dental clinic, word was passed down to me that Firebase 14 had been abandoned.

The marines at the firebase never did get their howitzer. The base was turned over to the villagers who lived nearby. The abandonment of the firebase neatly symbolized the futility of our effort in Vietnam. It was my prayer that the firebase hadn't lost any more marines.

Even though I still needed a cast, a month later my ankle was healing nicely, and it was a pleasure to have the rest of the officers and men rejoin the ship as it sailed for our home port in San Diego. I spent most days sitting on a dental stool, so my cast wasn't much of a factor.

Many of my shipmates helped me negotiate the multitude of ship's ladders and passageways, and I continued to be especially grateful to those operating the massive elevators that transported the aircraft to the flight deck. The petty officers operating the plane elevators would always give me a ride between decks. My commanding officer gave me every opportunity to transfer to a shore base, but a duty-bound closeness to my shipmates compelled me to finish my tour on the *Hawk*.

Regarding my being on the ship for what was to be my second "tour" of Vietnam, my commanding officer might have looked at me as a liability on a warship with a cast on my left leg. Perhaps he couldn't find anyone else who seemed agreeable to treating patients with impacted wisdom teeth.

The air wing rejoined our ship as we sailed out of San Diego for our return to Yankee Station. Although we had plenty of general-quarters emergency drills on our trip out, our band also had time to get in some practice. By the time we arrived at Cubi Point Naval Air Station at the huge Subic Bay Naval Base, we were pretty darn good. Daniel and the other band members from the air wing loved to play Dixieland and popular show hits. It seemed to relax them and ameliorate the stress of flight operations.

*****

As we arrived on Yankee Station in the Gulf of Tonkin, the US Congress was finally able to stand up to the president. In April 1970,

President Nixon had surprised the American people and Congress by announcing that in order to interdict the supply routes of the NVA and Vietcong into South Vietnam, he was sending a large contingency of US ground troops into Cambodia. The president's reasoning was that this would give the United States time to withdraw our troops from Vietnam.

Ultimately, the invasion and incursion into Cambodia had almost no effect on the steady stream of supplies and arms into South Vietnam from the north; however, it did cause Congress to act, citing a violation of the US Constitution.

The American Congress quickly passed a bill forcing the president to remove all ground and air forces from Cambodia by July 1, 1970. Although President Nixon continued to deceive the public and Congress by relentlessly bombing Cambodia, he did pull the troops out, proclaiming at the time "what a complete success" the whole operation had been!

On December 31 of that year, Congress repealed the Gulf of Tonkin Resolution, which President Johnson had used to initiate the war in Vietnam. Many members of our Congress had begun questioning whether the incident that had led to the "Tonkin Resolution" was actually a "false flag." By this time a majority in Congress wanted to end the financial drain and the tragic loss of our military personnel.

In February 1971, the ARVN (the Army of South Vietnam) launched a major invasion of Laos, called Lam Son 715. It was designed to sever the Ho Chi Minh Trail and interdict the flow of arms and munitions to the Vietcong in the southern part of Vietnam. Although President Nixon authorized the use of air power to protect these soldiers, the entire forty-five-day mission was an unmitigated disaster.

Fully one-half of the South Vietnamese troops involved in operation Lam Son 715 were killed or injured. The North Vietnamese probably knew about the entire invasion in advance through a sophisticated network of spies working with the South Vietnamese intelligence agents. The failure of this operation brought home the disingenuousness of Nixon's "Vietnamization" plan.

*****

On March 30, 1972, the North Vietnamese launched a major attack on South Vietnam through the demilitarized zone. This made the politicians in Washington very nervous. It was an election year, and President Nixon did not want to be the first president to lose a war. Within two weeks, the US bombing of Hanoi and Haiphong resumed. Haiphong Harbor was also mined. However, even this escalation did not solve Nixon's political problems. The resumption of air attacks on cities in North Vietnam did not stop the flow of war material into South Vietnam.

However, the resumption of air attacks did save the careers of aviators who had taken it upon themselves to bomb targets in Hanoi without authorization. Prosecution of naval aviators for bombing targets in the north came to an abrupt halt when President Nixon authorized an all-out attack on military and government targets north of the seventeenth parallel. Author Stephen Coonts has written an excellent account of this period in his historically accurate novel *The Flight of the Intruder* (Naval Institute Press, 1986).

On March 23, 1972, Lieutenant Commander Daniel Kirk was lost over Laos. Word was passed to me from one of the band members still on the ship. Lieutenant James A., who had been my roommate on the ship, also called me at my office with the sad news. Jim was in an orthodontic postgraduate program at the Temple University School of Dentistry at the time. Jim and I have kept in touch over the years, and it has been a pleasure to watch his wonderful family grow.

In addition to Lieutenant Commander Kirk, a top decorated naval aviator, the US Air Force losses over the prior Christmas bombing of Hanoi resulted in the downing of fifteen B-52s and eleven fighter-bombers, which increased the number of POWs held in North Vietnam by ninety-three. Daniel was not among them.

*****

President Nixon had two issues working in his favor for his upcoming political campaign. First, he was continually reducing our ground troops in Vietnam. We had gone from over 540,000 combatants and support personnel when he took office in 1969 to 70,000 troops in Southeast Asia by 1973. More importantly, instead of around three hundred American combat deaths per week when Nixon took office, fatalities were down to approximately one combat death per day. According to the president's point of view, "Vietnamization" was working.

The second issue in Nixon's favor was that his opponent in the upcoming presidential election, Senator George McGovern, was running a lackluster campaign on the primary claim that he would "get America out of the quagmire" that symbolized our efforts in Vietnam. Senator McGovern's primary issue had been neatly co-opted by the Nixon for President Campaign. Massachusetts was the only state that agreed with Senator McGovern during that presidential campaign.

*****

Nixon's "best" political ploy occurred on October 26, 1972. Within two weeks of the presidential election, Dr. Kissinger pulled a rabbit out of the proverbial hat, proclaiming that "peace was at hand" so that the president could claim his policies had brought "peace with honor." This fooled 60 percent of the American voting public and resulted in one of the largest political landslide victories in recent electoral history.

Over the next year, Nixon and Kissinger both tried to battle their way out of Vietnam. President Nixon battled with Congress and the public; Dr. Kissinger battled with the North Vietnamese negotiator Le Duc Tho. President Nixon ended active US involvement in Vietnam on January 23, 1973. That summer President Nixon signed a bill ending all American combat and support activities in all of Indochina. Without US support, the war continued as a civil war between North and South Vietnam until the end of 1975. Many observers claimed that the president had to relinquish control of the Vietnamization process because of his role in the Watergate scandal that was enveloping his presidency.

Chapter 19

Ending the Vietnam War—The Watergate Scandal

In June 1972, the Watergate Hotel complex in Washington, DC, housed the headquarters of the Democratic Party's national office. That month, five people were arrested for an attempted burglary of the Democratic headquarters. Nixon denied any connection with the burglary and was reelected that November.

In January 1973, during the burglars' trial, Judge Sirica discovered that three White House operatives had covered up the burglary. The operatives from the White House were H.R.Haldeman, White House Chief of Staff, JohnEhrlichman, White House Special Assistant on Domestic Affairs, and John Dean, White House Councel. These three men, along with the current attorney general, Richard Kleindienst, resigned in disgrace in April 1973. However, this sorry tale would get much worse for President Nixon.

The new attorney general, Elliot Richardson, appointed Archibald Cox as special prosecutor. Senator Sam Irvin led a special subcommittee to investigate the sordid affair. During the televised proceedings, Senator Irvin learned of the existence of taped conversations within the Oval Office that had bearing on the Watergate case. The attorney general and the senator requested, via subpoena, that the president turn over the tapes to the investigating committee. President Nixon refused to relinquish the tapes and ordered the firing of Archibald Cox. The date was October 29, 1973.

The attorney general, Elliot Richardson, a Republican, resigned in protest. However, public opinion, Judge Sirica's court order, and the repeated requests of the new special prosecutor, Leon Jaworski, eventually brought the tapes to light. The tape recordings were surrendered on December 8, 1973. Unfortunately for Nixon, the tapes revealed clear signs of his involvement in the cover-up of the break-in at the Watergate Hotel.

President Nixon's resistance in cooperating with the special prosecutor reinforced negative public opinion of his presidency and his administration. The subsequent spring, in 1974, the House of Representatives began an inquiry into impeachment of the president of the United States. In July 1974, its judiciary committee brought forth three articles of impeachment.

On August 5, the president released to the special prosecutor, Leon Jaworski, three additional tapes that clearly demonstrated his involvement in the cover-up of the break-in at the Watergate Hotel. Despite still insisting that he had done nothing wrong and declaring, "Your president is not a crook," President Nixon resigned on August 8, 1974.

In 1973, Vice President Spiro Agnew had resigned because of his involvement in bribery, extortion, and income tax violations during his terms as governor of Maryland. On Agnew's resignation, President Nixon had nominated Gerald Ford to fill the position of vice president. Ford had been a legislator from Michigan from 1948 to 1973. On Nixon's resignation, Gerald Ford became president of the United States.

Ford became the first president to reach that position without having been elected to the vice presidency or the presidency by the American people. Nixon was never convicted of any wrongdoing because of his resignation. However, Nixon was still pardoned by President Ford one month after the new president took office.

Operation Babylift

In the final days of the Vietnam War, in 1975, President Ford ordered the evacuation of over 237,000 Vietnamese anticommunist refugees from the country. One of the most astonishing and tragic accidents of the airlift seemed to epitomize the agony and despair that characterized America's involvement in that tragic war effort. The "Operation Babylift" evacuation began at four o'clock on Friday afternoon, April 4, 1975. An air force C-5A

Galaxy carrying 243 babies, many of them orphans, and 62 adult aides took off from Tan Son Nhut Air Base.

Thirty minutes after takeoff, the pilot noticed a blinking red light indicating decompression problems. As the pilot was returning to the air base, the aft pressure door exploded, causing the aircraft to crash moments later into a rice field near the Saigon River. Over two hundred children and all but one of the adult aides perished.

Those allies who couldn't get airlifted out of South Vietnam were destined to try to make it to Hong Kong by boat. Many of these refugees ultimately came to the United States. One of them, Dr. David H. (his American name), eventually took over and purchased the general dental practice in our office.

US Involvement in South Vietnam Ends

In a scheduled speech at Tulane University on April 23, 1975, the president of the United States, Gerald Ford, made an announcement: "America can regain the sense of pride that existed before Vietnam. But it cannot be achieved by refighting a war that is *finished* as far as America is concerned."

The second after the president uttered the word "finished," with emphasis, the audience of almost five thousand students erupted into thunderous applause and shouts of joy that went on for several minutes. This announcement was the president's way of letting the antiwar bloc in Congress and the American people know exactly where he stood on the war.

The last American evacuation helicopter left Vietnam on April 30, 1975. Except for the areas around the docks, where hundreds of people were still trying to evacuate by boat, Saigon seemed relatively quiet. It was hard for the residents to grasp that after twenty years of agony and bloodshed, the war with the North Vietnamese was finally over.

As the men, women, and boys of the North Vietnamese Army streamed into the city of Saigon, many were amazed and dumbfounded at the very large amount of luxuries and goods stockpiled at the South Vietnamese stores and Army PX (Post Exchange). Was this how the oppressed people of the South were living? Were these luxuries commonplace for the poor, downtrodden South Vietnamese they were there to liberate?

After the evacuation, the South Vietnamese government collapsed in 1976; the country was then united as the Socialist Republic of Vietnam. Saigon was renamed Ho Chi Minh City. Economic and political relations with the United States were not normalized until 1995.

Phone Call to MIA/POW's Family

During all this time the recurring question in my mind was, whatever happened to my friend Daniel from the *Kitty Hawk?* It was time to call his wife to see if there was any further news.

The call to Daniel's family was not easy. His wife and grown children were not at all convinced that Daniel had died when his aircraft went into the Laotian jungle in the spring of 1972. There were indications from the CIA broadcast from the mountains in Laos that Daniel was a prisoner of war somewhere in Laos. This is where the trail would have ended had it not been for encouragement from photographic images at the Stomatologic Institute in Moscow or the statements from actual prisoners of war such as Red McDaniel. Although the phone call to Daniel's family in 1978 was inconclusive, it gave me some encouragement to keep following any scraps of leads.

Captain McDaniel spent six long years in a Hanoi prison. The difficulties of his experience, including torture and indignities, and even humor come through in his book *Scars and Stripes*. His A-6 Intruder aircraft was shot down over Nam Dinh on May 19, 1967, on his eighty-first combat mission. He was listed as missing in action until 1970. He was finally released on March 4, 1973.

Captain McDaniel survived his ordeal because of his deep love for the Lord and his compassion for his torturers: "They were not the 'enemy' to me at all. They were people, part of the human condition, striving in their own way to arrive at some semblance of existence that would give them a measure of happiness."* Captain McDaniel is a true American Hero. He still speaks positively about his North Vietnamese captors and harbors no ill will toward any of them.

*McDaniel, E., Scars & Stripes, J.B. Lippincott, Co., Philadelphia 1975. P. 166.

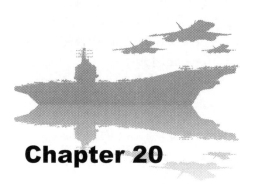

Chapter 20

EARLY BEGINNINGS—OUR INVOLVEMENT IN VIETNAM

The agony of our human, political, and economic expenditure in Vietnam really began prior to 1954, when the US financial backing of the French collapsed with the French defeat at Dien Bien Phu, a small French outpost in northwest Vietnam in the Muong Thanh Valley. Our president at the time, Dwight Eisenhower, knew that the American people had no taste for another Asian land war after our prolonged and difficult involvement in the Korean War.

The communist Vietnamese general Vo Nguyen Giap fought with the Viet Minh in order to defeat the French at this small mountain outpost near Laos. First, the general cut all the roads to the outpost at Dien Bien Phu, forcing the French to rely on resupply by air, and then he utilized heavy artillery to wear the French down. After the evacuation of all French troops, an international conference in Geneva, Switzerland, partitioned the country at the seventeenth parallel. The reunification elections that were scheduled for 1956 were never held, and the communists in the north established a government known as the Democratic Republic of North Vietnam.

Unfortunately, the Geneva Accords that were decided upon between April and July 1954 held true to the old adage: the seeds of the next battle are planted in the peace treaties. Had the Geneva Peace Conference never bowed to political pressure and partitioned Vietnam at the seventeenth parallel, the war between North and South Vietnam very possibly would have had a political solution.

The activities of the North Vietnamese guerrilla army and the South Vietnamese procommunist rebels (the Vietcong) led to US involvement in the form of so-called US advisors in the early 1960s and eventually to the Tonkin Gulf Resolution.

*****

On August 4, 1964, President Johnson announced that a US warship in the Gulf of Tonkin had been attacked by gunboats. A destroyer, the USS *Maddox*, had been fired on by the North Vietnamese. Very little or no discernible damage was evident to the US ship. However, the president then asked Congress to support a retaliatory strike by US aircraft on the North Vietnamese. On August 7, 1964, Congress overwhelmingly supported a joint resolution to "promote peace and security in Southeast Asia." Only two democratic senators, Wayne Morse of Oregon and Ernest Gruening, from Arkansas dissented. Presto! The Tonkin Gulf Resolution was born.

The USS *Maddox*, a Sumner-class destroyer, had been launched in March 1944. On August 2, 1964, while cruising in international waters twenty-eight miles off the coast of North Vietnam, this ship was attacked by three North Vietnamese patrol boats. These sixty-foot aluminum-hull patrol boats each carried two torpedoes packed with 550 pounds of TNT explosive warheads. The *Maddox* and F-8 Crusaders from the aircraft carrier the USS *Ticonderoga* counterattacked and successfully drove off the attacking patrol boats.

Both senators that opposed the resolution felt that the Tonkin Gulf Resolution was part of a ploy to aid our "advisors" who were already trying to help the people of South Vietnam. These two senators voted against the resolution because of the chance of our country being pulled into an Asian land war, the same caution shared by President Eisenhower over a decade earlier. The historical significance of this "resolution" was that it gave President Johnson the authorization to use conventional forces throughout Southeast Asia in order "to assist any member or protocol state of the Southeast Asia Collective Defense Treaty."

During the US involvement in the Gulf of Tonkin and in the country of Vietnam, the general feeling was that the North Vietnamese people were somehow to be underrated, discredited, or disparaged. Our disrespect and continued underestimation of the enemy combatants was a monumental mistake. How could these "primitive" villagers, with minimal modern weaponry, ever hope to be equal to the task of ridding their country of the mighty French or US forces?

*****

During the time I spent in Vietnam and throughout the years in my dental practice, all the Vietnamese people with whom I have ever come in contact or who have passed through our office have been kind, gentle, hardworking, and extremely bright. The kids in Vietnam were the best: very friendly and trusting.

My cousin Alan and his wife adopted an infant from a small village outside of Hanoi. Carrie is now fourteen years old and living in Manhattan. This bright and talented young woman is a treasure of enjoyment for her parents and to everyone who meets her.

Of course, there was never any idea whether the children who came to the hospitals or clinics for care in Vietnam were from the northern or southern part of the country. Politics never interfered in the treatment of any children.

My association with Dr. David H., who fled Vietnam by boat, has always been professional, caring, and trusting. He is a wonderful clinician and worked in our office for nine years until he got so busy that he had to move to a larger facility. At his wedding, it was my honor and pleasure to meet many of his extended Vietnamese family who had settled in the Boston area.

Chapter 21

A WORLD-CLASS WARRIOR AND LIFE POST-VIETNAM

It was delightful and relaxing to play music with Daniel and the Yankee Air Pirates Band. Every time we reminisced over that firefight northwest of Da Nang at Firebase 14, Daniel would just brush it off, saying, "That's what they pay us for doing." Our band played at the Subic Bay Officers' Club and officers' clubs in Sasebo, Japan, and in hotels in Singapore and Hong Kong; we loved playing Dixieland music all over Asia. Had I any idea of the possible difficulties, danger, and circumstances that Daniel would face in the future, I would have appreciated my time with him much more.

As my second tour of duty on Yankee Station wore on, my rotation came up, and the navy sent me back to the States and released me from active duty in June 1971. My reserve time ended in 1991. Daniel was lost over Laos in 1972. The circumstances of his aircraft crash have always been shrouded in mystery. In my one conversation with Mrs. Kirk in the mid-1970s, it seemed understandably painful for her to discuss the details. Did the navy truly not know the circumstances of his mission, or had the facts been deliberately hidden or obfuscated?

The American public was unaware of our activities in Laos in 1972. Even forty years after Daniel was lost, his wife still will not have a memorial service, even though the military has offered to help sponsor the service. Her response has been "Prove to me that he is dead, and then we will have a service!" Mrs. Kirk's loyalty and dedication has been inspiring for her family and all who have come to know her. The US Navy has never been able to prove that Lieutenant Commander Kirk is deceased.

*****

On the ship, Daniel loved showing all the antimissile technology in his aircraft. He would let me sit in the aircraft in the hangar bay as he stood on a ladder beside the plane, explaining what everything was supposed to do. He was a good-sized man, probably approaching six feet two inches in height and weighing at least 190 pounds. How he crammed himself into that cockpit was pure magic! He emphasized the importance of the antimissile technology, exclaiming, "Sometimes those damn SAM things are everywhere!"

Among the technology he showed me was what he called the "black box." Of course, this technology is ancient history by now, but it was the latest technology at the time. He explained that the surface-to-air missiles were particularly dangerous if your black box had a red light and a solid tone. If the box was blinking yellow, that meant that the SAM site had you on radar and was looking at you. If the yellow light was solid and the tone was beeping, the SAM had been launched. If your box had a red light with a solid tone, that missile was launched and locked on you! He said that if the missile looked like a flying telephone pole, you were probably going to be okay, as long as you took evasive measures.

However, if the launched rocket looked like a doughnut with a dot in the middle, you could be in real trouble. That missile was coming directly at your aircraft at two and a half times the speed of sound! Daniel would regale anyone who would listen with stories of some of the evasive maneuvers he had to take in certain hair-raising situations. The stories would often be absolutely terrifying. He would claim, "It was all in a day's work." He really loved flying.

On several occasions, Daniel actually showed his work. This was probably against all rules and regulations, but he would tape my Super 8mm movie camera to the inside of his Plexiglas canopy with duct tape. As he would zoom in to drop his ordnance, he would flick on the camera and film the entire episode. Some of that footage, with the secondary explosions, antiaircraft fire, and SAM launches, was quite heart-stopping.

Daniel thought of it as "rather routine." Although from the air, viewed on the Super 8 tape, the Vietnamese countryside and beaches of Hue were beautiful and spectacular, the defensive flying and incoming flack and missile fire were absolutely terrifying!

Daniel clearly thought a lot about his family because he talked about them all the time. His children must have had a difficult time growing up without knowing exactly what had happened to their father. They are all grown-up by now; they must be in their forties, or perhaps older.

After Vietnam, it was postgraduate school for me and specialization in a branch of dental medicine: pediatric dentistry and orthodontics. During the early summer of 1972, one of the band members still attached to the ship called to inform me that Daniel was "missing in action." It was a very sad day indeed.

Chapter 22

MISSING IN ACTION

"Missing in action" (MIA) is a casualty category assigned to armed service personnel who are missing or cannot be found. The assigned category can refer to killed or wounded personnel, prisoners of war, or deserted personnel. It basically means that the service branch, in Daniel's case the US Navy Department, cannot locate the serviceman or his or her remains.

What most people in the air wing—indeed, most people in the navy at that time, including the pilots themselves—did not know was that a small micro-locating device had been inserted into every flight suit of every pilot. The device nicknamed LOKATE had been initiated in 1966 and was initially stamped and then later actually sewn into the seam of the right-ankle zipper closure of pilots' flight suits. Even with the device embedded, the seam of the right-ankle zipper closure looked and almost felt exactly like the seam in the left-ankle zipper closure. If one was careful to fold and compare each seam, the right ankle seam would feel slightly stiffer.

When Daniel went down over Laos in March 1972, the LOKATE device was known only by a select few at the Pentagon. The loss of this highly skilled pilot and his valuable aircraft was immediately telegraphed to the fleet admiral and subsequently to the Pentagon. This device and the A7-E Corsair that Daniel was flying were now on the Pentagon's logistics map and immediately programmed into a defense department satellite-dedicated computer. The programming was slow by today's standards and took most of the day. The information gleaned from the satellite's position over Southeast Asia was coordinated with the pilot's last audio transmission and the visual observation of his wingman.

A wingman's job and duty is to fly behind and to the side of a flight leader. The wingman offers protection and support for the flight leader. Daniel's wingman was known as "Pinky." I don't know how he wound up with that handle or nickname; I could not even hazard a guess.

Pinky reported that he observed the A7-E aircraft after Daniel reported that a violent vibration had shaken his plane. The wingman's report indicated that the ejection seat had been fired because he observed a cascade of tinkling Plexiglas as the aircraft headed for the jungle canopy. The wingman's report included no sighting of a parachute from the detonated ejection seat. However, how long the wingman hung around to attempt a "location for rescue" is debatable.

Ejection Seat

Once the pilot reaches down between his legs and pulls hard on the ejection handle, everything happens automatically in sequence within a fraction of a second. First, the Plexiglas canopy is blown off, and an explosive charge under the pilot's seat detonates, flinging the pilot out of the aircraft in his seat with the parachute attached. The rocket-powered ejection seats were under redevelopment during the Vietnam War because too many pilots were being captured near where their planes were going down. Many of these pilots were then tortured and kept for long periods of time under deplorable conditions.

The AERCAB, or Aerial Escape and Rescue Capability, ejection seats were in the design phase and were to be developed to actually fly the pilot to a safe or safer location for rescue. The ejection seat would have been propelled by a small turbojet engine designed for pilotless drones, but the program was terminated at the end of the Vietnam War and never came to fruition.

If the aircraft is traveling too fast, approximating the speed of sound (750 miles per hour), the gravitational forces acting on the pilot's body can cause great physical damage and death. At that speed, approximately 20gs would be experienced, or the pilot's weight would increase by a factor of twenty.

Daniel's plane was traveling closer to 250 to 375 miles per hour, a speed considered very "doable" for ejection. Speeds of over 500 miles per hour are considered high-risk and unsafe. Important questions were then raised: How long did the wingman hang around to try to observe the result of the ejection? Was there continuing or *any* triple-A (antiaircraft artillery) fire or SAM missile activity?

Pentagon Sensitivities

The actual building of the Pentagon, which houses the US Department of Defense, occupies twenty-nine acres of land and sits on a total land area of 583 acres. Approximately 23,000 civilian and military employees work in the building and take care of the defense of the United States. In the late 1960s and early 1970s, the number of employees with full knowledge of the LOKATE program who oversaw all of the pilots and aircraft in our naval arsenal was exactly three: one rear admiral, one commander, and one senior chief.

Admiral Klonner thought up and designed the program with a senior program developer from IBM back in the early 1960s. The original program and device were quite crude by today's standards. The implanted device served more as a radar reflector and was effective only if the satellite was in a very narrow corridor overhead. The program and satellite surveillance were improved, refined, and put in place in 1966.

The original purpose of LOKATE was to get a better idea of what the defense department needs were for types of aircraft and trained personnel required for the fleet. After the program was implemented, it was discovered that LOKATE was a wonderful way of keeping track of the pilots as well as the planes they were flying. A LOKATE locating device was concealed and planted on the aircraft fuselage under part of the aircraft's designator number as well as in the pilot's flight suit.

There were two reasons for the top-secret designation. First, those in charge of the program did not want the air wing to feel that Big Brother was indeed watching them. The second reason was that the admiral at the Pentagon did not want any of this information available to our adversaries.

When the senior chief received the message from the fleet admiral concerning the A7-E Corsair II from VA-192, the Golden Dragons, piloted by Lieutenant Commander Daniel Kirk from the USS *Kitty Hawk*, a LOKATE program was immediately initiated. Over the next several hours three procedures were implemented in that small first subbasement office room, M1126, in the Pentagon.

First, the information was conveyed to Admiral Klonner, the naval commander and the senior chief in the LOKATE program. Second, the computer geeks at the Pentagon got busy programming information for upload to the satellite. Within twenty-four hours, Admiral Klonner and his staff were able to locate with fairly decent precision the location of the A7-E Corsair and its pilot, Lt. Daniel Kirk. In addition, a notice was sent to a special ops marine colonel for the possibility of an immediate search-and-rescue operation.

The Corsair II aircraft, plotted on the maps in room M1126 in the Pentagon basement, was located in eastern Laos. The pilot had been moved approximately twenty-five kilometers to the southwest to a possible Vietcong field hospital or prison camp. That's where they lost contact with the pilot for almost two months. This was extremely frustrating for the marine colonel, McNally, who was in charge of special rescue operations for Vietnam. His office was located in a military compound near Nha Trang. A rescue operation had already been planned when the signal from Daniel's flight suit seemed to vanish.

In late April 1972, the LOKATE device on the Corsair aircraft started moving north. Within a week it was in the outskirts of Hanoi. Its slow rate of travel indicated that it was being transported by truck or elephant. On May 20, part of or the entire Corsair aircraft was located at a military air base outside of Moscow. From the rate of travel, it was determined that what was left of the Corsair either had been flown or had flown on its own to the air base in Russia.

On June 19, 1972, the pilot's LOKATE device began reflecting a transmission from the satellite again. The staff in room M1126 were baffled until they decided that the VC or NVA hospital or prison must have been below ground in some tunnels. They decided that either the VC had put Daniel back into his flight suit, or they had just moved the flight suit. The LOKATE device recorded that the suit, Daniel, or possibly and hopefully both were now located about eighty kilometers north in a suspected prisoner-of-war encampment in Laos.

It was about this time, ten weeks after the disappearance of Lieutenant Kirk and his Corsair aircraft, that a clandestine, unconfirmed NSA radio-intercept located high in the mountainous region of eastern Laos picked up a message from the NVA that a Lieutenant Kirk was being held at a prisoner-of-war camp in Laos along with approximately seventy other prisoners from America.

There was no appreciable movement of the LOKATE device for almost a year. Had any of this information been public, critical questions would have been posed to the navy department: Is anyone out there looking for these seventy Americans? Has anyone from the State Department contacted the Laotian authorities about these POWs?

Miraculous!

One fine spring day in Washington in 1973, the commander working with Admiral Klonner noticed that the LOKATE device was no longer reflecting the signal from the suspected prisoner-of-war camp in Laos. It was nowhere to be found in Southeast Asia. It had just disappeared from the computer model and possibly off the face of the earth. Commander Ben Tillson and Senior Chief McMatton, both of whom were intimately involved in the LOKATE program from the beginning, searched furiously on computer screens in room M1126 for any signal from the satellite as it passed over Southeast Asia. They expanded their search on the next pass of the satellite to include the Middle East and China without success. Had the flight suit been destroyed?

The next day, the chief in room M1126 widened the satellite scan to include the northern hemisphere. He kept walking the search northward with every pass of the satellite. After four days of diligent searching, bingo, the signal showed up at a military airport—but not the one near Moscow that contained the A7-E Corsair II that Daniel had been flying on March 22, 1972, over Laos. The new location was a military airport called Uelkal in Eastern Siberia, with coordinates N 65°30′56″, W 179°182″.

The possibility that one of our valuable naval pilots could be in far eastern Russia at a Siberian military airport was so unexpected that the admiral at the Pentagon decided to consult with his commander and senior chief. Commander Tillson and Senior Chief McMatton both suggested that Admiral Klonner take this perplexing information to his military superior at the Pentagon. His superior told Klonner sternly, "Under no circumstance are we to pursue this information. If the Russians got word of the search for Lieutenant Commander Kirk in Eastern Siberia, it could compromise the entire LOKATE program, and we might never find Lieutenant Commander Kirk again."

This directive frustrated and depressed the three men directly involved in LOKATE, but they recognized and understood that the information had to be buried. It was May 1973.

The Sutton Factor

It never occurred to anyone involved at the time, or indeed over the last forty years, why the Russians would possibly want to keep one of our pilots for a prolonged period of time. After a researching into the problem of captured pilots, a couple of books written by Anthony Cyril Sutton, PhD, turned up.

Professor Sutton was a British-born economics teacher at California State University, Los Angeles, and a research fellow at Stanford University's Hoover Institute from 1968 to 1973. During his time at the Hoover Institute, he wrote a major study titled *Western Technology and Soviet Economic Development, 1917-1930.*[*] In this three-volume extensive study, Professor Sutton argued that the West played a major role in Russia's development of industry and technology, starting directly after Russia's 1917 revolution.

One of Professor Sutton's conclusions was that this technological knowhow was paid for by US taxpayers and US corporations, and the Russians funneled these advancements directly to our enemies, the North Vietnamese Army and the Vietcong. Sutton's 1973 summary of his earlier three-volume text was titled *National Suicide: Military Aid to the Soviet Union.*[*] This publication got him tossed out of the Hoover Institute.

---

[*] Sutton, A.C., *Western Technology and Soviet Economic Development,* 1917-1930. Hoover Institution, 1968.

[*] Sutton, A.C., *National Suicide. Military Aid to the Soviet Union.* Arlington House, New Rochelle, New York. 1973.

Professor Sutton wasn't finished. An update to *National Suicide* titled *The Best Enemy Money Can Buy** explored US technology transfers up to the 1980s. In Appendix B he summarized the conclusions of his research: pp. 199-210.

> In a few words, there is no such thing as Soviet technology. Almost all—perhaps 90–95 percent came directly or indirectly from the United States and its allies. In effect, the United States and the NATO countries have built the Soviet Union—its industrial and its military capabilities. This massive construction job has taken 50 years; since the revolution in 1917. It has been carried out through trade and sale of plants, equipment and technical assistance.

An even more damning quote appears on page 190 of Sutton's same book: "About 80 percent of the armaments and supplies for the Vietnamese War came from the Soviet Union. Yet a key part of President Nixon's policy was the transfer of technology to the USSR which aids Soviet war potential … Soviet military aid has been fundamental for the North Vietnamese."

If Sutton's conclusions are valid, it would make sense that the Russians would keep experienced pilots in order to fill in some gaps in their knowledge of our technology. It is painful to consider that the North Vietnamese Army used American technology given to them by the Russians to shoot down our aircraft and keep our pilots imprisoned up to seven years and perhaps much longer under the most difficult conditions imaginable.

The Cessation of Air Strikes in the Vietnam War

Retired Lieutenant Colonel Dan Hampton has written a compelling book* about a brave group of air force pilots who volunteered to fight back against the Soviet SA-2 surface-to-air missiles during the Vietnam War. This group of elite aviators, nicknamed the Wild Weasels, risked

---

* Sutton, A.C., *The Best Enemy Money Can Buy. Liberty House Press*. Billings, MO. 1986.

* Hampton, D., *The Hunter Killers*, HarperCollins, New York, NY. 2015. p. 345.

everything in order to blunt the effectiveness of the Russian-manned missile sites and eliminate them.

The last acknowledged aviators who went missing were lost on June 16, 1973. Captains Sam Cornelius and John Smallwood were flying an F-4E over Cambodia when their aircraft went down. Colonel Hampton writes, "There were persistent, credible rumors that they had survived, but since Washington never sought the release of Americans captured in Cambodia, no official action was ever taken. Their fate, as with so many others, remains unknown."

The Last Vietnam Battle

The last forty-one Americans whose names were etched into the Vietnam Veterans Memorial died on May 15, 1975, two weeks after the fall of Saigon.

On May 12, 1975, the cargo ship SS *Mayaguez* was on its way with an American crew from the port of Hong Kong to Sattahip, Thailand, when it was hijacked by the Khmer Rouge. The Khmer Rouge, a revolutionary communist militia, had overthrown the government in Phnom Penh, Cambodia, the previous month. The American crew of the ship was thought to be held on Koh Tang Island, about twenty-seven miles off the coast of the border of Cambodia and Vietnam. To this day it is still a mystery why the Khmer Rouge wanted to keep the crew of the ship in captivity.

No ransom or demand of any sort was ever communicated to the American government or to the owners of the ship.

President Ford sent the Second Battalion, Ninth Marines, which was stationed and training in Okinawa, to rescue the forty merchant crew members from the *Mayaguez*. The marines were told that resistance would be light, with only fifteen or twenty armed militants.

As with many operations during the Vietnam War, intelligence was sadly lacking, and the miscalculation was deadly. The marines flew onto the island and faced a heavily armed enemy force of between three hundred and seven hundred determined and armed soldiers.

All forty US crew members from the *Mayaguez* were rescued at the cost of forty-one US servicemen killed in the line of duty: thirty-eight marines, two navy corpsmen, and an air force copilot. Three marines were left behind—Lance Corporal Joseph N. Hargrove, Private First Class Gary C. Hall, and Private Danny G. Marshall—and marines will do almost anything to avoid leaving a fellow marine behind.

To say the entire operation was a disaster would be an understatement. The *Mayaguez* operation included all the errors that plagued our military throughout the Vietnam War: "miscalculation of enemy strength, incorrect intelligent reports, delayed decision-making from Washington politicians and the consideration of public opinion and politics in the decision-making process."*

---

* Stoffer, J., The Last Battle, *American Legion Magazine, August* 2012. pp. 16–22.

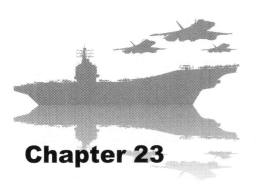

Chapter 23

THE RUSSIAN CONNECTION

By the late 1970s and into the 1980s, my dental practice was up and running, and a portion of my job was teaching part-time at Harvard's School of Dental Medicine, while trying to stay ahead of the bills. My first textbook, *Maxillofacial Orthopedics*, had come out in 1982, and my time was pretty much taken up with the dental practice and some minor research. But the question of what had happened to Daniel Kirk always remained in the back of my mind. There had been a tree-planting service but no memorial service. Mrs. Kirk, along with many others, was certainly not convinced that her husband was deceased.

This service for Daniel motivated me to write a short article about an experience I'd had during a recent dental conference in Helsinki, Finland. I was there to present a paper on early maxillary orthopedic treatment for children at the FDI dental society's annual meeting. Founded in Paris in 1900 as the Federation Dentaire Internationale, this is the world's oldest society devoted to dental research. Although that year's annual meeting was located in Helsinki, it included a side trip to the Soviet Union and the Stomatologic Institute, the university dental school in Moscow in August 1985..

A bright and talented woman had come into my life, and we married in the mid-1980s. My wife could speak a little Russian, so we decided to make a vacation out of the meeting and take the preconvention side trip to Moscow and Leningrad (now known as Saint Petersburg). Since we were all dentists, part of our time in each city was devoted to visits and exchanges of ideas with our Russian colleagues at the major dental institutes in the two cities. In Moscow, our spouses had the opportunity to visit the GUM department store, Red Square, or the Kremlin; in Leningrad, they could visit either the Winter or Summer Palace.

During our tour of the Stomatologic Institute, representatives from the oral surgical department gave us a brief description of some of their latest oral and plastic surgery techniques. As part of their presentation, they included before-and-after slides of some of their clinical procedures.

Concentrating on a lecture in a darkened lecture hall after lunch was always difficult. This particular afternoon, eight of us attended a lecture given by the academic chairman and faculty member of the Department of Oral Surgery at the university. The monotonous broken English of the presenter added to the usual after-lunch drowsiness. (Anyone who stayed at a Russian hotel—we were at the Cosmos—or who rode in a Russian bus in the mid-1980s can appreciate how one could be a little tired). The mattresses in the better hotels were thin, hard, and uncomfortable; they rested on a plywood frame. The "luxury" motor coach for sightseeing and travel was anything but luxurious: the travelers felt every bump, right through the metal seats. If you needed a restroom on the tour, you had to fight clouds of flies and an almost overpowering stench at the dilapidated wooden outhouses stationed along the route of the tour.

The academic chairman's discussion included remarks on Russian medical and dental research, orthodontics, and periodontal care. He explained the current state of Russian orthodontics by saying, "Russian children do not require orthodontic care like many of their Western counterparts because almost all Russian babies are breastfed." After some debate on the research cited for this orthodontic conclusion, it was pretty easy to evaluate the state of orthodontic care in Russia in 1984. Orthodontics was evidently not routine in Russia in the mid-1980s.

The second clinician to address us was a maxillofacial surgeon. Although Professor Jazinski spoke English with a heavy British/Russian accent, he was quite easy to understand. He was a slightly built man, approximately five feet nine, and in his midforties. His voice was much easier to listen to than the academic chairman's, and it had the force of his convictions behind it. You could tell by his enthusiasm that he enjoyed his research and clinical practice. He had short, very black hair that was just showing a hint of gray around the temples. His discussion centered on the treatment of facial trauma. I found it odd that even though he was excellent at describing the slides, he relied on an associate to explain the treatment and surgical procedures.

As expected, my eyelids got heavier and heavier as the lecture droned on. His slides were of marginal quality and clarity and reminded me of grainy black-and-white photos from the 1940s. Many of his slides were repetitious: mandibular fractures with external and internal fixation, zygomatic and orbital fractures, and some gunshot wounds. However, some slides were in color and easier to follow, and his passion for treating his patients came through very clearly.

Toward the end of his presentation, he showed us the before slides of a trauma victim who had suffered high bilateral fractures of the neck of the condyle from blunt facial trauma. The patient's face was distorted and discolored from bruising and swelling. Hematomatous splotching extended down the patient's neck. What made my eyes open wide to alertness was that the patient seemed vaguely familiar to me. Did he resemble a boyhood acquaintance? A patient from dental or postgraduate school? The following slides showed the radiographs pretreatment and immediately post-treatment.

The oral surgeon explained to us that the condylar fractures were old and had to be reset in order to achieve proper facial balance and harmony and to avoid occlusal and facial distortion. The six-week post-treatment facial photographs showed almost a complete reduction of bruising and swelling.

All of a sudden, my mind was immediately and totally alert. There on the screen in front of me was a remarkable likeness of Daniel Kirk! His face was covered with fine lines and healing scars that hadn't been there in the early 1970s, but the facial structure, hair, and eyes were very close. Was this what he would look like after more than fifteen years? As far as I knew, his MIA status hadn't changed since he'd been shot down over Laos in 1972. My heart wanted this to be Daniel, but my mind told me this couldn't possibly be the same man. As my mind and heart went through this tug-of-rope, I thought about how one would treat the facial scarring.

*****

Captain Jay Anastasi, my naval plastic surgeon acquaintance who worked at the Chelsea Naval Hospital near Boston, would certainly know how to minimize those scars. I had spent the summer of my third year in dental school following Captain Anastasi on the plastic surgery service at the hospital. He was a genius when it came to making the superficial scars from Vietnam disappear.

In addition to improving my surgical skills, I joined the other externs who were determined to enhance their skeet-shooting ability. At lunchtime we would all sign out shotguns from the Naval Exchange, purchase a box or two of twelve-gauge shotgun shells, and go down by the Mystic River to shoot skeet at the range. All the shot fell harmlessly into the river. Any of the naval personnel at the hospital could do that in the summer of 1967. I can't even imagine what would be the political, environmental, and criminal consequences of that fun activity today.

*****

Suddenly, the screen went blank, taking away that haunting scarred face. I had a million questions but knew I had to tread carefully; after all, this was the Soviet Union. The implications could be consequential.

Immediately after the presentation, I went up to Dr. Jazinski to ask him about the slides. Trying to control the excitement and enthusiasm in my voice, I kept the questions specific to the last patient. I first asked about the patient's eyes. "Why were the patient's eyes almost closed in all of the pre- and postsurgical photographs?"

"Oh," the professor explained, "this pris ... err, excuse me, patient, must be from a very snowy area where snow blindness would be common, possibly in the eastern part of our country."

"You mean Siberia?"

"Yes, it is possible," he explained. "Sometimes our countrymen are sent out to the east for reeducation or to work in factories or on farms."

"Would it be possible to see the patient's record? This is such an interesting case, and you have such a remarkably wonderful surgical result." I didn't want to appear too interested in this particular patient, so I concentrated on the surgical technique. The professor hemmed and hawed a bit, so I kept the compliments coming about the state of Soviet medicine and his particular expertise.

Eventually, in one slow and deliberate movement, the professor reached under a stack of papers and folders and handed me a manila folder with a red star stamped on the cover. Enclosed were more presurgical and postsurgical photographs and photographs of the actual surgical procedures.

Since the file was in Russian, I continued to nod as he spoke and kept furtively looking for some recognizable information on the patient. From the red star and cross, it looked like the record had been transferred from a military hospital. If only I knew a few Russian words.

Knowing I was running out of time, I pushed the professor a little harder. "Doctor, would it be at all possible for me to meet this patient to discuss his experience?"

All of a sudden, the professor's English wasn't so good. He said, "I have no particulates on that patient; it is government transfer file."

With this he snatched the folder out of my hands and declared, "We know the woman companion with you brought Bible into this country in luggage! Are you from your government? Are you military?"

At the airport, an inspector indeed had found a Bible in our luggage and had questioned us about it. How would this dental school professor hear about that insignificant incident? At the time my wife and I had both thought it was a little strange that an airline official would inspect our luggage on the way into the country, but we both thought it was just a little quirky and gave the incident no further thought.

Trying to buy time, I asked, "What do you mean, Dr. Jazinski?"

He started stammering in his British-Russian accent. "You … you people come into our country trying to spread religious propaganda and lies. You are from Sweden? You not really from America? Why you are spreading false information to our people?" The tone of his voice was getting more threatening, and he was shifting to Russian-language speaking. He then growled in Russian at our tourist guide Natasha and pointed to my camera.

Turning to our ever-present and comely tourist guide, I asked in a very calm and questioning voice, "Natasha, can you help me explain that I'm interested in the patient's wonderful results?"

"Doctor," she intoned in a sweet but businesslike way, "the professor believes you might be traveling in our country under false pretenses."

My explanation that some of my ancestors were indeed from the Stockholm area in Sweden but that my parents and grandparents had all been born in the United States didn't seem to end the problem.

She suggested, "Doctor, I would recommend that you get to your country's embassy as soon as possible in order to clear up this—what do you call it— little controversy."

*****

This whole charade was getting somewhat ridiculous. Some consternation on the part of the Russians was completely understandable. The week before our trip to Scandinavia and Russia, while responding to a reporter's question about how he was going to deal with the intransigence of the Soviet Union regarding international affairs, President Reagan had been recorded on an open microphone saying, "We will start bombing in five minutes!"

President Reagan's full comment was a sound-check parody prior to his address on National Public Radio: "My fellow Americans, I'm pleased to tell you today that I have introduced legislation that will outlaw Russia forever. We begin bombing in five minutes." The statement was never broadcast over the air but was leaked by a staffer at National Public Radio.

In America, the comment was clearly viewed as a humorous anecdote that, if anything, was meant to chide the Russians and prod them in a conciliatory direction. But there was no one in the entire country of the Soviet Union who found his comments even slightly humorous. The Soviet Far East Army was placed on alert after the statement got out.

The group of dentists who were with me at the lecture started edging toward the door.

*****

After filling in my "traveling companion" at the hotel, I headed straight for the American embassy. The cab took me to the Presnensky District in the center of Moscow, Bolshoy Deviatinsky Pereulok No. 8. Although I asked the driver to wait and tipped him two US dollars, as soon as I closed the cab door, he left me in a cloud of diesel fumes.

The building resembled a large glass and cement cube. The two marine guards at the entrance were gracious and accommodating. I introduced myself as a US naval lieutenant commander and asked to see the US ambassador.

One of the marine guards directed me to an administrative assistant's office for the deputy chief of mission. There, the admin explained that the ambassador was currently out of the country but the deputy chief would see me shortly. After I'd sat for a few minutes in a waiting area, Deputy Chief Shabrinski approached and introduced herself, gave me her card, and led me to a small conference room.

It was a little nerve-racking. This was my first inside look at an embassy, and I really didn't know what to expect. We exchanged a few pleasantries, and then I dove into my story about pilot Daniel Kirk from the *Kitty Hawk*. I finished by explaining what had happened at the local dental school with professor Jazinski in the oral surgery department.

Chief Shabrinski was very cordial and informed me that she would personally look into the situation and get back to me. She asked, "Where are you staying while in Moscow?"

*****

It took me approximately two minutes to find a cab near the embassy. When I arrived at the Cosmos Hotel and asked for my key at the front desk, the receptionist handed me a message from the deputy chief. *Wow, that was fast*, I thought.

The concierge helped me count out the correct number of rubles, and I called back from a phone booth in the lobby. After a short wait, Deputy Chief Shabrinski came on the phone. "Commander, I'm sorry, but there is no Professor Jazinski listed in the oral surgery department at the Stomatologic Institute in Moscow."

"Are you sure?"

"I did press them, but the administrator in the dean's office insisted that they had no one by that name on the faculty."

Now what? I thought. Flippantly, I replied, "Maybe we should be checking the local KGB faculty for that name."

To my astonishment she said, "That will take a few minutes. Do you mind holding?"

She was back on the line within five minutes. "Commander, there is a Sergey Jazinski on the KGB staff here in Moscow."

"Okay … is there any way you could find out if he moonlights as a dentist?"

"We do have an official bio and photo in our directory. It includes fluency in several languages, including English; it looks like he has short black hair and is of medium build. He is an official liaison for private industry."

"Well," I sighed, "we are taking a train to Helsinki tomorrow and will try to avoid your KGB operative who moonlights as a professor of oral surgery."

"I think that is recommended," she continued. "Russia is a complex mix of official and unofficial rules and regulations. The KGB is like any State Department and has a continuous interest in all visitors." After a brief pause, she continued, "And they don't appreciate too many questions."

Before leaving Moscow, I met with my fellow colleagues on the tour and asked what they thought I should do about these strange and mysterious developments. They all urged me to drop the whole episode. One of my dental collegues on the tour peppered me with, "Let's just get the hell out of Moscow and safely into Finland."

*****

The next morning, the first leg of our train trip took us to Saint Petersburg. We had one night and part of two days to spend in this city that had three name changes in the twentieth century: in 1914 the name Saint Petersburg was changed to Petrograd; in 1924 it was changed to Leningrad; and in 1991 it was changed back to Saint Petersburg.

Many areas in the city were absolutely beautiful. The city rests next to the Neva River, which empties into the Baltic Sea on the Gulf of Finland. Founded by Peter the Great in 1703, Saint Petersburg boasts many famous museums and historic landmarks, including the Hermitage or Winter Palace, one of the world's largest and finest art museums.

Catherine the Great founded the Hermitage and used it to house her own private art collection—thus the name Hermitage. Subsequent collectors have amassed over three million works of priceless art. To see it all would take more than nine years of continuous viewing. The city, the architecture, and the Summer Palace are a treasure trove of historical and cultural importance to all Russian citizens.

The most remarkable tribute to the population was their survival during the German army's siege beginning in 1942. Hitler planned on changing the city's name to Adolphsberg and kept the city under siege for 872 days in order to starve the population. At the height of the siege, six thousand people per day starved to death. There are 186 mass graves throughout the city, most of them today covered with beautiful gardens of flowers.

We were surprised to find a few small, independent stalls catering to the tourists as well as the local population. Private enterprise was creeping into the Soviet system in the form of fruit vendors, flower stalls, and vegetable kiosks. The colors and the cheerful vendors softened the bleakness of the city. Even in August a chill hung in the air, and the harsh cobblestone streets echoed loneliness. Many of us purchased fruit for our bus trip to the local Russian circus housed in a massive tent in the middle of a wheat field.

Russia is famous for its circuses. In addition to bears that danced and drove cars and dogs that attended school classes, there were high-wire acts that defied gravity. The lion and tiger trainers were fearless, or perhaps foolish. Why would anyone take a chance on placing one's head inside the mouth of one of these beasts? The ballet, pageantry, and beauty of the circus made for an entertaining evening.

*****

The next day, our tourist guide, Natasha, drooped us off at the train station. She took me aside to warn me, "Your train ride to Helsinki might not be exactly what you expect." In addition she took a note from her pocket and explained, "This was in your post box at the hotel. Don't open it until you have left Russian soil." She turned abruptly and left. It was curious that the folks at the hotel hadn't passed the note along to me. Even more curious, my hotel box had been completely empty at checkout time.

As the train started moving, the conductors appeared. They were the same officious types as those on the train we had taken from Moscow. They looked very stern in their uniforms and spoke harshly to all the passengers. Out the window the countryside flowed past, cold and dreary, even in late summer. I couldn't help but think that somewhere on this planet, possibly in this dreary country, was the US naval pilot who had gone down in Laos in March 1972.

Directly after we entered Finland, a strange and surprising phenomenon occurred. Those stern, officious train conductors who represented Soviet authority—strict, uncompromising, and meddlesome—abruptly changed. They removed their official hats and started smiling and joking with the passengers. They sold not only the official glass and silverware but also parts of their uniforms. They explained that the clothing under their uniforms would soon be switched for Western-style shirts and jeans in Helsinki. This instant switch from scowling officialdom to carefree, casual demeanor was unnerving and caught all the passengers by surprise.

I asked one of the conductors, "What is going on here? Why the abrupt change in attitude?"

He laughed briefly. "Look outside! We are in a free country now!"

Looking out the window, I saw that the scenery had also been transformed. There were herds of cows out in the well-tended fields, the forests were filled with beautiful birch trees, and the sun was shining. It was as if the entire train had traveled into another dimension. The frowns and strain on the passengers' faces gave way to smiles, laugh lines, and casual conversation. Popular music replaced the military dirge that had been broadcast over the train's speakers. It was almost a magical transformation for everyone on the train.

The envelope that Natasha had given me was addressed to me. Now that we were in Finland, I opened it quickly. Inside the envelope was a brief printed note: "Do not inquire about this patient again. Your health would be better served if you destroy this note and never say anything about it to anyone. C."

My mind started racing. I knew immediately that the note was from someone who must have known Daniel pretty well. His nickname in our band was Crock. We had given him this name for a couple of reasons. First, no one in the band like the nickname "The Magnet," and we all had nicknames that were pertinent to our band alone. I was "Banjo Man," the trumpet player was "Blowhard," and our bass player was "Boomer." Second, Daniel was by default our fearless band leader. He was one of the best musicians and knew all the songs. Often he would try to bolster our confidence before we played in front of a crowd of people. After he encouraged us, we would banter with him, saying, "Don't give us a crock of crap." "Crock" was a nickname that only those of us in the band would know. It was probably a stretch to think that the initial "C" could actually refer to Daniel, but it was possible.

But the mystery got even deeper. In the mid-1980s a movie about a crocodile man hit theaters: *Crocodile Dundee.* The plot was about an Australian man who lived in the Australian outback but could also survive in New York City. The comedy film was meant as an Australian commercial film that would appeal to an American audience. It proved to be a worldwide phenomenon, and the principal actor, the weathered Paul Hogan, was launched as Mick Dundee.

Soon after the film came out, anytime anyone in the band would communicate with each other, we would refer to Daniel as "Crock DunD." This communication was limited to no more than ten to fifteen men from our band. I placed the note back in the envelope, folded the envelope into three equal parts, and placed it in my back pocket. My insides were gurgling. I had an uncomfortable, eerie feeling that maybe I was being watched.

The note had only the letter "C" for a signature, but it was clearly some sort of warning. I had read about the Russians keeping some of our Vietnam-era veterans as prisoners of war, but I always thought this was more speculation than actual fact. My mind started racing. Could the note be from someone who actually knew Daniel?

I also asked myself, could I somehow ever get back into the Soviet Union and look for Daniel? It occurred to me that I could probably go back to the dental school and start asking more questions. However, the likelihood that the man in the photograph on the screen was actually Daniel was remote at best. I also wondered what sort of trouble the Russian authorities could visit on me if I started asking questions about one of our downed pilots from a war that had ended over twelve years ago.

I decided that I would wait until after my presentation on maxillofacial orthopedic technique at the FDI meeting and then inquire at the local dental school about giving a series of lectures in Helsinki and Moscow.

The assistant dean of the University of Helsinki, Dr. Shikolov, was employed by the medical school, and the Institute of Dentistry was a division of the medical school faculty. When I approached the assistant dean about lecturing, he asked why I wanted to lecture at the Stomatologic Institute in Moscow.

I carefully related my recent experience at the lecture at the dental school in Moscow. Dr. Shikolov was quite forceful in his response: "Going back to the Soviet Union could be a disaster for you if you asked questions about prisoners they may have from the Vietnam era. The KGB is very touchy about that subject, and it is possible you would never come out of the country!"

Dr. Shikolov had been the assistant dean of the Helsinki Dental Institute for over ten years. He had to be in his sixties, had graying hair going to all white, and seemed quite knowledgeable about my subject of maxillofacial orthopedics. He gave me what I thought was his honest opinion as he tried to fill me in on the Soviet mindset. "My parents fled Russia in the early 1940s as the Nazis were closing in on Moscow. They had to face many hardships, including very little food, during a dangerous trek across frozen land and sea during the winter of 1941. Although they were ostensibly fleeing the German army, the Wehrmacht, they told me in their later years that the Russian KGB was just as bad, if not worse than the German SS.

"I would never consider returning to the Soviet Union under any circumstance. Fortunately, you are from a free country and are probably unfamiliar with what can go on in a country that has closed its borders and sealed its population from the outside world. The Russian people get all their news filtered through the mindset of the KGB. You were very fortunate to leave when you did with the other members of your dental group."

The professor did offer me a small bit of encouragement: "Once you are back home and have resumed your teaching duties at Harvard, you might consider going public with what you do know. Keep in mind, however, that no matter what comes out in the American press, very little of it will ever become public knowledge in Russia."

These words were unsettling, and his final comment was unnerving. "Remember, Doctor, if you irritate the KGB too much, they can eliminate you in Boston just as easily as they can in Moscow!"

I decided to finish the conference, see a little of the dental institute and Helsinki, and return to my dental practice in Gloucester. On my return home, my calls to the Pentagon, the US Navy, and the news media were met with silence and derisive questioning.

*****

Years later, I started reading reports from Red McDaniel, a POW held in North Vietnam for several years. I also had the privilege of listening to one of his lectures at a Wardroom Club dinner in the spring of 2012 at the coast guard's function hall in Boston. I purchased his book, *Scars and Stripes*, and asked him if he had any knowledge of our POWs who might have been left behind after the prisoner release. His reply was chilling.

He stated that pilots had been of particular value to the North Vietnam POW camps. He referred me to a 2002 book by Joseph D. Douglass Jr. titled *Betrayed*. The preface of the book states that *"Betrayed* is an investigation into American prisoners of war (POWs) who never returned." Although Vietnam is the focus of the investigation, the book also studies atrocities and actions by the Russians, Chinese, and North Koreans after World Wars I and II and after the Korean War.

As I was reading Douglass's book, I kept thinking that most of his assumptions had to be impossible. But he kept referencing people who had defected from communist countries or people who knew or had seen the prisoners or their guards. One defector in particular, General Major Jan Sejna, came from Czechoslovakia to the United States in 1968. This high-ranking defector had personally seen "thousands of prisoners captured by the communists in Vietnam, taken by plane to the Czech prison camps and then on to the Soviet Union." Many of these prisoners were, according to Sejna, subjected to "medical and drug experimentation of the most ghastly nature."

Jan Sejna had been the chief of staff to the Czech minister of defense and was "personally aware of medical intelligence experiments using American POWs as human guinea pigs in both the Korean and Vietnam Wars."[*]

While reading the book, I kept remembering some of the comments made by Daniel and other pilots on the *Kitty Hawk* in 1969. A few of the pilots on the *Hawk* talked about the trucks they had targeted on the Ho Chi Minh Trail. They said they looked a lot like Ford trucks manufactured by the Ford Motor Company. After I read in Sutton's *National Suicide* about how the Ford Motor Company had built a plant in Gorky, Russia, these comments made a lot more sense to me.

Although the Douglass book *Betrayed* was frightening, a more recent book, *American Trophies* by Sauter and Zimmerlee, published in 2013,[*] is even more chilling. In the foreword, Sydney Schanberg, author of what became the Academy Award winning film *The Killing Fields*, states that in 1973 Hanoi returned 591 US POWs. "Our military and intelligence agencies showed there were at least 300—and likely more—still in captivity."

Since Schanberg had covered the Vietnam War extensively, he was curious about the country of Laos, which had joined the communists in North Vietnam. After the war the government of Laos "had admitted to holding hundreds of American captives." It is very likely that if he survived the loss of his aircraft, Daniel could well have been one of them.

*****

After getting back to my office following the FDI meeting in Helsinki, I wrote to the dean at the Stomatologic Institute in Moscow. The dean's responses to my inquiries about the professor of oral surgery were friendly but vague. It seemed quite plausible that he knew more than he was letting on. It was time to call Mrs. Kirk.

As I picked up the phone, memories of Daniel's worn, crumpled photos of his wife and their wonderful family came flooding back to me. I tried

---

[*] Douglass, J. D. Jr., *Betrayed*, First Books, New York, NY 2002, p. 268.

[*] Sauter, M. & Zimmerlee, J., *American Trophies*, Orcinus Solutions, Waltham, MA 2013. p. 5.

not to think about how emotionally wrenching this whole conversation could be. She was very gracious, and we talked about Daniel and the navy for a few minutes while I tried to get to the reason for my call.

When I told her about the slide show at the Russian dental shool, she went totally silent.

This was uncharted territory and harder than I expected. "LeeAnna," I said, quickly backpedaling a bit as I sensed her discomfort, "it has been over twelve years, and it is possible that the man I saw on the screen ..."

"Doctor, are you trying to tell me ..."

"It could have been anyone; it just had a likeness of Daniel. This is all just a theory, and I have no specific knowledge of what might have happened to him."

"You're not the first person who has mentioned our POWs could still be alive in Russia."

I didn't think it made sense to describe in detail my experiences in the Soviet Union. For Daniel's sake and perhaps my own, I thought it best to keep silent on any theories about the note. There was a pause on the line.

LeeAnna sighed. "I may have run out of options, but not hope."

On that sad note, I apologized for possibly upsetting her and said good-bye.

*****

The following day, I spent forty-five minutes on the phone trying to contact the right person to talk to at the Department of the Navy about the possibility that one of their highly trained A-7 pilots might still be alive in Russia. My inquiries got me nowhere. It turned out that there were several well-intentioned groups still trying to find information on soldiers, sailors, and airmen who were categorized as missing or killed in action. Even more curious, no one at the Pentagon had any idea what I was talking about when I mentioned the LOKATE system. Everyone claimed ignorance.

Because of the anguish it might bring to the Kirk family, I pushed Daniel's story and my time on the *Kitty Hawk* and at Firebase 14 into the back reaches of my brain.

The Pentagon Connection

The Garwood Affair

I kept doing some minor research and looking into different articles and books about POWs and MIAs. An interesting article from 1984 on the front page of the *Wall Street Journal* by Bill Paul caught my attention. The article featured an interview with a POW who had been released in 1979. Robert (Bobby) Garwood had been captured by the North Vietnamese on September 28, 1965, approximately one week before the scheduled end of his tour of duty. Garwood had earned a degree of freedom in North Vietnam because he had learned the language and talked like a native and was useful to the North Vietnamese because he could repair cars, trucks, and machinery.

He made two attempts to escape. In 1977 he was able to pass a note describing his condition to a New Zealand journalist. Although the journalist passed the note on to the US embassy, it was summarily ignored.

Garwood's second attempt was more successful. He was able to pass a note to a Finnish World Bank official, Ossi Rakkonen, who was in Vietnam on business in 1979. The bank official went public with the note, and the Vietnamese immediately released Bobby Garwood because of the adverse publicity.

Mr. Garwood's troubles, however, were not over. When he arrived in Bangkok on March 15, 1979, he was met by a Marine Corps representative who immediately read him his rights. The next representative of the Corps informed Garwood that he had been retained as counsel and told him not to talk about his time in Vietnam to anyone.

Within a year Garwood was tried on minor charges and stripped of his rank, his allowances, and $148,000 worth of back pay. The US government's attempt to discredit Garwood was complete. No one would listen to his story of being a POW or his eyewitness accounts of seeing other American POWs in Vietnam. Many have tried to discredit his story of captivity. One of his main problems was the long period of time he spent with the North Vietnamese and Vietcong without a meaningful attempt to escape. The actual story of marine Bobby Garwood may never be known completely.

*****

Thinking back over the roughly forty-five years that have passed since I left Vietnam, I have concluded that it had to be impossible for that man in the slide presentation at the Stomatologic Institute in Moscow to be Daniel. There could not be any valid reason that his location would be a secret after all these years, nor would there be any reason that the Russians would not disclose information about our captured or deceased airmen. It just seems odd that nothing except a helmet was recovered from the crash site. It also seems odd that a KGB agent would be in one of the Russian dental schools. In addition, who sent the note warning me to make no further inquiries about the patient?

It was later learned, through the Freedom of Information Act, that Daniel might have survived in Laos after his plane went down. The NSA (National Security Administration) operative who was listening to radio transmissions from a secret location atop a mountain in Laos listed Lieutenant Kirk as being held in a Laotian prison camp after the crash of his Corsair A7-E aircraft. If any of the subsequent information from the LOKATE program is credible, then the defense department in room M1126 of the basement in the Pentagon knew exactly where Daniel and possibly his aircraft were located.

This operative had a list of seventy-five names of US service personnel who were missing and presumed captured or deceased. Unfortunately, this information cannot be confirmed. As an electrical engineer, Daniel had intimate knowledge of his aircraft and aeronautical engineering science. He would have been a very valuable captive for any of our adversaries.

There are several possibilities regarding what might have happened to Lieutenant Commander Kirk. The first and most probable is that Daniel was lost in March 1972 when his plane crashed in the Laotian jungle. Another speculative possibility is that he survived the crash and died in a Laotian prison camp. A third speculation was that he survived prison camps in Laos or North Vietnam and was brought to Russia so scientist there could understand the technology in the Corsair. The forth and least likely possibility was that Daniel was alive, and living somewhere in the Soviet Union; and that the Russian government fabricated the note given to me by the intourist guide to ensure that no more inquiries about this particular pilot would surface.

Probably for a good many politicians in America at the time, the only thing worse than Lieutenant Commander Kirk spilling his knowledge of aeronautical science and engineering under torture to our enemies would have been his testimony as to what he knew about Nixon's secret war before the Congress of the United States.

THE PEROT REPORT

It came to the attention of the Reagan White House in 1980 that there was a distinct possibility that American prisoners of war were still being held in Laos. The Vietnamese offered to trade prisoners for cash. Reagan felt that might start a dangerous precedent and asked his advisors for help in finding information for the release of POWs.

One of those advisors was Ross Perot, the head of Electronic Data Systems. Perot was an independent advisor and would not rely on information from Washington or the Pentagon. He went directly to Southeast Asia and talked to businessmen and officials from the government.

According to Brown* in *Moscow Bound: Policy, Politics and the POW/MIA Dilemma*, Perot's report contained the following conclusions: (1) the US forces left behind POWs at the end of the war; (2) the US government knew POWs were being left behind; and (3) substantial evidence showed that at least 343 MIAs were still alive in Laos.

Much secrecy surrounding the MIA/POW problems exists in the governments of Laos, Vietnam, and Russia. What is even more troublesome is the amount of secrecy that our own US government has placed as a roadblock for families and the news media who wish to find information about what happened to their much-loved and missed family members and friends.

In the early 1900s, Senator Smith, who had been looking into the MIA/POW issue for several years, finally "achieved his goal of forming a Senate Select Committee on POW/MIA Affairs." This committee was formed on August 2, 1991 and lasted until January 2, 1993. Its purpose was solely to investigate the fate of U.S. service personnel listed as missing in action during the Vietnam War. The following is a quote from Sauter and Zimmerlee:*

---

* Brown, J.M.G., *Moscow Bound*, Veteran Press, Kansas City, MO, 1993.
* Sauter & Zimmerlee, p.255.

In its main focus on American POW/MIAs from Southeast Asia, the efforts pitted Smith against Senators John Kerry (former Secretary of State) and John McCain, who sought to limit the probe in an apparent attempt to put the issue behind America and move to normalize relations with Vietnam.

Ultimately the Committee stated: we acknowledge that there is no proof that US POWs survived, but neither is there proof that all of those who did not return had died

"There is evidence moreover, that indicates the possibility of survival, at least for a small number, after Operation Homecoming."[*]

The problem of US government secrecy was addressed in the much-heralded "McCain Truth Bill." This was passed in the 1990s in order to make information on those who were missing in action or possibly prisoners of war more accessible. But this piece of legislation did nothing to enhance access to secret records and actually made accessibility more difficult. There were provisions in Senator McCain's legislation that created wide areas of information that government officials not only could hold back but were directed to keep secret from the public.

Presidents Clinton, Bush, and Obama have also issued executive orders that were supposed to open up tremendous amounts of previously classified material. The documents released have been heavily censored and even blacked out with black markers. Much of this censoring and blacking-out of information has ostensibly been done in relation to POWs long declared dead "in order to protect their privacy."

---

[*] Sauter and Zimmerlee, *American Trophies*, p. 255.

Chapter 24

AMERICA'S EFFORT IN VIETNAM—A HISTORICAL PERSPECTIVE

Between 1956 and 1975, over two and a half million Americans served in Vietnam. About one-third were drafted, and about two-thirds were volunteers. The mix included eleven thousand women. In racial terms, 12.5 percent of the troops were African American, and 85 percent were Caucasian. The average age was twenty-one. During World War II, the average age had been twenty-six. The following famous men, along with scores of others, served their country in Vietnam: Senator John McCain, Vice President Al Gore, film director Oliver Stone, FedEx founder Fred Smith, and Secretary of State John Kerry.

Unfortunately, many Vietnam-era veterans and indeed anyone who was politically aware at the time remember John Kerry's testimony before the US Senate Foreign Relations Committee in 1971. In that testimony, Kerry, wearing tattered fatigues but presenting no evidence of war crimes, stated that his fellow soldiers had "personally raped, cut off ears, heads and limbs and randomly shot at civilians as they generally ravaged the countryside of South Vietnam reminiscent of raids by Genghis Khan."

Kerry's testimony helped Congress later defund the war. Members of our military who were prisoners of war at the time had to listen to Kerry's testimony as it was played for them in their cells by their North Vietnamese captors twice a day. It was terribly demoralizing for our POWs.

*****

Another demoralizing scenario was played out by antiwar activist Jane Fonda. Since she was a North Vietnamese sympathizer, she was allowed to travel to North Vietnam and see firsthand the remarkably "humane and kind" treatment the army of North Vietnam rendered to our prisoners of war. A handful of American prisoners were selected, cleaned up, and given clean pajamas in order to meet and shake hands with Ms. Fonda. At least one prisoner, a civilian contractor, was beaten severely for three days for not wanting to meet with her.

Many American prisoners were held in the "Hanoi Hilton," the most infamous North Vietnamese prison. Former prisoners such as air force pilot Colonel Jerry Driscoll (who still suffers from double vision from the beatings he suffered) and Chief Master Sergeant Ronald D. Sampson often refer to Ms. Fonda as an excellent example of an American traitor. It is up to the reader and the Almighty to make these judgments.

Many of the prisoners of the North Vietnamese encouraged viewers to skip the 2013 movie *The Butler*, in which Ms. Fonda plays the role of Nancy Reagan. Survivors of the North Vietnamese prison camps cannot easily forgive "Hanoi Jane's" blatant traitorous actions against their fellow prisoners.

*****

It has been over forty years since the last American combat troops departed from Vietnam. There were many reasons for our pullout of troops and loss of tactical victory, including lack of political will and unpopularity of the war in America. In addition, Soviet and Chinese technology for North Vietnam was almost unending.

It is also possible that even with an American victory, our efforts to bring the safety of a political system such as a democracy or republic to the people of Vietnam could have been in vain. Politicians of every stripe often have difficulty fighting evil forces of greed and power. Financial greed and political power can be all-consuming for many people.

In the late 1700s, the majority of settlers in America realized that loyalty to one king was not the form of government they wanted and was not going to lead to political or religious freedom. The American

Revolution brought about our constitution and a shared representative form of government with three branches: executive, legislative, and judicial.

It is up to the people of Vietnam to decide the best form of government for their country. Despite the good intensions of the American government and our allies for the people of South Vietnam, there was overwhelming military and political support for the people of North Vietnam from communist China and the Soviet Union.

Approximately 50 percent of all Soviet foreign aid between 1965 and 1968 went to North Vietnam. Dozens of US aircraft were brought down by teams of Soviet-trained or actual Soviet missile experts and antiaircraft gunners. Many of the North Vietnamese aircraft were flown by Soviet pilots.* The Chinese government supplied almost 30 percent of all North Vietnamese armaments.

The foot soldiers endured many harsh conditions in Vietnam, and few had adequate training: jungle warfare included incredibly wide swings in climate conditions with heat, rain, mud, wild animals, and countless forms of mines and booby traps set up by an enemy that was indistinguishable from the population we were there to protect.

During World War II, the average number of days in combat for our soldiers was forty days over four years. In Vietnam, it was close to 240 days in combat in *one* year. One in every ten men who served in Vietnam was either killed or wounded. The total number of Americans killed in the years 1956–75 was 58,214. Almost seventeen hundred Americans are still missing. My pilot friend from the *Kitty Hawk* is still among those listed as missing in action.

---

* M. Lind, "Why We Went to War in Vietnam," *American Legion Magazine* (January 2013): 20–30.

Epilogue

Many of the interviews for this project were conducted long after the war had ended, and many of the interview sessions were unsatisfactory and somewhat troubling. Almost 100 percent of the interviewees were uninterested in rehashing the experiences they had lived through during the Vietnam War. Most of the men I spoke to were retired, disabled, or both. Those who were willing to discuss some of their experiences were nervous, distrustful of the government, or terrified that their name might become public.

None of them would place any trust in our government. They were afraid of some sort of (perhaps imagined) retribution or retaliation from a government that either had lied to them or had let them down during the postwar years. Many were afraid of losing whatever meager veterans' benefits they had accumulated. Some were afraid of losing their physician or medical benefits.

It was distressing to see how many of the brave soldiers who had spoken so openly three or four decades ago were now decidedly hostile toward our government. It makes one think that the most powerful and wealthiest nation on earth should be able to run a professional and trustworthy plan for national defense and care of our veterans. Veterans' care in America is a disgrace.

Although this is not true in all veteran hospitals, there are too many instances where veteran men and women who gave everything for their country languish because of long wait times for treatment or even proper diagnosis. What does it say about the heart of a nation when it cannot provide first-class treatment for its veterans?

Entrepreneurial Spirit

The US government has, however, done a better job in staying out of the way of entrepreneurial spirit and technological development. For example, it has been an interesting journey for aircraft development from the 1870s in America to the 1970s in Vietnam to now.

In the 1870s a college president suggested to his church bishop that "man would someday fly through the air like birds." The bishop was enraged, claiming that "flight is reserved for the angels." The college president, Milton Wright, went home to care for his children, two of whom were Wilbur and Orville. These bicycle mechanics used "Pride of the West" ladies' underwear cloth to cover the wings of the world's first airplane. The Wright brothers' first successful flight lasted twelve seconds and traveled only 120 feet on December 17, 1903, at Kitty Hawk, North Carolina. This section of the Outer Banks was chosen for its soft, sandy landing site for their delicate aircraft.

In the 1960s and '70s, the air power used in Vietnam was frightening and awe-inspiring. During that time period, the human race experienced flight to the moon and back. In the spy world, the years 1962–90 were known as the era of the Black Bird (SR-71). This aircraft, retired because of budget cuts to the air force in 1990, could travel one mile in 1.6 seconds! It could land and take off from the flight deck of the USS *Kitty Hawk* or any aircraft carrier and fly almost straight up to 85,000 feet. The US Air Force had forty of these aircraft, not one of which ever received a scratch from the almost 4,000 enemy missiles they outran.

In the battlefields of the future, unmanned drone aircraft will be capable of soaring quietly and almost invisibly over enemy territory and delivering photographs or destruction from a remote location.

December 17, 2015, was the 112th anniversary of the Wright brothers' first flight. The record air speed the brothers accomplished was thirty-one miles per hour. It is interesting to speculate what the next one hundred years might bring for the transportation industry.

*****

Another addition to modern warfare is the computer. Many folks alive today have lived through a dramatic computer revolution. The first electronic digital computer, ENIAC, in 1946 could accomplish fourteen ten-digit calculations per second. The machine weighed over thirty tons and was one hundred feet long. IBM's newest supercomputer, Blue Gene Q, is capable of doing over a quadrillion calculations per second and is the size of two large refrigerators. A pentaflop machine is capable of speeds up to a thousand trillion (quadrillion) floating point calculations per second! Most current cell phones contain much more computing power than the first spacecraft.

*****

People from all around the world would like similar advances in our current diplomatic efforts in order to stabilize markets and governments. A strong, capable, and well-equipped military with current technology should be able to make the Vietnam War experiences ancient history for future generations.

*****

When we examine the situation with our disabled war veterans, we realize that there is much important work to accomplish. Returning veterans are a treasure trove of value for businesses and industry, regardless of any disabilities they may have received while on active duty.

These returning men and women of our armed forces who have given so much are an indispensable source of expertise, energy, and leadership for the next generation. We cannot afford to squander their valuable leadership, technological, and organizational skills. Our businesses and corporations require and will thrive on their knowledge. The Walmart Corporation has recognized the expertise of returning service personnel, with plans to hire up to 100,000 of these veterans beginning in May 2013.

*****

Although new inventions and small companies are forming every day all over America, one small example is in a cellar workshop in Bedford, Massachusetts. Here an MIT graduate and polio victim, Phil C., and his team of engineers, helped by electrical engineer Wallace A., are developing intelligent braces for disabled patients' legs that will help them walk and descend stairs. These "supplemental legs" are strapped directly to the patients' own legs and are a major breakthrough with far-reaching implications for our disabled veterans, older people with knee problems, or anyone limited by problem knee joints.

What advances in technology are going to be welcomed during this century? It can only be hoped that the technology will be used for good more than evil. Humans' ability to create should outweigh humans' ability to destroy. Reducing buildings to ruins or killing our fellow human beings does little to advance the idea that we have learned from our mistakes in Vietnam. Future generations will judge our success or failure.

General Giap, our main communist adversary during the Vietnam War, really left his country in ruins—as communism usually does. Giap had no problem sacrificing thousands of his countrymen (40,000 during the Tet Offensive), a trait he shared with other communist dictators such as Stalin, Lenin, and Mao. He passed away in the fall of 2013 at 102 years old.

Market reforms were instituted in Vietnam in 1986, and a fierce reformer, Vo Van Kiet, took charge in 1991. The government of Vietnam today, although it still pays attention to the communist form of governing, is beginning to act like a capitalist country. The United States is its largest trading partner.

Author's Note

The writing and retelling of the stories of many brave men who experienced the Vietnam War has on occasion been painful. Some of these veterans have been brushed aside by a government not interested in their experiences. However, many more of the men whose stories are retold here have become successful and stable members of their communities. If some brave soldiers have exhibited symptoms of post-traumatic stress syndrome, it is certainly understandable.

Salty language seemed to be a part of the life of the sailors and ground troops in the war zone. Although this language is not part of the author's vocabulary, no judgments or admonitions are directed at anyone.

Many of the interviews for this book were conducted years ago. Any errors in positions, titles, locations, and family ties are entirely the author's. The novel focuses on the years 1969–71. For an excellent first-person look at life in the bush, I recommend Frederick Downs's *The Killing Zone*, Robert Tonstic's *Days of Valor*, Phil Caputo's *A Rumor of War*, and Karl Marlantes's *Matterhorn*. These brave men survived some of the bloodiest battles of the Vietnam War. Their stories are well worth reading and are historical treasures.

For a later look at the fate of the South Vietnamese Army and people (1973–75), I recommend a terrific book by George Veith called *Black April*. This well-researched book chronicles the plight of the courageous men and women of South Vietnam who fought for their country's freedom after the Americans left.

Printed in the United States
By Bookmasters